THE
SUBWAY
GIRLS

ALSO BY SUSIE ORMAN SCHNALL

On Grace
The Balance Project

THE
SUBWAY
GIRLS

SUSIE ORMAN SCHNALL

ST. MARTIN'S GRIFFIN ☒ NEW YORK

THE SUBWAY GIRLS. Copyright © 2018 by Susie Orman Schnall. All rights reserved. Printed in the United States of America. For information, address St. Martin's Press, 175 Fifth Avenue, New York, N.Y. 10010.

www.stmartins.com

Designed by Anna Gorovoy

Library of Congress Cataloging-in-Publication Data

Names: Schnall, Susie Orman, author.
Title: The subway girls / Susie Orman Schnall.
Description: First Edition | New York : St. Martin's Griffin, [2018]
Identifiers: LCCN 2017056741 | ISBN 9781250169761 (trade paperback) |
    ISBN 9781250169778 (ebook)
Classification: LCC PS3619.C446545 S83 2018 | DDC 813/.6—dc23
LC record available at https://lccn.loc.gov/2017056741

Our books may be purchased in bulk for promotional, educational, or business use. Please contact your local bookseller or the Macmillan Corporate and Premium Sales Department at 1-800-221-7945, extension 5442, or by email at MacmillanSpecialMarkets@macmillan.com.

First Edition: July 2018

10 9 8 7 6 5 4 3 2 1

To the real Charlotte and Rose, my grandmothers,
whose names I borrowed for this book
and whose memories I will forever cherish

I learned this, at least, by my experiment:
that if one advances confidently in the direction of his dreams,
and endeavors to live the life which he has imagined,
he will meet with a success unexpected in common hours.

—Henry David Thoreau

THE
SUBWAY
GIRLS

CHAPTER 1

CHARLOTTE
THURSDAY, MARCH 3, 1949

After extensive research and considerable internal deliberation, Charlotte had submitted employment applications to five advertising agencies, their prestigious footings in Madison Avenue's most glimmering and stalwart buildings having nothing to do with her choices. Four rejected her expeditiously. The deliberately worded and carefully typed missives were diplomatic: the standard *We are unable to offer you employment at this time. We wish you well in your continued pursuits* sort of baloney.

Charlotte was convinced, however, that the true reason for the rejections was her advanced age. That the hiring executives took one look at her, with her impressive-but-unnecessary-for-a-typist education from Hunter College and her twenty-one-year-old vestal womb on the verge of decay, and assumed they were better off with girls fresh out of high school. Charlotte, they had most wrongly assumed, in her eyes at least, was one stockinged step away from the maternity ward, which would leave them with a typist seat gone cold and the terribly inconvenient need to recruit a new girl mid-season.

But as Charlotte and JoJo made their way out of Professor Finley's econ class, the March air stinging their exposed skin, Charlotte hoped that the news from advertising agency number five would be imminent. And positive. "It should be today, JoJo. I don't know how much longer I can hold it together if it doesn't come today," she said, shielding herself from the cold wind with her woolen scarf and fierce ambition as they walked toward their favorite coffee shop, a well-lit number on the corner of Seventy-First and Lex.

"I don't know if I can eat a thing," Charlotte continued once they had sat down. "I feel like that Hawaiian tsunami from a few years ago is gaining momentum in my stomach."

"She'll have a tea, and I'll have an egg salad on white, please," JoJo told the waitress.

"That letter better be bursting with good news. Another rejection and I'm heading straight to the high point of the Brooklyn Bridge."

"Charlotte!" JoJo scolded. "Don't talk like that. You're gonna get the job. And if you don't, there are better options than a swan dive."

"Like what?"

"J. Walter Thompson is not the only advertising agency in all of Manhattan, you know."

"Easy for you to say. You have a job, Miss Copywriter at McCann Erickson," Charlotte said, taking a sip of her tea.

"I realize how important this is to you. And I know things aren't great at home. It's as if every day you're still living in Bay Ridge is like another ragged breath into a balloon. And you're on the verge of combusting."

"Ain't that the truth? And I don't know whether to laugh or cry."

"Laugh, Charlotte. It's good for digestion."

Charlotte gave JoJo one of her what-are-you-talking-about-JoJo looks and then laughed. How lucky she was to have a best friend like JoJo. A girl who relied on truth as much as humor, realizing that the former was essential and the latter was what made life bearable. A far cry from most of the other girls in their class, who relied more on flattery and gossip, neither of which was essential nor made life bearable, and resulted in the type of girl Charlotte and JoJo had neither time nor patience for.

"Lookin' like spring might finally be on 'er way," the optimistic-as-eggs postman said as he and Charlotte both approached the front walk to her house.

"I sure hope so," Charlotte said politely, smiling and accepting the small pile of mail. Waiting for the afternoon post had punctuated Charlotte's days the last couple of weeks. Anticipation. Disappointment. Anticipation. Disappointment.

Flipping fervently through the envelopes, Charlotte spotted a J. Walter Thompson return address. Anticipation? Check. Disappointment. She hoped not. Charlotte's stomach dropped. An elevator with a broken cable.

J. Walter Thompson, the most prestigious agency in Manhattan, had been Charlotte's first choice all along. It was the perfect place for Charlotte to begin her dream career in advertising, despite the distressing fact that the decade insisted upon that career, for young ladies at least, be confined to the typing pool. But Charlotte was used to feeling confined, and preferred the metal-desk-and-Smith-Corona sort of confinement to the sort she was presently enduring amid the silence and the sadness that was her parents' home in

Bay Ridge, Brooklyn. So while the other firms' rejections were disappointing, they weren't the worst outcome. The worst outcome would be a rejection from JWT. Charlotte didn't have a backup plan.

Ignoring the cold, Charlotte sat on her stoop and examined the envelope. *Miss Charlotte Friedman.* Clear black type. The shipshape handiwork of an earnest typing pool girl.

She would have preferred to die—JoJo enthusiastically claiming the cemetery plot immediately to her right—than be like most of the Bay Ridge girls, who wanted to get married and have babies straightaway. A girl who settled for being a typist or a teacher temporarily, if at all, while waiting for Mr. Right to sweep her off her loafers, bring her home to his mother for a thorough once-over (*Nice teeth,* she'd say), and then straight to a tidy railroad apartment in the boroughs where she could carry on with the housekeeping, the cooking, the mothering, the drudgery of it all.

Girls today had choices. Charlotte had choices. She would get a college degree. She would be a professional. Together, she and JoJo were going to make names for themselves. And one day, and this they discussed only on nights when Coca-Cola wasn't the only dark liquid in the tumblers, they'd open their own agency. It was all decided. Charlotte could barely contain her excitement that her life was truly about to start. And that soon she'd be able to afford an apartment in Manhattan with a couple of the other girls. A life worth living, indeed.

She took one last look at the envelope and ripped it open. Her heart raced as she unfolded the single page and read its contents in haste. Once she got past the "We are unable to offer you . . ." Charlotte lowered her head to her knees and cried. There was so much anticipation and emotion in every tear dropping onto the cracked concrete.

She had spent hours fantasizing about what it would be like to ride the elevator with purpose each morning; the way she'd spread her hands across the desk, absorbing the firmness and stability of the job; the skirts and blouses she'd hang according to outfit; and the journal she'd keep to ensure she didn't repeat an ensemble within a given week. So much time fantasizing about learning everything she could about advertising by reading the memos she would be asked to type, by listening extra carefully during the meetings for which she'd record notes, by lifting trade magazines from reception on her way out the door on Fridays. Those images flickered out like lightbulbs that had died emitting too much brightness.

Charlotte had anticipated that when she got her first job, she'd feel desired in a way no mother or lover ever could make her feel. She had little to no experience feeling desired by either a mother or a lover, so the disappointment in having to wait even longer felt almost violent. An assault against everything she had longed for. A barricade blocking her emergence from childhood to adulthood. The sense of relief that Charlotte had hoped to feel as a result of opening the letter was as long overdue as a forgotten library book wedged behind the sofa.

"That *was* the option. There are no other options, JoJo," Charlotte whispered into the phone so her mother wouldn't hear. She was crammed into the hall closet, smoking, the phone cord threaded under the door.

"I don't even know what to say."

"I know what my parents would say. *You're too ambitious, Charlotte. Why don't you just marry Sam and settle down, Charlotte?* Maybe they're right."

"Is that what you want?"

"No."

"I didn't think so. I thought you were done worrying about what you think you're *supposed* to do."

"I thought I was too."

"So what's your plan?"

"Brave Charlotte would start an entirely new job search and apply to more agencies. There has to be an empty typewriter somewhere on Madison Avenue."

"That's my girl. J. Walter Thompson doesn't know what they're missing."

"Hmmm. That's a great idea, JoJo. Thanks."

"What—" JoJo started. But Charlotte had already hung up.

Charlotte stubbed out her cigarette into the juice glass she'd brought into the closet. She knew her mother could smell the smoke, but Mrs. Friedman accepted the inevitability of Charlotte smoking as long as Charlotte didn't smoke directly in front of her. She had smoked herself for years before—well, before her hands had started trembling so terribly from grief that she once dropped the cigarette onto the rug and almost caused a fire. Since then she hadn't smoked, but Charlotte found it gave her own hands something to do. And that was helpful.

Luckily, Charlotte had her satchel in the closet and dialed the number on the JWT rejection letter. *What the heck?* she thought. Though not typically in her nature to be so forward—with boys, her parents, hemlines—Charlotte felt she had nothing to lose, everything to gain, and an obligation to her future self to give it a shot.

"Mr. Hertford, hello. This is Charlotte Friedman. I was an applicant for the typing pool?" she explained once the switchboard operator connected her to the man who had both interviewed her and broken her heart.

"Of course, Miss Friedman. What can I do for you, dear?"

"Mr. Hertford, I received your letter of rejection, and I wanted to convey my disappointment. I felt I was extremely qualified for the job, and working at J. Walter Thompson was far and away my first choice. Sir, I'm calling to ask if there's any chance you would reconsider." Charlotte took a deep breath.

"Well, well, Miss Friedman. It's not every day I have a girl calling like this. I must say I admire you for being a go-getter. But unfortunately we don't have additional opportunities available at this time."

"How about as a receptionist? I'm quite adept at the telephone, Mr. Hertford."

"I'm sure you are, dear. But we're fully staffed up front and on the switchboard, as well."

Charlotte was quiet.

"I promise to keep you in mind should anything change."

"Please do, Mr. Hertford. I wouldn't let you down. I absolutely promise."

"I'm sure you wouldn't, dear. Good day."

Charlotte slowly returned the handset to the receiver. She was proud of herself for making the call, but disappointed in its outcome. Perhaps this was one of those signs she had heard people talking about. Some universal force wagging a stumpy finger in her face and saying, *You didn't get this job because you're not supposed to be working, you young, impressionable girl. Who do you think you are, anyway? You've completed almost four years of college. We gave you that. Now get your wits about you, child, and do what you're supposed to do. Reproduce!*

After shutting the closet door behind her and replacing the telephone on the hall table, Charlotte walked to the kitchen to rinse out the juice glass. Her mother was working a crossword puzzle in pen and sitting at the small kitchen table, which was covered with Charlotte's grandmother's well-worn floral cloth.

Charlotte often caught her mother staring out the window, her lips moving but no sound coming out, something she'd been doing ever since they'd received the dreadful telegram that told them that Charlotte's brother, Harry, wouldn't be returning home from the war. Harry, in Charlotte's opinion, had been the only good thing about their family.

"Would you like some tea, Ma?" Charlotte asked.

"Just had some, but thanks."

Charlotte sat down and looked out the window.

"There's mail for you, Charlotte," Mrs. Friedman said, not looking up from the puzzle.

"There is? Where?" Charlotte, surprised she had missed it when she was looking through the mail pile earlier, immediately thought there must have been another agency she applied to that she hadn't heard from yet. Or maybe, J. Walter Thompson had sent her the rejection in error and this was the actual letter offering her a position and Mr. Hertford had simply forgotten. In the couple of seconds it took her to get from the kitchen to the hall table where her mother had left the envelope, Charlotte had considered the entire spectrum of possibilities. How wrong she was.

The return address bore no name, and the number on Park Avenue didn't provide a clue. Charlotte, certain it was a job offer, ripped the envelope open, pulled out the piece of heavy-stock cream paper, and read its contents. As shocked as a kite in a thunderstorm, Charlotte had to read the letter twice.

CHAPTER 2

OLIVIA
THURSDAY, MARCH 1, 2018

"Did they call yet?" Thomas asked, rushing into the conference room, an extra-large coffee in one hand, a scrunched Starbucks bag in the other.

"You have a hair out of place, Thomas," Olivia said, smirking.

"Not yet," Matt said from his perch at the head of the large table. "They said nine o'clock." He glanced at his watch—he had chosen his great-grandfather's gold Rolex today, Olivia noticed—and then looked from Olivia to Thomas.

"They must just be tied up with pathetic consolation calls to the losers," Thomas said, stuffing an English muffin sandwich in his mouth.

"Classy," Olivia said, and gave Thomas a look.

"Come on, you two. Not now," Matt said.

"I didn't say a word," Thomas protested, his mouth a cavern of mangled egg.

"I heard from a friend at Y&R last night that Boss & Bates dropped out," Olivia said, looking at Matt.

"Really, why?" Thomas asked.

"Apparently, they weren't happy with their final presentation yesterday, so they withdrew rather than face an inevitable rejection. I guess they thought it would make them look better on the street," Olivia said.

"I guess they thought wrong, since it only makes them look like bigger losers," Thomas said, laughing and staring at Matt.

Matt didn't look up. He was typing into his phone.

The conference room phone rang with the internal tone. Matt grabbed it.

"Matt," he said into the receiver.

"Put it on speaker," Thomas said in a loud whisper.

"Great, thanks, Layne. Please put him through." Matt looked up at Olivia and Thomas and gave them a thumbs-up. "It's him."

"Speaker, Matt," Thomas said.

"Steve, good morning! It's Matt Osborne," Matt said, suddenly all smiles and bellowing voice.

"Speaker," Thomas hissed.

"Shut up," Olivia whispered to Thomas.

They both looked at Matt. He was still smiling.

"Thank you. We put our best into the concept and the storyboards. I'm really happy to hear you liked it," Matt said. He looked up quickly and smiled at Olivia and Thomas.

Olivia's stomach was in knots and had been since they'd gotten the invitation from Nike to pitch their new energy bar business. She had led the pitch and couldn't have been happier with their strategic direction and creative. The presentation seemed to have gone perfectly. "Seemed" being the operative word.

"I see," Matt said, and Olivia snapped out of her worry to look at him. His voice had changed. Olivia knew that voice too well, the you-liked-our-pitch-but-you're-not-going-to-award-us-the-business voice. "Can you tell me what it was that gave you reservations?" Matt was drawing circles with his pen on the pad in front of him, his mouth in a half smile. That mouth.

"Damn it!" Thomas shouted. "I knew it."

Matt looked up, gave Thomas an angry look, and put out his right hand in a calm-the-fuck-down gesture.

"I see. Well, thank you for your time, Steve, and for the opportunity to pitch the business. If things don't work out with JWT, give us a call. I know we'd be able to make you happy."

Matt placed the handset down and put his face in his hands.

"Shit! We needed that business," Thomas said, banging his fist on the table.

Matt looked up at Thomas and didn't say a word. Then Matt gave Olivia a sympathetic look. Or was that a smile? She'd never been able to read his expressions accurately when he was angry.

"Let's meet back here in an hour. Be prepared to discuss all of your accounts and billings down to the dime. We need to figure out our next steps," Matt said. He stood up and left the conference room, letting the door slam behind him.

"Jesus, Olivia, I told you to go with the first creative Pablo came up with."

"That was the wrong creative, and you know it, Thomas. The second creative was much stronger," Olivia said, and stood up, grabbing her phone and her latte. Walking toward the door, she stopped and looked back at Thomas, who was picking spinach out of his teeth. "You could say, 'Nice work,

Olivia.' That would have been the smarter thing to do, because who knows where we'll all end up? It's pretty likely you'll be begging me for a job one day." She threw open the door and walked toward her office.

Olivia slammed her office door behind her. She woke up her computer and saw 117 emails waiting, their bold font an aggressive affront. She turned up the music on her computer, the Coldplay she'd been listening to when she got into the office that morning, early. She hadn't been able to sleep.

"Damn it!" she yelled to the ceiling. But that was the only indulgence she allowed herself. She immediately began compiling a document with all her accounts and billings in preparation for the meeting with Matt, who decided at that very moment to make an appearance.

He never knocked.

"Sorry, Liv," Matt said when he opened the door. He stood in the doorway, the morning sun from the window behind Olivia shining into his eyes and making them glow. He was about six feet tall and had *the look*. The look shared by successful men up and down glorious Manhattan island: investment bankers, mergers and acquisitions attorneys, media executives. The look that said, shouted, really: *I'm confident. I'm successful. And I would be lying if I pretended I had no idea I could have any woman I wanted.*

"Thanks, Matt. This isn't the first time I've lost a piece of business, and it probably won't be the last."

"True. But it still stings. You nailed that pitch. Best I've seen you do," he said, walking toward the chairs across from

Olivia's desk. "JWT? How could they have chosen JWT? They're so . . . corporate." The word made his mouth look like it had bitten hard into a lemon.

"Don't know. I really thought I was going to pull it off for us. Sorry about that."

"Stop that, Liv," Matt said, reaching for her hand. She didn't pull it away.

"Fine, but those billings were the only way to make up for losing the Green Goddess account. I don't blame her, but I still wish Katherine Whitney hadn't left the company. That awful woman who replaced her, Maggie, never gave us a fair chance."

"Hopefully we'll be okay."

"Do the numbers work out at all?" Olivia asked with a worried expression, finally pulling her hand back.

"I'm not sure. I was working on that all night. Not"—he gave a kind smile—"that I wasn't confident in you and thought we wouldn't win the business, but just in case."

"Turned out to be a prudent exercise."

"I didn't have all the updated billings with me last night, so once you and Thomas and I meet, I'll be able to see where we stand."

"I'm trying not to be pessimistic," Olivia said, pressing the palms of her hands to her forehead.

"Ha!" Matt said, laughing at her.

Olivia managed a smile. "I know, I know. I'm terrible at not being pessimistic. But I know if the numbers don't square, you're going to have to let Thomas or me go."

"Liv, there are loads of things we can do to cut costs before I would have to let you or Thomas go," Matt said, raising his left eyebrow. Always his left.

Olivia had been concerned that Thomas's and her salaries were too high. She didn't think Matt could justify keeping them both with so little business in the agency. He had been bleeding the reserves dry keeping things afloat, hoping they'd win this account. She had been so worried about this eventuality. She hadn't expected them to lose, but now that they had, Olivia was nervous in a way that felt foreign to her. Extreme, as if she were visiting another planet and not one thing, the color of the sky, the feel of the earth, the taste of the air, was familiar.

"You know I'll work harder for you than Thomas ever will. I still can't understand why you asked him to join the agency, Matt. Really. Possibly the worst decision ever."

"Okay, okay, old news, Liv. I'm going. But I'll see you in the conference room in"—he looked at the Rolex—"fifteen minutes."

"Remember when you took that guy home and he decided he didn't like you, so he stole all of your small kitchen appliances when he snuck out of your apartment early the next morning?" Olivia asked. She was on her phone, walking home from work. All she wanted was to take a bath, eat the whole box of frozen corn dogs in her freezer, and get into bed with a glass of wine and her remote.

"Um, yes," James said on the other end of the line.

"It was worse than that."

"Oh, honey. I'm sorry. Where are you? Meet me for a drink."

"I'm spent. I'm going home."

"No, you're not. Meet me at Barcanto's."

"You mean that pretty little bar I'm standing directly in front of right now?" Olivia smiled to herself. She could use a bit of James right now.

"Be there in a flash. Tell Ian to make my mojito strong."

"Olivia, gorgeous, sit down," the bartender, Ian, said as soon as he saw her. She and James came to Barcanto's frequently, and she came on her own sometimes on her way home from work when she wanted to have a glass of wine and unwind. She'd also come a few times with Matt.

"Hi, Ian," Olivia said, giving him a kiss as he leaned over the bar.

"What can I get you?"

"Pinot Grigio."

"You got it," Ian said, taking a wineglass and wiping the rim with his towel.

"And James will have a mojito. A very strong mojito, he said," Olivia said, smiling.

"Oh, he will, will he? That tease." Ian and James had dated for a year or two back in the day when James was comfortable letting his boyfriends treat him kindly.

Olivia answered emails while she waited for James. She noticed a trio of businessmen come in and sit at a four-top in the back corner. One of the men smiled at her as he passed. Olivia smiled back and took a sip of her wine.

"Well, look what the cat dragged in," Ian said, and Olivia looked up.

"Hello, Ian," James said. "And hello, Olivia," he said, planting a kiss on her cheek.

The three chatted and laughed about work, James's new guy, and their mutual friends. Olivia and James decided to order dinner at the bar. Lamb chops and sautéed spinach for Olivia. A Barcanto burger and fries for James. When Ian handed over a second glass of wine to Olivia, she protested and said she was stopping at one.

"Compliments of the gentleman," Ian said, winking at Olivia and directing her gaze to the table in the back of the restaurant.

The man Olivia had noticed when he walked in lifted his glass in the air and smiled. She did the same.

"Are you still dating that gorgeous boss of yours?" Ian asked Olivia.

"Matthew Osborne?" James said in a dramatic voice, making a sweeping motion with his hand and ending it by smoothing over his hair. Or lack thereof. James was completely bald, but he did it for effect.

"Matthew Osborne of the perfectly coiffed hair and glinting azure eyes," Ian said, a dreamy look in his eyes.

"Come on, guys. He's not my boyfriend. Never was and never will be."

"Well," James said. "Forgive me, dear friends, but a certain blond investment banker is waiting for me right now in his apartment, so I'm going to go, even if he is most likely going to take advantage of me and break my heart."

James took out his wallet and handed Ian a hundred-dollar bill. "That should cover Olivia and me, Ian. Whatever's left, use it to pay a barber to shave off that awful goatee. It's so . . . *expected*. And if there is nothing left, well, then remind me next time, and I'll make up for it."

Ian smiled and they gave each other a kiss over the bar. James gave Olivia a hug and he was off.

Olivia sat for a minute and finished the second glass of wine as the businessmen walked by the bar toward the door.

"Thank you for the wine," Olivia said to the one who had bought it for her. He was tall, with salt-and-pepper hair and green eyes. Late forties. Olivia immediately looked down at his ring finger. Bare.

"I hope you enjoyed it. I almost sent you a glass of my favorite Pinot Noir, but I saw you were drinking white. I didn't want to impose my tastes on you."

"How refreshing," Olivia said. "A man who doesn't want to turn a woman into what he wants her to be, but rather lets her be who she is. Quite revolutionary."

The man stared at Olivia for a moment. Without a word, he joined his friends who were waiting for him at the front of the restaurant. Olivia turned to see. He shook hands with them and came back to where she was.

"They have to be on the next train back to Westchester. But I don't. So will you let me buy you another glass of wine?"

"That's so nice of you, but I really have to be getting home."

"If I told you I just had the most boring dinner of my life and I could use ten minutes of pleasant conversation, would you reconsider?"

Olivia was weakening. The wine was smoothing lines and lessening urgencies.

"How do you know my conversation would be pleasant? I've had a shitty day."

He laughed. "See what you did there? I don't even know your name and you've already made me laugh."

"Olivia."

"Jack."

"Nice to meet you, Jack."

"So will you stay for another glass?"

"Sure," she said, deciding it couldn't hurt to flirt for a bit with a man who she'd most likely never see again. She'd been working so hard lately that her dating life had been nonexistent. And however much she objected, James told her that her mostly one-sided infatuation with Matt did not, thank you, count as a dating life.

"So, this shitty day, tell me about it."

"I thought you were in need of pleasant conversation."

"I was. But vent away, Olivia. I'm all ears."

"Okay, fine," she said, sinking into her seat and enjoying the smile Jack was directing her way. The third glass of wine was going down a little too easily, and Olivia placed the glass on the bar to slow down her rate of consumption. "First tell me: What do you do, Jack?"

"I'm in transportation."

Olivia loved when men said they were "in" and then named an entire industry. How much vaguer could they be? Like one of the first guys she dated when she moved to New York. "I'm in hospitality," he had said. It had sounded glamorous to Olivia until she found out he refilled the mini bars at the Plaza.

"Would you like to be more specific?" Olivia asked.

"Not really. It's pretty boring." Jack smiled. "And what do you do? Let me guess: you're in fashion."

Olivia tightened her smile and turned her head. "No," she said. "Why was that your first guess?"

"My bad. I hope that didn't offend you in any way. You just, I guess, look quite fashionable."

"Thank you, but no. I'm in advertising. I'm an account director at a firm called The Osborne Agency."

Luckily the bar had gotten crowded and Ian was busy, so Olivia didn't feel self-conscious that he was listening to their conversation. But she did notice out of the corner of her eye that he had refilled her wineglass.

"What led you into advertising?" Jack asked. "Don Draper?"

"You mean Peggy Olson? Actually, I've always been creative, and for some very strange reason, as a little girl, I used to make up ads. I created my own magazines in my bedroom out of construction paper. I wrote a few articles, but there were mostly ads," Olivia said.

"You started young."

"I've worked very hard to get where I am."

"Where did you grow up?"

"In a little coal town in Pennsylvania, just outside of nowhere."

"But you seem to fit in quite nicely in the big city."

"Smoke and mirrors, Jack. Smoke and mirrors," Olivia said, taking a sip of her wine.

"And how is the advertising industry treating you?"

"Well, not the best day to ask," Olivia said with a sarcastic smile.

"That bad?"

"Worse. We'd been pitching a piece of new business and we lost it. It was my presentation, and it didn't go nearly as well as we had all thought. It was a big blow to the agency, and I feel totally responsible."

Olivia sat with Jack for the next hour. They ordered dessert and, when he offered her another glass of wine, she asked for club soda instead.

"You know, I don't usually talk about myself as much as I did tonight. I'm also usually a lot more restrained about accepting wine from strangers. I can't believe I told you all that about my life and career." Olivia was starting to feel exceptionally tired and was angry at herself that she'd been so open.

"What if I told you I have a very bad memory and I've already forgotten everything you said?" Jack asked.

"I would say that I appreciate that very much," Olivia said. "But I also think it's time for me to go home. I need to get some sleep."

"Can I put you in a cab?"

"No, thanks. I'm nearby. I can walk."

"I'm happy to walk you home."

"That's okay. I'm just around the corner. I'll be fine. It was nice meeting you, Jack."

"You as well, Olivia. Keep up the good work. I think you're going to be a tremendous success."

"Thanks," Olivia said, a little confused by Jack's suddenly avuncular behavior. She had found him attractive and was thinking it might be nice to see him again. And not one to shy away from giving a man her card and suggesting he call, Olivia also knew that in a situation like this, if the man didn't make some sort of overture, he probably wasn't interested.

Not the first time and probably won't be the last, Olivia thought, realizing the day was taking on a rather depressing theme.

Jack gave her a kiss on the cheek, told her the pleasantness factor of their conversation had exceeded his expectations, and said good night.

Olivia shouldn't have been so convinced she'd never hear from Jack again.

CHAPTER 3

CHARLOTTE
THURSDAY, MARCH 3, 1949

Dear Miss Friedman,

We are pleased to inform you that you
have been selected as a finalist for Miss
Subways. Please report to the John Robert
Powers Modeling Agency at 247 Park Avenue,
New York City, on Monday, March 7, at 1:00
P.M. sharp for your interview. We are
unable to reschedule this appointment.

Sincerely yours,

Diana Fontaine
Director of Model Services
John Robert Powers Modeling Agency

Charlotte had forgotten all about Sam's cockamamie
idea to enter her into the Miss Subways contest. Thinking
back now on that night a group of them had been out for

ice cream, she remembered it was actually Martin who had raised the flag.

"Say, what do you think of submitting Charlotte's photograph for Miss Subways?" he had said to Sam and Charlotte while the others in their group heatedly debated the Dodgers' prospects for the upcoming season.

"You're a regular Jack Benny!" Charlotte said. "I could never be chosen for Miss Subways."

"Well, sure you could, Charlotte," Sam said. "You're just as pretty—scratch that—*prettier* than any of the girls I've seen on those posters."

"My agency runs the whole program and my boss told me that they're always looking for pretty girls. Let me enter you, Charlotte," Martin said. "What's the worst thing that could happen?"

"Whatever you say, Martin. As long as you get me an interview at your agency."

"You can be sure of that, Charlotte. J. Walter Thompson would be lucky to have a girl like you in the typing pool."

Let's just see what happens, they had said to her. Live a little, Charlotte. "Why not?" she had ultimately told them, trying, though it wasn't easy, to be game and easygoing. Charlotte had been 99 percent certain that nothing would ever result from them entering her besides a curtly worded letter thanking her for her interest and sending her on her pleasant good-luck-ever-being-a-model way. Make that 100 percent.

But, she now realized, she was wrong. Something *had* come of it. Charlotte laughed aloud at the cruel irony. Two letters in one day. The first denying her entrée into the industry she so desperately wanted to be part of. The second inviting her to participate in one she couldn't care less about.

How she wished their contents had been switched. *Yes, Miss Friedman, we'd love for you to type our memos and fetch our coffee. We're terribly sorry, Miss Friedman, you're not lovely enough to be featured in our subway beauty pageant.*

Charlotte crumpled the letter at the inanity of it all.

"Who was it from, Charlotte?" her mother called.

Charlotte returned to the kitchen and threw the balled-up letter into the garbage. "Miss Subways. Sam's friend entered me. And they chose me as a finalist."

"How about that?" Mrs. Friedman met Charlotte's eyes for the first time that day.

"It's ridiculous," Charlotte said, waving her hand dismissively.

"Your father would never allow it."

"Which is fine, because I would never do it. I have no time for silly things like Miss Subways. Speaking of having no time, I'm going to JoJo's to study and then I'm meeting Sam for dinner."

"Miss Subways! That's marvelous, Charlotte!" JoJo said when Charlotte told her. The girls were sitting on JoJo's bed, their econ books and notes strewn across JoJo's matelassé.

"Did you pinch a shot of your father's whiskey again?"

"I'm serious. Miss Subways is a big deal."

"Maybe. For silly girls who have nothing better to do than fuss over their looks."

"You do realize that you can be smart and serious and still fuss over your looks. It's not a crime in this country."

"I do realize that, but thank you for pointing it out,"

Charlotte said sarcastically, folding her legs under her and opening her textbook.

"Why wouldn't you give it a go, Charlotte? Life is all about collecting experiences, and this seems like a pretty exciting one. I'd do it in a second if someone ever gave me the chance."

"I'll tell you the time and place. You can go in my stead. How will they know you're not Charlotte Friedman reporting for duty? Model duty." Charlotte giggled.

"Have you looked at me lately?" JoJo asked, tilting her head.

"I have. I look at you all the time, and each and every time I do, I see a beautiful young woman with dazzling chestnut-brown hair, the cutest nose this side of the East River, and hazel eyes that burn with a zest for life and the confidence to take on the world."

"That was so nice," JoJo whimpered, pretending to wipe a tear from her eye.

Charlotte threw a pillow at her head and laughed.

"Opportunities come when you least expect them, Charlotte."

"Are you trying to say that there's an opportunity for me in modeling, and I just have to report to John Robert Powers on Monday, where my true destiny will be revealed?" Charlotte held out her hands, pretending to look into a crystal ball.

"Would that be the worst thing?" JoJo asked, lifting her left brow.

"Perhaps."

"I hope you know I say this out of love, but it's not like you have job opportunities knocking down your front door. I know tons of girls, including myself, who would do anything to be Miss Subways."

Charlotte sat against the headboard and thought for a moment about what JoJo was telling her. "How nice for them," she said. "It's time to study."

Sam was waiting at their regular corner table in the back of Thompson's Drugstore and he waved Charlotte over. Immediately her shoulders softened and a smile came to her face.

Sweet, stable, reliable Sam. Tall, reddish-haired, sparkling blue-eyed Sam. The pair were set up by a mutual friend during Charlotte's freshman year of college, when Sam was home from law school over winter break. That was nearly four years ago, and they'd been going together ever since. Sam worked at Linden & Linden in Midtown. His hours were decidedly horrendous, required for future partners of important Manhattan law firms. But trying for courting. And though Charlotte knew Sam wished he had more time for their relationship, wished that his face didn't look so gray due to lack of sunlight and sleep, she also knew that his career was important to him and she found that a redeeming quality. One on a list of many.

"Darling," he said as he rose to give her a kiss on the cheek. He pulled out her chair and she plopped down. Drained. Sighing. "What is it, Charlotte?" Sam asked.

"I heard from J. Walter Thompson."

"And?" Sam asked expectantly.

"They don't want me either. Nobody wants me, Sam."

"Oh, Charlotte, honey. I'm so sorry. And you know that's

not true. *I* want you. In fact, I wish you'd reconsider my proposal," Sam said.

"Sam, you know I don't want to get married yet. I have so many things I want to do. Besides, how would that change anything?"

"We can elope. The sooner the better. And then you'd feel less of an urgency to start a job right away because I'd have you out of your parents' house."

"Sam," Charlotte said, tilting her head.

"What's so awful about marrying a guy like me, anyway?" Sam asked as he took a sip of his Coke.

"We've been through this a million times. There's not one itty-bitty, tiny, little thing wrong with marrying a guy like you. In fact, there are a trillion things right with marrying a guy like you, and someday it will happen. Just not now. I'm only twenty-one. There's time."

"But I'm twenty-six. I think the older partners think there's something wrong with me that I'm not married, and when it's time for me to be up for partner, I don't want them to overlook me because they think I'm not a family man."

"Well, you tell those hoity-toity partners that your future wife is making a name for herself. They'll put you right at the top of that partners list knowing you snagged a girl who had something going for her." Charlotte lifted her chin and smirked.

"Okay, okay, Miss Confident. I'll call a meeting first thing Monday morning to announce to all who will listen that I have the smartest, most ambitious girl in all of New York City, and that if they don't make a partner of me, I'll open my own firm and sue 'em all."

"Now that's more like it," Charlotte said, and squeezed

Sam's hand. "But what will they think when you're not a family man in the traditional sense of the word?"

"Sorry about that, Charlotte. I wasn't thinking."

"It's okay. I guess I've kind of gotten used to it. But I still can't believe you'd be okay with it."

"My first choice is you. If we can't have children together, then that'll just be how it has to be. Or we can adopt. Either way, I love you, Charlotte. You know that. Babies or not."

"I love you too. And thanks for saying that." They stared into each other's eyes. Perry Como swooning, seemingly just for them, in the background.

Charlotte did want to marry Sam. Just not yet. She had told him that the first time he had proposed during the summer after Charlotte's freshman year of college. There was no ring, of course; she was only eighteen. Not like girls at eighteen didn't get rings from their boyfriends. But Sam told Charlotte he knew she had plans. He told her he wanted to make sure she knew he was serious about her. That he had his own plans and they included her. He had proposed a few times since, always sincerely but never entirely seriously because indeed there was no ring. Charlotte knew that when a man was truly serious about proposing, there was a ring. And a bent knee. And that's what she would have. With Sam. Someday, when the timing was absolutely right.

"What am I going to do about a job?"

"J. Walter Thompson isn't the only game in town. Why don't you send letters to some of the other concerns?"

"I've thought of that. I even called J. Walter Thompson and told them they were making a grave mistake."

Sam smiled, reaching for Charlotte's hands over the table and enclosing them in his own. "You're such a go-getter."

"That's what the JWT man said. But look how far that go-getting got me."

"Something will turn up. Any one of these agencies would be lucky to have a girl like you working at it."

"You think? Why?" Charlotte asked coyly.

Sam saw the bait clearly and took it anyway. "Well, you're the most beautiful girl in all of New York City, and you know how those account men like to stock their lakes with the pretty ones. You're the smartest girl I know. And I've seen you type. Boy, do those fingers dance."

Charlotte smiled dejectedly.

The waiter delivered their food, the grilled cheese glistening and the perfect shade of golden brown that Charlotte liked.

"When is your graduation ceremony?" Sam asked.

"June twenty-second."

"You have three months to find something. That's plenty of time, Charlotte."

Charlotte took a bite of her sandwich and, a thought occurring to her, looked up at Sam. "What would you think if I became a model?"

"A model?" Sam exclaimed. "I'd support you in anything you chose to do, but I never knew you were interested in modeling."

"Remember the night Martin suggested entering me into Miss Subways? I got a letter today saying I'm a finalist."

Sam slammed his Coke down on the table harder than he had intended. Enough so that the couples nearby broke their necks looking. "That's terrific!"

"You really think so?" Charlotte couldn't imagine Sam would take Miss Subways seriously.

"Sure I do."

"JoJo thought so too, but I don't know. It seems so 'look at me, look at me.' And it certainly promotes celebrating a girl's looks instead of her talents."

"I don't think you need to dissect it so conscientiously. Seems like the girls in those pictures are having a lot of fun. Go for it, Charlotte. I'd love to tell the guys at work that my girl is Miss Subways."

Charlotte laughed and leaned over to give Sam a kiss. She appreciated his enthusiasm, but something about it still didn't feel right.

In bed that night, Charlotte couldn't stop thinking about what Sam and JoJo had said. Why wouldn't she go to John Robert Powers? Just for the experience, at least. If life, as JoJo claimed, was all about collecting experiences, then she didn't yet have a life worth bragging about, her most exciting experience to date having been a full day at the 1939 New York World's Fair when she was eleven.

At the time, and for several years after, Charlotte thought that nothing would ever compare to the terrifying parachute jump, the synchronized swimming show (that Johnny Weissmuller!), and especially those darling monkeys. She'd thought there would never be anything in life more thrilling.

She and Harry had talked about that day for years. And each time, their memories made the shiny shinier. Charlotte was even more terrified of the parachute jump, and Harry, of course, was even braver. Harry was even more certain he would grow taller and swim faster than Johnny Weissmuller. (Perhaps, Charlotte would say, but she'd insist he'd never be as handsome.) And Charlotte was even more smitten with Monkey Mountain and its hundreds of inhabitants. They'd spent hours re-creating the spectacles in their living room on cold winter days, forcing their parents to sit in the audience. Their father, without fail, would leave their show before it was over.

But memories fade. And those, despite their impact, had faded like the photo of her brother in its frame on the mantel. Perhaps it was time for a new experience.

Charlotte tiptoed down the stairs and felt her way into the dark kitchen. Opening the garbage can, she sifted through the scraps and eventually found what she was looking for. Smoothing out the paper, which luckily had somehow been protected from the dregs of dinner, Charlotte reread its contents. She still had a few days to make her decision, and figured she'd sleep on it. But after scrutinizing the letter more carefully, with its self-important tone and affected presentation—undoubtedly an extension of the John Robert Powers models themselves, Powers Girls, as they were pretentiously called—she scoffed and tossed it back where it belonged.

CHAPTER 4

OLIVIA
FRIDAY, MARCH 2, 2018

"What the hell did you say to him?" Matt asked Olivia as she ginger-stepped into the conference room the next morning.

Every Friday morning at nine, the three of them had a state-of-the-agency sort of whirl: Olivia; Matt, the founder and CEO of The Osborne Agency; and Thomas Cameron, the other account director, whom Matt had brought along with them from Young & Rubicam at the eleventh hour.

"What the hell did I say to who?" Olivia asked defensively, taking off her scarf and coat but leaving her sunglasses on. The lights in the conference room were so bright, she thought, so very, very bright.

"To whom," Thomas corrected her.

"Shut the fuck up, Thomas," Olivia said, giving him a nasty look. Olivia dialed her assistant on the conference call phone in the middle of the table. "Chloe, a trough of black coffee, please."

"Done," came Chloe's voice from the speaker.

"John Haldon," Matt said, looking happier than she'd seen him look in quite a long time.

"I don't know who that is, and I also don't know why you have to talk so loudly," Olivia said, putting her head down on the table and covering her ears with her hands.

"John Haldon is the chief marketing officer of the MTA," Matt said.

"He's great. I've known him for years," Thomas added, clearly trying to prove, yet again, his worthiness to Matt. "Jack and I go way back."

Olivia's head shot up. "Ow," she said, rubbing the back of her neck. "Did you say Jack?"

"I did," Thomas said. "Is it fair to say you've come to work today in a state incapable of actually, um, working?"

"Oh please, Thomas. Put your flappy tongue back in its slimy holster and leave me the hell alone. The last time I came to work with a hangover was when you were still a brown-nosed assistant account exec at Y&R, texting your mommy every time you had dirty laundry. So give me a break. I needed to blow off some steam."

"And it seems, if the phone call I received this morning is any indication, that you blew that steam in precisely the right direction," Matt said.

Chloe knocked on the door and walked in. She placed an urn full of coffee in front of Olivia, along with a tall paper cup, two sugars, and three Advil. "This is the biggest vessel I could find."

"Perfect, thank you," Olivia said, smiling at Chloe. Olivia took a sip of the coffee and sighed. "I did meet a Jack last night. He said he was in transportation."

"Jack in transportation," said Matt, "is none other than John Haldon from the Metropolitan Transportation Authority. He called me this morning and told me he was quite charmed by one of my account directors last night. Sorry, Thomas, but I didn't for a second think it was you."

Olivia threw a saccharine smile at Thomas.

"He invited us," Matt continued, "to pitch the MTA business, which happens to be up for review."

"You've got to be kidding!" Olivia stood up, her mouth wide-open.

"No, ma'am," Matt said.

"That's amazing news!" Olivia said. "I had no idea he worked at the MTA. Come to think of it, we didn't really talk much about him. I kind of dominated the conversation."

"Shocking," Thomas said, rolling his eyes.

"Anyway, we're coming in late. He said other agencies have six weeks on us. So we need to mobilize fast."

"Did you sleep with him?" Thomas asked, looking smugly at Olivia.

"Thomas, please," Matt said.

"Really, Thomas. It's only nine o'clock. I don't think you've ever revealed your misogyny so early in the morning before. But sure. Yes. How could I have relied solely on my intellect and professional experience to convince an advertiser to include our agency in his pitch lineup? Certainly only my womanly wiles would be able to do that." Olivia turned back to Matt. "You were saying."

"The pitch is in two weeks. They're looking for a new agency of record, but their immediate need, the one they want us to address, is a revamp of their on-subway advertising. A new CEO just started and he's chopping heads."

"On it. I'll put together a starting brief, and I'll spend the weekend brainstorming. Let's meet at eight o'clock on Monday, and I'll tell you what I have," Olivia said to Matt.

"Good plan," Matt said.

Olivia smirked at Thomas, stood up, and walked to her office. The renewed sense of purpose energized Olivia, and she was thankful for the adrenaline rush. It was her resting state. Olivia only felt like herself, the self that was authentic, when the pressure was turned up all the way to the point that would make most people explode.

"Can you hold that?" Olivia called to the person in the elevator as she entered her apartment building.

A hand reached out. The doors jerked and slid back open.

"Thanks," Olivia said.

"Sure thing."

Olivia went to press eleven but noticed it was already lit. She glanced at the guy standing next to her but didn't recognize him as one of her neighbors. She looked at her phone.

"Olivia, right?" the man asked.

"Yes, do I know you?" Olivia asked, puzzled.

"Ben. My grandma lives next door to you," he said, nodding. His hands were in his pockets, and he was rocking forward and backward. His energy, both precise and unassuming, didn't take up much space.

"That's right," Olivia said, only partially lying. "I haven't seen you in a really long time."

"I've been away. Working."

The elevator stopped at eleven. Ben held the door and Olivia walked out. She turned right and Ben followed a couple of steps behind. He knocked on 11D, while Olivia turned the key for 11E.

"I'm back now, clearly, so I guess I'll be seeing you around," Ben said.

"Okay," Olivia said, smiling politely as she walked into her apartment.

Olivia kicked off her shoes and dumped her mail onto the cluttered hall table. She hung up her coat and dropped her work bag onto the floor. After filling a glass with white wine, Olivia plopped down on the couch and put her feet up. The exhausting week had begun to loosen its grip.

A couple of years ago, when Matt had approached Olivia about leaving Y&R with him to start a boutique agency, she was all in, despite the embarrassing cliché of it all. She had begun her career at Y&R as an assistant account executive right out of college (no sketchy hostels and overstuffed backpacks in Europe for Olivia; she had four years of crushing student debt to pay back), and Matt had been her first boss.

They had worked together for seven or eight years, and Olivia admired and respected him. Fed up with all the acquisitions and corporate headaches at Y&R, Matt burned to build an agency that would elevate the agency-client relationship and produce a unique type of creative. Not that any of that was unusual for a start-up in their industry, but Olivia trusted Matt and didn't think twice about going all Jerry Maguire with him when he asked.

Together they hired Pablo, an outside-the-lines creative director in San Francisco, and the three of them approached agency-building with the fervor of an eight-year-old with a new box of Legos.

As they started to accrue clients, Matt needed another body on accounts. And even though Olivia presented a determined display of red flags, Matt hired Thomas, who they had worked with at Y&R. He was an unmitigated asshole, but he was also the most effective account executive they knew.

Olivia spent the weekend poring over everything the MTA had sent: descriptions of their recent campaigns, memos outlining their marketing goals, spreadsheets with ridership data, and a timetable for the pitch. Olivia had a paltry two weeks to come up with her strategy, the creative, and a coup de grace presentation.

By the end of the weekend, Olivia had torn through massive amounts of takeout, wine, and coffee. As well as a healthy measure of self-doubt, frustration, and long stretches of inability to process. Ultimately, she renewed her confidence through half-assed meditation and a quick glance at some lousy motivational Instagram feeds stuffed with stylized quotations set against backgrounds of skinny girls jumping off cliffs. By Sunday night, she felt supremely proud of what she'd accomplished. With that start, she'd be able to go into the office the next day and start working closely with Pablo and Priya, the only Osborne Agency account exec Olivia would save in a hot New York City flood, to decide on their strategic direction. But she already had one idea that lit her up.

James had been calling all weekend to get together, but Olivia hadn't wanted to quell her momentum. They decided on an early dinner Sunday night at an Italian place between Olivia's apartment and James's place in the Meatpacking District.

Once they had ordered, James told Olivia all about his weekend with the cheeky blond investment banker who had an adorable name: Chase. It had gone swimmingly (James's word), and James reported he was well on his way to having his heart broken.

Olivia told James about her ideas for the pitch, which James absolutely loved. And then she told him about her most recent email from Jenna, who had been the third in their threesome in college.

"She and Chris are in some small village in Spain, living it up, visiting churches and fairs and naval bases."

"Tough life, that one," James said, taking a sip of his Pellegrino.

"I know. But thank God she still needs me to take care of her apartment. If it weren't for that, I'd be living in a dank basement studio with an atrocious commute."

"I know this is sensitive, Liv, but do you have any savings?"

Olivia shook her head. "I'm still paying off my student loans and my mom's hospital bills, so I'm pretty much broke."

"You did the right thing."

"I know that in my heart, but on some level I feel like I'm just enabling my father."

"Because she went back to him?"

"I've read everything about women who are abused. I get it. I know what she tells herself to allow her to go back. But as I'm getting older, I get less and less tolerant of her behavior. I feel like I've done everything to help her. I've invited her to live with me. I've told her about support groups. I've even tried to physically remove her, but she goes back. While she was in the hospital this time, I told her that if it happens again and she goes back, I'm not helping her anymore. And now it's a waiting game to see what happens next. But at some point I have to be an adult and live my own life, and that includes me getting to decide that just because they're my parents, it doesn't mean I have to continue to act like their child."

"Well said, Liv."

"That's a lot of Google therapy talking."

"I get it. You've done so much, but you have to stop feeling like any of this is your responsibility."

"I hear what you're saying, but it's hard. This is my family, after all. I may sound strong, but the truth is, when I let myself think about it, which I try not to do, it wrecks me."

"I'm so sorry."

Olivia smiled sadly and took a sip of her wine.

"I hope I'm not being insensitive by changing the subject, but I think you would feel a lot better about your life in general and it would be a good distraction if you would go on some dates."

"Right, because I have so much time and bandwidth to develop a healthy relationship right now."

"You have to make time."

"I know. I actually had thought there might have been something with that guy from Barcanto's. Little did I know at the time that the something could save my job."

"I'm not sure which is more important to save right now: your job or your woman card. You know you have to have sex once in a while to get that thing renewed."

Olivia laughed. "It hasn't been that long. But I'm a career woman, James. And I'm only thirty-one. I can do the husband and baby thing later on. Plus, I need to make my own money. I don't ever want to depend on anyone else financially. So now that, thanks to my disgrace of a father, I'm back to almost square one with my savings, I really have to focus on work."

"Your parents really did a number on you," James said with a sad expression.

"Perhaps. Or perhaps they did me the biggest favor of all.

Because while our dear Jenna is traipsing through Europe on her daddy's dime, I'm learning resilience and grit and all those other things those psychologists write about on the *HuffPost*. I can take care of myself, and no one can take that away from me."

"Except Jenna," James said. And then: "Sorry, that was awful. That just slipped out. Didn't mean it." He held his hands out in surrender and made a sad face.

"No, it's true. You're right. I am at the mercy of Jenna's travel plans. Which is why I have to win this MTA account. And pathetic Thomas has to sit on the sidelines and watch it all happen."

CHAPTER 5

CHARLOTTE
MONDAY, MARCH 7, 1949

Charlotte pushed open the large glass door, its height and heft trumpeting its importance (or at least ensuring its regard as such), and approached the reception desk, which was staffed by three exquisitely cheekboned young women: a bevy of rouged birds answering telephones. The middle creature made eye contact. "Welcome to John Robert Powers. How can I help you?"

Charlotte held her letter aloft, her gilded ticket to the ball. "I'm a Miss Subways finalist?" she asked more than said, her nerves threatening to overtake the calm she had so carefully, along with a full palette of makeup, arranged on her face.

On Friday night, after Charlotte had mercilessly rerelegated Miss Diana Fontaine's ridiculous letter to the garbage, she put herself to sleep ransacking the backcountry of her brain for memories from the World's Fair: the feeling that she was finally someone, the hubbub of the crowd, the cloying stench of the monkeys, the sundry bits and bats that hung like frayed tassels from the edges of her memory. But she could not recall much. The details, which had once been so vivid, had hazed over like a mirror too close to the bath.

Thus, early the next morning, decidedly and with the urgency of a late-summer hurricane barreling toward an out island, she salvaged Miss Diana Fontaine's gracious letter and brought it upstairs to her bedroom. After rereading it two, three, maybe sixteen times, Charlotte decided that a) depositing a new experience into her memory bank was cardinal and b) despite—perhaps because of?—her father's certain disapproval, she would see what this Miss Subways stir was all about.

Because Charlotte's wardrobe was judiciously suitable for her college courses, the occasional wedding, dates and groups at the soda shop, and not a turn of hem more, she owned neither top nor bottom chic enough to wear to the John Robert Powers Modeling Agency on Park Avenue. Eventually, due more to lack *of* than confidence *in* choices, Charlotte settled on a will-just-have-to-do navy skirt and striped blouse.

As soon as she'd found a seat on the subway into Manhattan that morning, she'd looked up. Next to the placard advertisements for cigarettes and life insurance, for shaving cream and shoes, there she was: Miss Subways.

"Meet Miss Subways Vivacious Thelma Porter," the poster announced in its distinctive clipped voice, next to a photograph of a smiling beauty. "Psychology student at Brooklyn College and part-time nurse receptionist in dentist's office. Is active in social welfare work and ardent church worker. Sings in a choral group and is a Gershwin devotee."

Though confused by her curiosity and fascination, Charlotte had stared at these posters since they began appearing

seven or eight years ago. In a way, the Miss Subways winners seemed so glamorous to her. So out of reach but also not,
since Miss Subways could be the girl sitting to her right or
across the aisle. Charlotte simultaneously looked up to and
down upon these girls who were brave enough to go for it and,
in at least part of Charlotte's mind, silly enough to bother.

Charlotte didn't know much about how the Miss Subways
process worked, only that each month there were rumored
to be hundreds, maybe thousands, of applicants and only
about ten finalists. What she did know was that, despite the
part of her that derided the whole enterprise, this was one of
the most exciting things she'd ever done.

"Your name, please?"

"Charlotte Friedman."

The exquisite bird checked her list, nodded, and pointed
Charlotte in the direction of a large, bustling waiting room.
There must have been thirty girls in there, many who looked
as frightened as children. Some were in the latest fashions,
holding portfolio books. Others were more confident, most
likely already Powers Girls. There were a few actual children,
too, all dressed up—not appearing the least bit frightened—
mothers tending, wiping imaginary smudges off their faces
with saliva-dampened thumbs.

Charlotte found an empty seat and sat down.

"Miss Subways?"

Charlotte turned to the girl on her right who had asked
the question. She was a petite blonde with cartoonishly large
blue eyes, and she stared intently at Charlotte, a huge smile
across her face. "I'm Bella London. Not my real name," she
whispered. "But I thought it sounded more cosmopolitan.
And you are?"

"Charlotte Friedman," Charlotte said, extending her hand to Bella's.

"Isn't this just the most exciting thing ever? My girlfriend Marge was a finalist three months ago. A Powers man plucked her off the street. Can you imagine? But she didn't win. She was devastated, poor girl. Says her life was ruined. I'm not so sure of that. It wasn't much to begin with. Where are you from, Charlotte Friedman?"

"Brooklyn."

"I'm a Bronx girl."

"Have you been waiting here long?" Charlotte asked.

"No, just a few minutes. I asked the girl up front and she said that when all the finalists arrive they're going to speak to us about the contest and what we should expect moving forward. I can hardly believe it!"

Charlotte smiled and looked around, trying to guess which of the other women were there for Miss Subways. The ones she decided were finalists all looked approximately her age and were beautiful. Charlotte couldn't fathom being considered among these girls. Though she never believed it, she'd always been told she was pretty. Not by her parents, of course, but by JoJo and her other friends. And, of course, by Sam. Always by Sam. Her green eyes were clear and bright, her porcelain skin had a rosiness of its own accord, and her light brown hair was glossy. She watched what she ate, so she was slim—she'd never had to reduce—but had curves in the right places.

Bella continued yapping in her ear and Charlotte nodded politely. But she wasn't listening. She was lost in her own thoughts about what becoming a Miss Subways could mean.

Just then, Charlotte noticed a striking brunette sashay by in a stylish, cinched-waist, emerald-green dress and a fashionably curled hairstyle. Charlotte straightened in her seat, assuming that was the woman from the modeling agency who would be giving them instructions.

But the brunette sat down across from Charlotte. She removed her gloves, opened her clutch, and took out lipstick and a compact. Charlotte couldn't stop staring. The woman (she was no girl compared to the others clutching their finalist letters) must have felt Charlotte's eyes, because she glanced up. Charlotte looked away quickly and turned to Bella, feigning interest in her interminable chatter.

"Ladies, hello, may I please have your attention?" It was the middle bird from earlier. "Will the Miss Subways finalists please come this way?"

Charlotte was surprised to see the brunette stand up. They walked down the corridor, heels clicking on the gleaming floor, and stopped in front of a closed door.

"Miss Fontaine will address you in our conference room." She opened a door, a portal to a new world, and directed them inside. A statuesque woman—she could have been Rita Hayworth's towheaded twin—wearing a stylish navy suit, a blond chignon, and an air of influence, stood just inside the entrance to the conference room and silently watched the finalists file in, nodding, assessing them like so many gussied-up horses at a farm auction.

Charlotte had never been in a room like this. It was massive, with a long gleaming wood table in the middle and upholstered white fabric chairs with wooden armrests all around. There was coffee and tea service on a wooden credenza lining the back wall, but neither the bird nor Rita's twin offered. Charlotte couldn't have swallowed a sip even if they had. Her stomach was raw.

"Please sit down," the woman said curtly, with a tight smile. Unfortunately, Bella was still to her right. Charlotte looked around to see where the procession had deposited the brunette: across the table and a couple of seats down.

"I'm Diana Fontaine," Rita's twin continued. "I'm the director of model services here at the John Robert Powers Modeling Agency. And part of my job is to oversee the Miss Subways program. Now first, congratulations are in order," she said, visibly softening. "This is a highly competitive contest, and you should all give yourselves a little clap for making it to this room." She clapped softly while the finalists looked around at each other uncomfortably until the brunette starting clapping. The rest joined in.

"You have been selected as finalists for Miss Subways July 1949. Today, I will tell you all about the Miss Subways program. If, after learning about it, you're interested in pursuing the opportunity further, you'll need to return to this office on Friday at ten o'clock to meet Mr. Powers. During that interview, he'll ask you questions—"

Charlotte felt, before she even saw, Bella's hand shoot up with the velocity of a rocket, startling Miss Fontaine.

"Yes?" Miss Fontaine looked at Bella sternly, seemingly affronted by the interruption.

"What kinds of questions?" Bella asked.

Charlotte heard a *hmph* and looked over to see the brunette rolling her eyes. Charlotte looked back at Bella, who had also heard it, and noticed Bella glaring at the brunette. My goodness.

"Questions about your school or your job," Miss Fontaine said. "Questions about your family and what becoming Miss

Subways will mean to you. Nothing to worry about. Just be yourself."

"Or not, in some people's case," the brunette said under her breath. Miss Fontaine didn't seem to hear. Or if she did, she agreed.

"I'm now going to give you a little background about the Miss Subways program."

"See, this is what I was telling you," Bella whispered in Charlotte's ear.

"Shhh," the brunette said, shooting daggers at Bella.

Bella straightened in her seat, raised her eyebrows haughtily at the brunette, and turned her attention back to Miss Fontaine.

"As I was saying. The J. Walter Thompson advertising agency developed Miss Subways for the New York Subways Advertising Company, which is responsible for selling advertising space in all the subways and elevated trains. The thought was that it would be a good morale boost for subway riders to see a pretty face on their commute each day, and the posters would draw attention to the neighboring ads. The campaign began in 1941, and some of you might know that our first Miss Subways was—"

"Mona Freeman," Bella piped in.

"That's right. Thank you, Miss . . . ?"

"Miss London. I'm Miss Bella London."

Miss Fontaine stopped to write something on a small pad. While she was looking down, the brunette whispered loudly in a mocking lilt, "*Bella London,* I'm sure."

Miss Fontaine looked up like a third-grade teacher to see who had said that but not before the brunette lowered her eyes demurely. Miss Fontaine glanced from girl to girl but only found Bella with a scowl on her face and the rest of the girls smiling innocently and attentively in Miss Fontaine's direction.

"Mona Freeman went on to Hollywood and is finding great success, having already appeared in over a dozen pictures, including *Isn't It Romantic?, Black Beauty,* and *Mother Wore Tights.* And many of our past Miss Subways have gone on to exciting careers as models." Miss Fontaine surveyed the room, as if expecting another interruption. Charlotte would have enjoyed stuffing a sock in Bella London's big cosmopolitan trap.

"Since John Robert Powers is New York's preeminent modeling agency, J. Walter Thompson hired us to manage the program. It's clear by taking a quick glance at all of you that we are looking for attractive girls. But it's also important that the winners have a New York story, which is why we don't just use professional models. As Mr. Powers likes to say, he's not looking for 'glamour-gal types or handpainted masterpieces.' He likes to connect with the Miss Subways on a personal level, to feel as if they could be any New Yorker out and about riding the train. That's why he takes the time to personally interview each finalist.

"If you're selected, your poster will be seen for an entire month by over five million riders each day. And as you know, it's a huge honor to be chosen. You'll be interviewed for magazine articles, and you'll most likely be recognized not only when you're riding the train, sitting under your own poster, perhaps, but also on the street. So we look for respectable girls, girls who will uphold the dignity of the contest."

Charlotte could have sworn Miss Fontaine looked directly at Bella.

"Now, that's all for today. How many of you plan to return on Friday?"

Bella's hand shot up, and each hand in the room followed. An energetic formation of unanimous enlistment.

"Capital. Thank you all for coming, and I look forward to seeing you on Friday."

"What's your problem?" Bella asked aggressively as soon as Miss Fontaine left the room. She was standing and looking directly at the brunette. The other girls stuck around for the show.

"I don't have a problem, dear," the brunette said condescendingly. "Why don't you lower your voice and start walking so we can all get on with our afternoons?"

"Well, I'm sure!" Bella said.

"Well, I'm sure your name isn't really Bella London," the brunette said.

"And what's your name, if I'm allowed to ask?" Bella asked.

"It's a free country. And my name, my real name that is, is Rose Grant."

"Can you believe her?" Bella said, turning to Charlotte.

Charlotte shrugged, not wanting to get involved. It wasn't her thing, had never been, to be confrontational. But still, when Bella turned away, Charlotte looked straight at Rose Grant, dazzling Rose Grant, and smiled. Rose winked and made Charlotte feel like a million bucks.

A few girls left but most stayed. After introducing themselves to each other, they talked about how excited they were, about what they would say to Mr. Powers, about how they were chosen. Charlotte learned that Mr. Powers himself had invited Elizabeth Connor, the girl who had been seated to her left, to be a finalist (skipping the general entry selection process entirely). Apparently he was quite taken with her when she checked his hat and coat at the Stork Club. And

Annabella Duarte, who had been directly across the table from Charlotte, had a cousin who worked in the mail room at John Robert Powers and he had entered her picture into the contest.

There was one Negro girl among the finalists: Angela Nelson. She was a classmate of Thelma Porter's. Thelma had been the first Negro Miss Subways, and Charlotte was pleased to see that the Miss Subways contest honored the diversity of the city by including all ethnicities, especially since even the Miss America pageant didn't have any Negros competing. At least, Charlotte thought, there had finally been a Jewish Miss America. Charlotte and all her friends had felt such pride when Bess Myerson won a few years ago. And Charlotte was quite aware that if she were to become a Miss Subways, she wouldn't be the first Jewish girl to do so.

Charlotte found herself getting caught up in the lovely fuss. And she was pleasantly surprised by the other girls. They weren't silly at all. They were students. And office workers. And nurses. Besides Rose, not one of the girls would've been mistaken for a high-fashion model. More than a few wouldn't have even turned a fellow's head if they'd just been ordering at the automat. Instead, as a whole, they could've been any group of coeds lolling on their sorority house porch, trading class notes, drinking limeade, and mulling over hemlines for that night's social.

A small clutching took hold of Charlotte's stomach, and she felt the heat of it radiate toward her fingers and toes. A tingling sensation that she could do this. That she would do this. That, in fact, she wanted to do this very much. Plus, Charlotte realized, she couldn't think of one good reason not to.

"Let's go, Charlotte," Bella called imperiously as the girls eventually began to file out.

"I'll see you later," Charlotte said lightly, waving goodbye. Then she whirled around and headed straight toward Rose.

CHAPTER 6

"Is he ready for me?" Olivia asked Matt's assistant, Layne, at eight on the dot.

"He told me to wait until you're both here and then send you in together," Layne said.

"Both? Who's the other person?" Olivia asked.

"Well, top of the morning, ladies. You're both looking radiant today. Olivia, did your girlfriend James choose that fetching blouse for you?" asked Thomas, Starbucks cup in hand.

"You're deplorable," Olivia said, scrunching her eyes at Thomas.

"He's ready for you both," Layne said.

Olivia purposefully pushed her way ahead of Thomas and walked into Matt's office.

"We had an eight o'clock," Olivia said to Matt, who had just stood up from his desk and was walking toward the couch and chairs on the opposite side of his enormous and sparsely decorated office.

"Good morning to you too, Olivia," Matt said, amused.

"Matt," Thomas said, nodding.

"Good morning," Matt said to Thomas. "I hope you both had nice weekends."

"Stellar weekend, actually," Thomas said. "Julia and I took the kids to our house in East Hampton. It was cold, but we had a lot of fun just playing indoors, if you know what I mean."

"Olivia?" Matt asked, turning to her.

"I was working on the MTA brief all weekend, which is what I thought we were meeting about, alone, this morning."

Olivia and Thomas were sitting as far apart as they could on the sleek black leather couch. Matt sat across from them in a matching black leather chair.

"That's what I wanted to talk to you about," Matt said. "Both of you."

Olivia looked at him with a puzzled expression and sat up straighter toward the edge of the sofa. Thomas took a sip of his coffee and leaned back into the cushion.

"We're going to have a little contest," Matt said, clapping his hands together.

"What kind of contest?" Olivia asked, tilting her head to the side and squinting her eyes.

"I'd like you both to come up with a strategic and creative direction for the MTA. The person whose approach I like best will give the presentation at the pitch, and if we win the business, that person will head the account." Matt sat back in his chair, a smirk on his face.

"No way, Matt. There's no way," Olivia stood up and stared directly down at Matt. "This is my pitch. I brought it in, and I'm going to bring it home." She was furious.

"I can understand how you would feel that way," Matt said, a bit of condescension in his voice. "But our ultimate goal, our shared goal, I'm sure you'll both agree, is to win this business. And if I have to up the stakes with a little healthy competition, then I think it's worth it."

"It actually makes a lot of sense, Matt," Thomas said, nodding.

"Shut up, Thomas!" Olivia shouted, and glared at him. "Actually, can you give Matt and me a minute?" She stared at Thomas, tapped her foot, and waited for him to get up.

"This is ridiculous and you know it," Olivia said once Thomas had left. She sat on the edge of the coffee table right in front of Matt. "We wouldn't even be in this pitch if it weren't for me. I'm fine with Thomas contributing some creative ideas, but I'm doing the presentation. Do not take this away from me."

"Liv, Liv, calm down," he said, enclosing both of her hands in his and lowering his voice. "I hear what you're saying, but you're not hearing what I'm saying. I looked at the numbers. I spent all weekend looking at those damn numbers, and unless we win this business or some other miracle happens by the end of this month, we're in big trouble. So I'm desperate here. And you're angry."

"You're damn right I'm angry," Olivia said, yanking her hands away and standing up.

"Good. Because when you're angry, dear Liv, you deliver the goods."

Olivia glared at Matt. "You've got to be kidding me. So this is some little psychological fuck fest? Nice, Matt."

Matt stayed silent and raised his eyebrows.

Olivia sighed, realizing Matt wasn't going to budge. "I get Priya."

"Deal."

Olivia stood tall and stared at Matt for a second. "You suck," she said, and headed toward the door.

"I love you too," Matt said.

Olivia walked out and slammed the door behind her. Thomas was standing next to Layne's desk.

"Are you and your panties okay there, Olivia?" Thomas asked. "You look a little hot and bothered," he said.

She gave him a look of disgust and headed straight to her office. On her way, she passed Priya's cubicle. "Priya, come with me."

When they were in Olivia's office, Olivia at her desk and Priya in one of the chairs across from her, Olivia gave her the download on the MTA business and Matt's game plan.

"Shit," Priya said, when Olivia had finished. "Now I get why you're so pissed."

"Are you in?"

"Unconditionally and wholeheartedly," Priya said emphatically.

"Great," Olivia said.

"So what now?"

"I'd like you to go to the New York Transit Museum in Brooklyn. I emailed one of their archivists yesterday and made an appointment to look through historic campaigns to see if anything sparks an idea. If you can do that for me, I'll start developing the game plan back here. And, actually, I have one idea. Still a seed. But I've been tossing it around since Saturday."

"Go ahead," Priya said.

"Long-term, the MTA wants to increase ridership on all its buses, subways, and trains; take share back from the app cabs; and better communicate its values of improving its environmental impact, rider experience, and safety. Short-term, however, they just want to increase ridership. So how do we do that? How do we get people on the subways?" Olivia continued. "Well, you give them something to look at. My idea is to create a promotion where we invite influential New York City tastemakers from the worlds of entertainment, art, fashion, and the media to essentially take over a subway car and imbue it with their personal style or brand."

"I'm liking this," Priya said, nodding.

"Like Anna Wintour. Anna Wintour would be given a car on, say, the E train because that stops at the station where the Condé Nast offices are. So, Anna gets together with her creative team and they come up with a concept for the car. Maybe they create subway ads on fake covers of *Vogue* and post those up in the car. Or they re-cover the seats in fur, faux of course. And they put a skin on the outside of the car with, I don't know, Anna's face on it. Whatever. She would have full creative control to make that car her own. And then people would flock to see it."

"Or how about Beyoncé?"

"Exactly. Beyoncé could have her music piped into her car, videos of her concerts streaming on screens, lemons hanging from the ceiling," Olivia said, laughing. "Really anything. We could do all the cars at once for a month or roll out one car each month for a year and then make reproductions of them and put them on display somewhere like a museum exhibit. We could do it in Vanderbilt Hall at Grand Central, for instance. And people could pay an entrance fee, which would be a donation that would go to the MTA's charitable endeavors. Or there could be an app where we devise a voting system so people could vote for which car they like best and then we would award the designer of that car money for the charity of his or her choice. I don't know exactly. I'm just thinking out loud here."

"It's a great idea, Liv. There's so much potential, and the buzz would be off the charts. I could see the different celebrities doing launch parties for their subway cars. The PR and merchandising opportunities are enormous."

"Anyway, it's just one idea. We need more than that and then we'll figure out the best approach."

"Knock, knock."

Olivia looked up to see that not only was it dark, but Matt was standing in her doorway.

"Oh, hey," Olivia said, stretching her arms above her head.

"How's it going?" Matt asked.

"Well, Priya's out doing research and I'm finalizing strategic direction briefs and hashing out a creative idea."

"What is it?" Matt asked, and sat down in one of Olivia's chairs.

"Oh, no. It's not yet ready for public consumption," Olivia said, smiling and shaking her head.

"I'm not public," Matt said, his arms spread out. He had a playful grin on his face. Olivia knew what was coming.

"Trust me, Matt. It needs a bit more time. And then I'll fill you in."

"Fine. Dinner?"

"What about it?"

"Would you like to eat some? At a restaurant? With me?" He sighed and tilted his head.

"Sure," Olivia said matter-of-factly. "But I can't. No

dinners in restaurants with the boss until this pitch is over. Too much to do."

"How about we pretend I'm not the boss?" Matt stood up and came around behind Olivia. He placed his hands on her shoulders and began to knead.

She wanted to let out a moan. She actually wanted to turn around and pull him onto her desk and make loud and passionate love to him.

"Matt," she said with a warning tone in her voice.

"Yes, Liv."

"Good night, Matt."

He stopped massaging her shoulders and walked back around to the other side of the desk. "Would you like me to send you dinner from whatever restaurant I end up eating at all by my lonely self?"

"That would be nice, but I have some yogurt in the fridge, and I'm not really that hungry. Plus, don't give me your pathetic line about having to eat all by yourself. What about Lily?"

"Lily and I are done," he said with a tight smile.

"Oh, sorry," Olivia said somewhat sincerely. "I didn't know."

"She decided that I was too old for her," Matt said slowly, and started to quietly laugh.

"Ouch," Olivia said, a pained expression on her face.

"I know, right?"

"You'll have no problem finding the next Lily," Olivia said, and then whispered, "and the next, and the next." She paused and suddenly became lost in her thoughts. "Anyway," she said, "have a good night. I'll see you in the morning."

"Good night, Liv," Matt said, and walked toward the

door. "I know you're gonna hit the ball out of the park with this one."

"Olivia. Hi," Ben said.

Olivia was waiting for the elevator, flipping through her mail.

"Oh, hey, Ben. How are you?" Olivia asked, changing places with him as she entered the elevator and he exited.

"Good. Great, actually. Long night at work?" he asked, still holding the door open.

"Yeah, working on some new business."

"Great. Exciting," Ben said, pushing the hair out of his eyes.

"Long night at your grandma's?" Olivia smiled.

"Yes," Ben said, his face lighting up. "After a delicious and filling dinner," Ben said with a flourish, "Grandma and I debated the vagaries, at great length I might add, of the women on *The View*. She's quite knowledgeable, my grandma, on *The View* ladies' political leanings and relationship dramas. And don't get her started on the inter-host relationships."

Olivia laughed. "Yeah, whenever I see her, she's like, 'Olivia, did you see *Ellen* today?' And I always have to remind her that I was at work. She tells me to tape it, which in and of itself is so cute, because who's taped anything in years?"

"My grandma," Ben said, laughing.

"It's so sweet that you two have such a great relationship."

"We're all we have left from our family," Ben said as the elevator began to make a dinging sound.

Olivia stepped out, back into the lobby, so the doors

would close and the elevator would stop ringing. She really just wanted to go upstairs and go to bed, but after a statement like that from Ben, she knew that would be too rude.

"I'm sorry. I didn't know that."

"Yeah, we lost my parents in a car accident back in ninety-five. I was ten."

"My God, that's awful. I'm so sorry."

"Thanks," Ben said, stuffing his hands into his pockets. "My grandma raised me. She moved into the house I had lived in with my parents. So, yeah, we're really close."

"I don't know her that well. We pass each other in the hall sometimes or share an elevator ride, but we've never had more than a cursory conversation."

"That's exactly what she said."

"You guys talked about me?" Olivia asked with a teasing lilt in her voice.

"Maybe a little. But she's the one who brought you up," Ben said, smiling, his palms in the air.

"Okay," Olivia said, nodding. "Don't worry. I'm not accusing you of anything." She laughed.

"No, I know. I mean, not that I wouldn't bring you up. It's just that . . . Well, whatever. I don't even know what I'm saying," Ben said, laughing and shaking his head.

"Yeah, I know. It's late," Olivia said, pushing the elevator call button. "Well, I guess I'll see you around." The elevator door opened and Olivia stepped in, turned around, and pressed eleven.

"Okay, I'll see you," Ben said, and stood there, still smiling, as the doors closed.

Olivia's phone pinged and she looked down to a text from Matt.

Matt

I'm at Thai Paradise. Got caught up with something at work, so just eating now. I know you love it here. Reconsider my invitation?

Olivia sighed loudly and thought for a moment. Why did she pine after men like Matt? Men who were as averse to availability, emotional intimacy, and commitment as they were to their annual grab-and-cough appointments. Why, Olivia thought, riding up in the elevator, when there were men who she might actually have a shot with? Mature men who didn't require the instant gratification, the novelty, the shiny newness that their lesser brothers sought in their women and their iPhone games. But the truth was she did pine after Matt. And she was starving.

Olivia's fingers danced over her phone, deciding how to answer. She could say yes and sit across the dinner table from Matt. She'd clearly be substituting for Lily. He'd act interested in what she'd tell him about Jenna and her MTA pitch. He'd order her a second glass of wine without asking. He'd walk her home, even, Olivia's mind exploring the idea of what could come after. She could also say no, retaining her dignity, not having to see herself reflected in Matt's eyes as an older, heavier, less seductive substitute for Lily. She could heat up leftovers from the weekend, put on her coziest sweats, and avoid the emotional acrobatics that dinner with Matt would incite. She weighed both options and began to type.

Olivia

Well, I am starving. Office-fridge yogurt had
expired. I'll be there in five.

Olivia was about to press send when the elevator stopped
at her floor. She pressed the lobby button and the doors began to close when she suddenly reconsidered. She quickly
stuck her hand between the closing doors and stepped out
onto her floor.

After deleting her prior text, Olivia tapped out a different one.

Olivia

Already in my pj's. Thanks anyway.

She clicked send, felt relief course through her body, and
realized that though she wasn't living her life on the edge
and pushing the envelope with respect to the relationship
she would like to have with Matt, she was also preserving
her self-respect and drawing a firm boundary between her
professional and personal lives. Why then, she wondered,
was she unconvinced that she had made the right decision?

Olivia and Matt had a complicated relationship. It had
started off entirely professional, when Olivia had first started
at Y&R. After they'd worked together for four or five years,
they developed an easy friendship. It was a bit flirty, but
nothing blatant. Nothing that made Olivia cringe or feel uncomfortable or require forms to be filled out up in HR. Matt
was nothing like Thomas or some of the other boneheads
whose respect for and tolerance of women were as pathetic
as the job society had done teaching them to be men.

Olivia and Matt's level-one friendship changed, though,

when they left Y&R and were working long hours starting the new agency. One night, Olivia, Matt, and Pablo went to Barcanto's after work. Ian was generous with the alcohol, as was his normal way, and Matt ended up walking Olivia home.

They drunk-stumbled into her apartment, and Matt told Olivia he thought she was beautiful and had always imagined what it would be like to kiss her. She decided to let him find out.

They slept together that night and things had existed in a tolerable limbo ever since. Matt continued his professional dating career and Olivia worked her ass off and sometimes had erotic thoughts about Matt. Only James, Jenna, and Ian knew that she was secretly in love with him. She could tell that sometimes he thought about her in that way too. But as long as they were working together, she was going to keep it strictly professional. Well, mostly.

There had been other men throughout the years. Sweet men. Men who asked her out with sufficient notice on proper dates that required advance reservations. Men who walked her to her door and didn't expect another drink or, worse, expect to gain intimate knowledge of her waxing predilections. Men whose next-day follow-up involved an actual phone call instead of just texted acronyms and emoji. But none of those men had ever had the ability to distract Olivia from her single-minded focus on her career. When Olivia imagined her life with all those predictable men, she couldn't see past the stereotypical gender-roled, routine-sex, so-so married life she knew they'd have together.

While most of her friends were married or dating the guys they would probably end up married to, and some were already on their second kid, Olivia was fine, at least most of the time, working hard and rebuilding her savings account. Chasing the dream, she would tell them when they asked. And in return, her friends would look at her with a sad smile as if they knew something she didn't. Once in a while, at her weaker moments, Olivia thought maybe they did.

CHAPTER 7

"Over here, Charlotte," JoJo said, waving from the back table where she and Sam were already drinking milk shakes.

Sam stood up to kiss Charlotte and pull out her chair. "How did it go?"

"I've never experienced anything like that in my entire life!" Charlotte said excitedly, and then told them the whole story, filling it with a million adjectives: about the process, the other finalists, the intolerable Bella London and the exciting and gorgeous Rose Grant, and how each girl raised her hand when Miss Fontaine asked who would be returning on Friday for the interview and photo shoot.

"So you're really gonna do this?" JoJo asked.

"I am," Charlotte said with a wide smile. "You know, I was ambivalent at first, but I had a lot of fun today, and I want to see this through. Who knows what doors it could open for me?"

"But are those actual doors you'd be interested in walking through?" JoJo asked, doubt creeping into her voice.

"Don't give her a hard time, JoJo," Sam said. "This is a good opportunity. Why wouldn't she give it a try?"

"Thank you for your support, Sam," Charlotte said, sticking her tongue out at JoJo. "Plus, J. Walter Thompson is actually the advertising agency that created Miss Subways, so you never know who I might meet in this process."

"I support you, Charlotte. I just don't want you to lose sight of what you really want to do."

"That would be impossible," Charlotte said. "Participating in this Miss Subways process won't stop me from pursuing advertising."

"Unless you win and get discovered and become a famous model," JoJo said.

"Well, yes, there's that," Charlotte said, raising her nose in the air. "But I'll try to remember the two of you if that should happen."

"Please do," Sam said, giving her a kiss.

"If you're off in Paris or London or wherever it is you high-fashion models roam like overpaid gazelles, don't get all weepy and jealous if I claim Sam for my very own. He's the last good one out there."

"As long as you return him unsullied."

"Of course!" JoJo said, and the two girls giggled. "But let me be serious for a moment. Sam and I just want for you what we know you want for yourself. And I wouldn't want you to get distracted by something because it's new and shiny. Remember what you told me the other night about the window closing on advertising opportunities?"

"What window?" Sam asked.

"Once the agencies have finished their hiring efforts for this season," Charlotte explained, "it'll be nearly impossible for me to get a job in the typing pool. I'm already way too old as it is. They just love those eighteen-year-old freshies with their crisp typing school certificates pinned to their Peter Pan collars and their minds unaroused by college. I was lucky to get the interviews I got, and those were all by personal connections through professors and through Martin. If I can't convince JWT to hire me or if I can't find an opening somewhere else before graduation, which at this late stage is agonizingly and highly likely, I may never get my foot in the door at an advertising agency."

"It sounds so grave, Charlotte."

"It's the truth, JoJo, and you know it."

JoJo looked down at the table and took a sip of her milk shake.

"Looks like the clock is ticking and you've got some work to do contacting all those other agencies," Sam said.

"That sounds dreadful and overwhelming," Charlotte said, putting her hands over her face.

"Sorry, darling. Just being realistic."

"I know. I'm just feeling discouraged. Here I have this fun opportunity to pursue Miss Subways. Best outcome, I think, is that I become Miss Subways and potentially have an opportunity to become a Powers Girl."

"My goodness. The confidence! What happened to my Charlotte?" JoJo asked, her mouth wide-open.

"Snap it shut, JoJo. Let me dream here for a second. Worst outcome is that I just enjoy the lovely fuss and then move on with my life. The only question is, does pursuing Miss Subways distract me from finding another job in advertising? That's what I need to figure out."

"I think you can do both. Keep looking for a job. And stay in the running for Miss Subways. No reason not to," Sam said.

"I agree," JoJo said.

"Well, in that case, I'll go with counsel's suggestion."

When Charlotte got home, all the lights were off, so she tiptoed upstairs so as not to wake her parents. Charlotte noticed the note on her bed as soon as she turned on her bedroom light. *Come see me at the store in the morning.* The note, in her father's calculated scribble, revealed nothing more. He wasn't the most communicative person, and Charlotte, though she didn't know what he wanted to discuss with her, couldn't imagine it was anything good.

Charlotte felt her stomach tighten as she approached Friedman's Paint and Wallpaper, her father's store on Third Avenue in Bay Ridge, Brooklyn, Est. 1932. The large plate-glass windows seemed grimier than usual. Charlotte had stood in front of this store a million times, she and Harry marking their growth by where their eyes lined up with the carefully etched letters spelling out the name of the store on the glass. The store suddenly looked worn-out, like an old man whose trousers sag as he shuffles, eyes cast downward to the public chess tables in the park.

Preparing for bed the night before, Charlotte had tried to figure out what her father wanted to discuss with her. Perhaps he was finally ready to listen to her advertising ideas. She'd been trying to persuade him to place ads in circulars and do in-store promotions, to modernize his marketing plans to keep up with the times and bring in new customers.

Each time she'd brought up her concepts, however, he'd shot her down. *I've been doing it this way for years, and this is how I'll keep doing it.* She had tried to convince him that she was right and he was wrong—to be absolutely sure, she had never succeeded in that endeavor in the past—but she had failed.

"Hello, Charlotte!"

"Hi, Donald," Charlotte said to the manager. "Is my father around?"

"Upstairs in the office."

Charlotte approached the closed office door tentatively. Her father wasn't mean, but he wasn't the adoring type. Not like JoJo's father, who took them fishing and told them hilarious stories about growing up with his four sisters. Charlotte was a little afraid of her father; since Harry had died, his moods were unpredictable.

"Come in!" Mr. Friedman yelled when Charlotte knocked.

Charlotte took a deep breath, smoothed her skirt, and opened the door. Her father was sitting behind his wooden desk, which was choking to death in piles of paper.

Mr. Friedman sat back in his chair and took a draw from his pipe, the same one he had smoked Charlotte's entire life. The earthy smell of the tobacco, the sounds of the throaty inhalation and exhalation, the feel of the rubbed wood. Those senses were rooted as deeply in her consciousness, in her profound and penetrating knowledge of him, as the sound of his voice. He stared at her.

Charlotte sat down and then shifted in her seat uncomfortably. She thought about the Miss Subways letter in her purse and whether she should share the news with her father despite her mother's belief that he wouldn't allow her to participate. Considering now didn't seem like the opportune time, she pulled her purse closer and concentrated on the family-of-four photograph, dated and dusty, on the corner of her father's desk.

"I'm not sure if you're aware because I haven't wanted

to worry you and your mother, but the store hasn't been doing well."

"I didn't know."

"Well, I met with the bank yesterday, and things are worse than I thought."

"I'm so sorry to hear that," Charlotte said sincerely. "What are you going to do?"

"It's more like what are *you* going to do?" Mr. Friedman leaned back farther in his chair and paused.

"Do you mean my advertising ideas?"

"No, Charlotte. I mean that I need you to work at the store. I can't make payroll, and I need to let Donald go."

"But I can't," Charlotte said, suddenly standing. As she rose, her purse dropped to her feet and she didn't bother picking it up.

"Nonsense," Mr. Friedman said gruffly. "You'll do as you're told."

"Can't you just work here by yourself?"

"You're fully aware that there are too many days when I have to be out of the store consulting with contractors and giving estimates at customers' homes. I need someone here."

"But I have school. And I'm graduating. And then . . ."

"And that will have to wait because I need you here, Charlotte. And that's the end of it."

Charlotte grabbed her purse and ran out of her father's office, down the stairs, and out onto the street. Donald, still unaware of the fate the tyrant upstairs had in store for him, called after her, but Charlotte didn't turn around.

With tears stinging her eyes, Charlotte walked the mile and a half home and tried to sort out the maelstrom, which had been borne whole in her brain the moment her father had dumped his plan on her shoulders.

"How dare he!" Charlotte said. And though she hadn't intended to say it aloud, the startled glance from a suit rushing by confirmed she had.

It was perfectly clear to Charlotte *why* her father felt comfortable with her taking over Donald's job. She'd worked at the store during the summers and on weekends since she was a little girl. First, as a child with her brother, sweeping the aisles, helping her father hang paintbrushes on the pegs, greeting the customers: *Hello, Mr. Davenport. Welcome to Friedman's Paint and Wallpaper, Mr. Cavanagh.* Later, as a teenager advising the neighborhood ladies on the latest wallpaper styles for their dining rooms, delivering small parcels to construction sites, tending the till. And more recently, on weekends and when she could take a break from her studies, helping her father with the ordering and coming up with cleverly worded signs for the aisle endcaps.

As she reached her house and decided to pretend she wasn't feeling well so she didn't have to discuss any of it with her mother, Charlotte scolded herself for running out of her father's office. *You should have stood up for yourself and dealt with it like a woman.* At least, she knew that's what JoJo would tell her. But Charlotte wasn't JoJo. Charlotte had never been one to throw back her shoulders, stick her fist in the fight, and state her position with purpose and confidence. But she'd just done so with Mr. Hertford at JWT, hadn't she? Charlotte realized she'd have to make this a regular thing and stand up to her father too, or she could kiss her dreams good-bye.

Charlotte put her coat back on and retraced her steps to

her father's store. She couldn't imagine giving up everything she'd worked so hard for at Hunter over the last four years and the opportunities in advertising that she wanted more than anything to discover.

As she walked, she heard her brother's voice in her ear. He was always so supportive, encouraging Charlotte to follow her dreams to go to college, to push beyond her father's low expectations. She felt a spring in her step and knew she partly owed it to her brother to make something of herself, something outside of what her father had dictated for her. It wasn't her fault her father's store wasn't doing well. She shouldn't have to pay such a serious price. No, she would talk to her father and put her foot down. He would understand. He just had to.

The courage that had been building as she walked east from her house on Seventy-Fourth Street and then north on Third Avenue slowly dissipated with every tread on the stairway to her father's office door.

"It's all decided," he said. He was surprised that she'd returned, but he seemed more resolute than he'd been before. "I even discussed it with your mother last night while you were out, and she agreed."

Charlotte sat, shocked, trying to come up with a way to convince her father to change his mind. But she was the girl in her nightmares: paralyzed and unable to say a word.

"Charlotte, I realize working here isn't what you had planned. But this is life. It should have been your brother. But it's you."

"But I need to finish school. And I'm starting my career," Charlotte said, throwing her fist in the fight.

"Did you get a job?"

"No," Charlotte said firmly, challenging her father to say

a word. "But I have several prospects and an offer is imminent."

"You're just going to have to accept the reality and move on. When things turn around at the store, you can finish your degree and find a job then."

"It doesn't work like that!"

"Don't be so dramatic, Charlotte," he said with a dismissive wave. "You know how I felt about this college thing when you started. Stop being such a dreamer."

And there it was.

Her father continued, "Advertising is no place for a young lady. You'll start working here and that's that. I'm planning on letting Donald go today."

"Don't you have to give him some sort of notice?" Charlotte asked incredulously. Her father was nowhere near kind, but he wasn't a tyrant.

"Of course I'll give him notice. You can stay in school for two more weeks, but then I'll expect you here."

"I don't know why you have to ruin my life like this," Charlotte said, standing up.

Mr. Friedman was silent. She matched his silence and waited for him to speak. Implored herself to not say another word until he did. She stared at the walls, covered haphazardly with tacked-up purchase orders and wallpaper swatches. She had spent hours in this office as a girl, watching her father. Thinking he was so powerful. Commanding the empire that was Friedman's Paint and Wallpaper. Now she realized how small that empire was. And how sad its sovereign. Needing to disrupt her life because he couldn't succeed at his own.

Even when she was little, Charlotte tended to avoid her father when she could. He had no time for little girls and their attendant ribbons and dolls. He was tolerable to her when she was in the store, but he addressed her as he would any employee, not his darling daughter learning her father's trade at his work boots. He put all he had, what little love and support, into Harry. Harry was, after all, what mattered. At least for the store. So she retreated into her studies, earning exemplary marks and securing a place at Hunter without any help—or encouragement—from either of her parents.

Harry, who Charlotte felt was her only ally in the family, didn't get along with their father at all. *Harry, don't waste your time with sports. Harry, you have a duty to take over my business. Harry, come straight to the store after school. Harry, did you hear me?*

Finally . . . "I'm your father, and you'll do as I say."

Charlotte took a breath and decided to adjust her approach. "I understand the predicament you're in, and I'm sorry you're dealing with all of this, but I'm twenty-one years old, and I don't have to follow your rules anymore," Charlotte said, feeling badly for disrespecting her father, but knowing she had to give this argument her best Joe Louis. Charlotte saw her father's eyes soften for a moment. She'd never witnessed anyone standing up to him and was shocked at his response.

"So what do you propose?" he asked, drawing on his pipe.

Charlotte thought quickly. She stood and lifted her chin. "I propose that I finish school. I have two and a half months until I graduate. Perhaps you can save money by having Donald come in only on the busiest days of the week. I can work here on Saturdays so you can essentially cut his salary in half, which will save you on payroll. Between now and then, we'll both try to think of ways to bring in more customers and cut costs. I also propose that you hear me out on my advertising ideas—"

"Absolutely not."

"And what about the first half of my plan? About letting me finish school?"

"I'll think about it and tell you tomorrow."

Charlotte knew that was better than a no, and went around to her father's side of the desk to give him a peace-treaty hug. "Thank you, Papa," she said. He returned her embrace stiffly but not reluctantly. Perhaps that was a start.

CHAPTER 8

OLIVIA
TUESDAY, MARCH 6, 2018

Olivia walked to work the next morning in a daze. She was thinking about Miss Subways, the historic MTA campaign she had come across the night before in her research. She was fascinated by the history. And by the women.

She kept wondering where these women were now. How had being Miss Subways affected their lives, if at all? Was it just a blip in time, an exciting but fleeting side excursion on their life's journey? Or did it actually have an impact on them and inform their future lives? Did they display their posters in their homes as they got older? Was being Miss Subways a lasting part of their identities?

Still deep in thought as she approached her desk, she didn't notice at first that Priya was sitting in one of the chairs in her office.

"Good morning," Priya said. "I brought you a latte."

"Thanks. That was so nice of you."

"I have good news. I found something at the Transit Museum you might find interesting." Priya started unfolding a piece of paper on her lap.

"I have a feeling I know what you're going to show me," Olivia said, taking a sip of her latte.

"You do? How?"

"I was searching around online last night and I found something I thought was interesting. I wouldn't be surprised if we found the same thing. But please, go on."

Priya finished unfolding the paper and held it up to Olivia. It was a photocopy of a Miss Subways poster from 1946.

"I knew it!" Olivia said, and clapped her hands.

"No way!"

"Yes, it's a fascinating campaign, isn't it?" Olivia leaned forward in her chair, anxious to hear exactly how Priya felt and how she thought they could utilize Miss Subways in their MTA pitch.

"Amazing," Priya said. "I was blown away by these women's stories. I couldn't stop reading about them. The archivist at the Transit Museum just kept bringing me more and more."

"I felt the same way. I loved reading about all the different jobs these women had. I always assumed they were all teachers or secretaries back then, or didn't have any professional ambitions at all, but that couldn't be further from the truth."

"When I meet women in their eighties and nineties, it's easy to forget that they were living these vibrant lives when they were younger. It's awful, but I admit that I underestimate older women. I don't give them the credit they're due. I mean, I realize they paved the way for us and all, but still, not enough credit. We could probably learn so much from them." Priya's eyes were lit up.

"I know what you're saying," Olivia said. "You just assume that the times they lived in were so different that they couldn't possibly know what it's like for us. But you know what, from reading those posters, and all the other articles, those women were going through the same shit we are. All the conflicts with work and personal lives—that is nothing new."

"So what are you thinking?" Priya asked, taking a sip of her coffee.

"Well, a few things. First, if *we* found this, then there's a chance that one of the other agencies—"

"Or TomAss," Priya interrupted, raising her eyebrows.

"Or TomAss," Olivia said, laughing, and continued, "could have found it too. So I think we need to put this on the list of possible concepts to use. There's a lot of rich history here, but I'm not sure that means we should make this our top choice just yet."

"Right," Priya said, taking her pad and pen from the chair next to her so she could take notes. "A dissenting voice in my head can't let go of the fact that the whole thing seems a little sexist. I mean, a beauty pageant on the subways? It's only redeeming when you think about how ambitious these women were. And I can't stop wondering where they are now—"

"Me too!"

"But how do we reconcile this campaign—developed by men more than seventy-five years ago, written by men, photographed by men—that essentially exploited women so that other men would look at subway ads?"

"All true. But we're also looking at it from the lens of today. At the time, the sexism wasn't interpreted that way."

"But it was. You watched *Mad Men*."

"I did. And I still do, over and over and over again." Olivia laughed.

"Don't tell me that Peggy and Joan and Betty and even poor Trudy didn't realize that the boorish behavior of those men was keeping them in gender roles that they had to fight tooth and nail to escape from."

"Or not," Olivia said, tilting her head.

"Yes. Or not. And then that led to all kinds of other behaviors and solutions to their problems."

"True," Olivia said, glancing at the emails that were piling up on her computer. "So we can agree that there was a lot of sexism going on in Miss Subways. But these women did it willingly. From all that I read, it seemed like a huge honor. Some were lauded as local celebrities. In other instances, it propelled their careers. How's that for the women playing the men at their own game? Playing by the men's rules to actually get what they wanted all along. And thousands upon thousands of women tried to become Miss Subways. So it couldn't have been all bad."

Priya proceeded to tell Olivia about other historic campaigns, which were portals to a seemingly simpler zeitgeist, the campaigns themselves an almost quaint reflection of the ideas and ideals of travel, work, capitalism, and marketing from the century before.

Olivia looked out her window in thought.

"What are you thinking?" Priya asked.

"I'm feeling like the MTA killed those old campaigns for a reason. I wonder if we're better off coming up with something new and fresh rather than trying to rehash history and then having that approach possibly backfire."

"That makes sense," Priya said.

After Priya left, Olivia returned calls and emails, but couldn't get Miss Subways out of her mind. She typed "Wikipedia Miss Subways" into her browser and scrolled down the resulting page to the chart listing the Miss Subways title holders.

She loved the names. Mona Freeman, May 1941. Dorothea Mate, June 1942. Rosemary Gregory, August 1942. Enid Berkowitz, July 1946. Dorothy Nolan, March 1949. Saralee Singer, February 1950.

Those names sounded like music to her. Melodies of a different time floating through the air. Olivia had always felt sentimental about old movies. The voices those actresses had. Olivia knew it was unfair to ascribe entire personalities to women solely because their voices sounded old-world and they wore dainty gloves to the supermarket. But it seemed deserved.

Olivia's grandmothers had died before Olivia was born. And her mother wasn't any kind of role model. Olivia longed for an older woman in her life. And the women from all those old movies she watched became her surrogate mothers and grandmothers. They comforted Olivia when, curled up in sweats with a glass of wine in her hand, she had only her television for company.

Her curiosity for the women suddenly overtaking her, Olivia started Googling them one by one, typing in their names followed by "Miss Subways."

It was past seven. They had brainstormed with Pablo for a few hours and had several new ideas. But Pablo also loved the Miss Subways concept. To him there was an element of *Casablanca* mystique. He talked about the older women in his own life and how he had learned a great deal from them. That they had so much wisdom and that perhaps by finding some of these Miss Subways winners, they could get some nuggets of an idea to use for the new pitch.

That turned out to not be as simple as they had thought. For one thing, the majority of the posters used the women's maiden names, as most weren't yet married when their posters ran. Olivia found an archived *Collier's* magazine photo spread showing some of the women on an outing to Jones Beach, and several gossip columns by a journalist named Walter Winchell that mentioned Miss Subways. But she was having trouble finding anything that led them to current phone numbers or email addresses. Unfortunately, she did find a number of obituaries. She was starting to get depressed when Priya came rushing in.

"I found one! July 1949!" Priya said.

"Nice work! How did you find her?" Olivia asked.

"She wrote a magazine article a while back about the path of her career and she mentioned Miss Subways, so it came up on Google. I did a Whitepages search and found a phone number for her. So, I called," Priya said, smiling wide.

"And?"

"And—she didn't answer," Priya said. "But I got a machine and it sounds like an old lady voice, so chances are it's her."

"Did you leave a message?" Olivia asked.

"Of course. I told her I worked for an advertising agency and we were interested in talking to her about her experience with Miss Subways. I left my number and asked her to call."

"You are absolutely worth those big bucks we're probably not paying you, Priya."

"Let's land this business and then you can give me a monster raise," Priya said, tilting her head.

"Done. Okay, go home. I know that cute boyfriend of yours is probably waiting for you. Hopefully our Miss Subways will call you back. Text me if she does, and tell me everything."

"You again. Why do you keep following me?" Ben asked as Olivia got off the elevator on the eleventh floor. He was standing outside his grandma's apartment.

"You caught me," Olivia said, lifting her arms in surrender. When she did that, the plastic bag holding her Thai takeout spilled its contents all over the floor. At the same time, Ben's grandma opened her door. "Shit!" Olivia said.

"What happened?" Ben's grandma asked.

"Hi, Mrs. Glasser. I'm so embarrassed. I dropped my dinner," Olivia said. "Sorry for the mess. Let me go and get some paper towels from my apartment."

"Nonsense," Mrs. Glasser said. "I'll grab some. Come. Come. Both of you, come in. Olivia, I haven't seen you in so long. Please, you'll have dinner with us."

"Oh, I couldn't," Olivia protested, looking at Ben as Mrs. Glasser was already walking into her apartment to grab the paper towels.

"She gets mean when people don't do what she wants them to do," Ben whispered, pointing at his grandma.

Olivia laughed.

"I made plenty of food. Salmon. We're having salmon!" Mrs. Glasser shouted from the kitchen.

"She makes a killer salmon," Ben said, nodding and putting his work bag on the floor.

Mrs. Glasser returned with the paper towels and handed them to Olivia. Ben took them out of her hands and told her he'd take care of it.

Olivia stood in Mrs. Glasser's living room, looking around. She had never been inside the apartment. It was not what she had expected. All of the furniture was modern and sophisticated. Again, Olivia got mad at herself for assuming that all old ladies liked to live among chintz and aging Queen Anne dining room sets with needlepoint seat coverings.

Mrs. Glasser's living room looked like a page out of a Restoration Hardware catalog, with really interesting and eclectic touches and accessories. The art on the walls was colorful and modern. Not an oil painting of Central Park in sight.

"Your apartment is beautiful," Olivia said to Mrs. Glasser, who was setting another seat at the dining room table: white lacquer with white leather chairs.

"Thank you. Ben helped me fix it up when I moved here. We had some beautiful antique furniture in our old house, but he convinced me to get rid of it all. I think I like this look better. It makes me feel youthfull," Mrs. Glasser said, smiling.

"I really hate to impose," Olivia said.

"That's silly, dear. I'm always happy to have young people enliven my dining room table."

Ben walked back into the room, stuffing the soiled paper towels into the plastic bag that used to hold Olivia's dinner.

"Mission accomplished," he said.

"Thank you so much. That was so nice of you," Olivia said, suddenly feeling both uncomfortable for intruding on some other family and close to tears with yearning, realizing how much she was missing in her life by not having dinners like this more often. Or ever.

"Is there anything I can do to help you, Mrs. Glasser?" Olivia called into the kitchen.

"Yes, dear. You can open this bottle of sparkling water and pour glasses for the two of us. Ben, the savage, insists on tap."

"Again," Ben whispered, "you have to do what she says or you might never get invited back."

Olivia smiled at Ben, who was dressed in a suit. She still didn't know what he did for a living. But she was curious.

"Do you mind showing me where the bathroom is so I can wash my hands?" Olivia asked.

"Down that hall, second door on your left."

Olivia made her way down the hall, which was covered in framed photographs. She found a large frame filled with about ten smaller photos in different sizes. They were all of a little boy, around six years old, and a man and a woman. Olivia assumed it was Ben and his parents. She felt a pain in her heart. So unfair that a little boy who had parents who loved him, good parents, had to grow up without them. There were no family photos like this lining halls in her own home. Neither her mother nor her father had ever taken photos. It was like Olivia's childhood never existed. All that remained were memories that clouded her thoughts like black smoke from a fire, aches buried so deeply within Olivia's soul that it felt like they would never go away.

Olivia noticed a black-and-white wedding photo with an imprint of a photography studio name on the lower left corner. It must have been Mrs. Glasser and her husband. Mrs. Glasser was beautiful. She looked like the leading ladies in Olivia's favorite movies: a cross between Katharine

Hepburn in *The Philadelphia Story,* Grace Kelly in *High Society,* and Ingrid Bergman in *Casablanca.*

Another photograph on the wall caught Olivia's eye. She gasped and inadvertently took a step back as if she'd been punched in the stomach.

CHAPTER 9

Charlotte woke up early so she could catch her father before he left for the day. He was in the kitchen, ingesting that morning's coffee and the prior night's news.

"I wanted to finish our discussion. Have you thought more about what I said?" Charlotte asked as she entered the small kitchen.

"You'll finish school and then work at the store once you've graduated."

Charlotte let out a sigh of relief and smiled tentatively at her father. At least this was a start.

"It was your mother's idea," Mr. Friedman said, waving her off dismissively.

"The good news is, he's going to let me finish school." Charlotte and JoJo were standing on the platform, waiting for the Fourth Avenue subway to take them, along with the patchwork masses, into Manhattan.

The train arrived and they boarded the packed car.

They jostled their way into the back corner so they could hear each other over the babel, the newspapers, the humanity.

"And the bad news?"

"I have to work full-time at the store after graduation."

"At least you can graduate."

"It's the last thing I expected, but somehow my mother convinced him, and I wasn't going to ask questions."

"Give yourself a little credit, Charlotte. Perhaps you convinced him too."

"Doubtful. I have about as much influence on my father as the First Lady has on foreign policy."

"I'm sorry, Charlotte."

"Why should he have the right to make decisions about my life?"

"Because he's your father and that's what fathers do."

"Says who?"

"Says fathers."

"Oh, JoJo. It's not fair."

"Neither are broken heels and broken dates, but they both happen on a regular basis. To me, at least. It's called life, Charlotte."

"It doesn't mean I have to accept it."

"What if you say no?"

"It's not that simple."

"I guess, family obligation and all. But part of me thinks you're giving up too easily."

"What do you expect me to do?" Charlotte asked, the anger in her voice rising. "It's not like I even have a job offer that I can throw in his face. I have no money to move out. And, let's be honest, the chances of me becoming Miss Subways and then a famous model are pretty slim."

"There's got to be something you can do. I know. Let's pretend your father's store is our first advertising client. How are we going to help him drum up business?"

Charlotte kissed JoJo straight on the mouth. "You're a genius. That's just it. We'll find a way to bring business into the store, the cash register will sing its lungs out, and I'll be off the hook."

"What are the store's biggest problems?"

"My goodness, where do I start? It looks like it hasn't had a proper bath in a decade. A bright, new competitor just opened down the block and customers have been, according to my father, leaving him by the droves to luxuriate in its wide aisles, capable lighting, uniformed and competent sales help, and competitive prices." Charlotte suddenly sprang to attention and looked JoJo in the eye. "Wait a minute," she said, grabbing JoJo's arm. "I just thought of something." Charlotte tilted her head mischievously.

"What?"

"Winning Miss Subways could be the answer. Think of all the stories we hear about Miss Subways and the boatloads of attention the winners get. The proposals they receive. The gifts suitors send. It happens to each and every Miss Subways. If I win and they mention my father's store on the poster, which is free advertising throughout the entire subway system, then people will come to see me—well, not *me* per say, but Miss Subways—which will bring more business to my father's store and hence, more money. My father can take that money, ring up Donald, and everything will be back to the way it was. That's what I call a fine way to solve a Brooklyn problem."

"Huh, Charlotte, that's not a terrible idea," JoJo said, nodding.

"It's a long shot."

"But it's a shot."

"There's one small problem."

JoJo looked at her questioningly.

"I have to actually *win* Miss Subways."

"So win." JoJo put her hands on Charlotte's shoulders and looked her in the eye. "Promise me that from this moment on, you'll believe that you can win Miss Subways."

Charlotte's shoulders slumped. "I wish I could borrow a teaspoon of your confidence, JoJo."

"You've got loads of confidence in there, Charlotte. You just have to find it under those layers of self-doubt you're wearing like a fur coat."

"Easier said than done." Her mother had always taught her to keep her expectations in check. That way she'd never be disappointed. *Yes, Mother dear,* Charlotte thought, *but that way you can never dream.*

"But it's showtime, so take off that coat. It's not doing you any good."

"You're absolutely right. And I'm going to try."

"Atta girl."

"Do you really think this could work?" Charlotte asked, biting her lip.

"Sorry. I didn't hear that. Say that again?"

Charlotte laughed nervously. "I said, I really think this will work. I'm going to go back there Friday and knock the trouser socks off Mr. John Robert Powers. I'll kick those other girls in the knees if I have to." Charlotte took a deep breath and looked up at Miss Subways Thelma Porter smiling down on her. "I just have to win."

———

Charlotte knocked hesitantly on Professor Oldham's door. He was the chair of the economics department, and though Charlotte had never had him as a professor, she had heard him speak on numerous occasions.

"Come on in," a warm voice said from within.

"Professor Oldham, hello, sir," Charlotte said, still standing in the threshold, holding the door. "I'm Charlotte Friedman. I'm a senior, sir, an econ major."

"Of course, Charlotte, please come in. Have a seat." He set his pen down next to the notebook he was writing in and smiled at her. There was a large window behind him, and the light streamed in, a sunbeam landing on the seat of the wooden chair he motioned to.

"Thank you," she said, still standing.

"What can I do for you?"

"I hope I'm not being too presumptuous, but I've heard you say that you welcome students to come in and discuss anything with you. Sir, I've come to discuss my future."

Professor Oldham leaned back in his seat, put his hands behind his head, and adopted a serious expression. "I'd be happy to discuss your future with you, Charlotte. But only under one condition."

"Yes?" Charlotte asked, a hint of worry in her voice.

"You must first sit down," he said, a smile returning to his face.

Charlotte laughed, sat down, and told him about her interest in advertising and the predicament she was in, trying to find a placement before the end of the term. "I am doing everything I possibly can, and I thought you might have some advice."

"Why advertising?"

No one had ever asked Charlotte that. She had always

just told people that's what she wanted to do and they accepted it. She sat for a moment and collected her thoughts. "Well, that's a very good question. And I have a few answers. I've always been intrigued by advertisements I see, whether on the subway, in a magazine, wherever. And each time I see one, I try to imagine what went into the making of it. From the first idea that the account man must have had to the actualization of that idea into a full-blown ad. I'm fascinated by the creative process that goes into coming up with a strategy to help a company's business. Plus, it all seems so exciting and glamorous. It's an environment I want to work in." As she was speaking, Charlotte's voice took on a gauzy quality. She was lost in the dream of it all.

"You do realize, though, that you'll be doing none of that, right?"

"Excuse me?" Suddenly Charlotte was brought back down to earth.

"The typing pool, which I assume you know is where you'll work, won't give you much access to strategic conversations and advertisement actualization."

Charlotte was surprised by the condescension creeping into Professor Oldham's voice. "Yes, I'm aware of that," she said confidently, trying to remain respectful.

"The chances of you getting anywhere near an ad are slim. You're more likely to get bitten by an alligator."

Charlotte paused, then said, "I understand, but I still feel it would be exciting to be part of the machine that produces the ads even if, at the beginning, I'm not the one actually producing them myself."

"At the beginning, the middle, and the end, I'm sorry to say. Why don't you work for a women's magazine? There's more opportunity there. You could get some writing experience, and then there'd be more of a chance you could work for any agency as a junior copywriter doing ads for beauty and fashion and other things that would interest you."

"With all due respect, Professor, I'm not interested in copywriting as a career, nor am I interested solely in beauty and fashion. My plan is to start in the typing pool, as girls do, and earn my way up by working hard."

Professor Oldham laughed. "I'm sorry, Charlotte. I don't mean to discourage you. But you girls need to be realistic. The closest you'll get to an account executive is to marry one."

Charlotte stood up, thanked the professor for his time, and resolved that she'd add him to the list of people—presently just her father—she looked forward to proving wrong.

"Charlotte, get down here right now!"

Charlotte was in her bedroom, doing homework, when she heard her father yell. She sprang up, opened her door, and ran down the stairs.

"What is it?" she asked, alarmed.

"What is this?" Mr. Friedman was holding a piece of paper in his hands. They were shaking, so Charlotte couldn't focus on what the paper was.

"I don't know. I can't see it." Charlotte was standing on the stairs, debating whether she should approach to see what the paper was or if she should keep her distance from her enraged father.

"*Dear Miss Friedman,*" he began, cruelly imitating a woman's voice. "*We are pleased to inform you that you have been selected as a finalist for Miss Subways. Please report*

*to the John Robert Powers Modeling Agency at 247 Park
Avenue, New York City on Monday, March 7, at 1:00 P.M.
sharp for your interview. We are unable to reschedule this
appointment."*

"Where did you get that?" Charlotte asked, her tone
bitter.

"It doesn't matter. Were you going to keep this from me?"

Charlotte decided to tell the truth, hoping her father
would see the value in her plan. "I was, because I didn't
think you'd allow me to do it. But—"

"But nothing, Charlotte. You will not do Miss Subways."

"Why? What's wrong with Miss Subways?" Charlotte
asked, switching her weight from foot to foot on the stairs.

"It's not something nice girls do," Mr. Friedman said, his
face turning red.

"That's not true at all. I met these girls. And they're all
nice. And—"

"The answer is no, and my decision is final."

"Father, please! Just hear me out!" Charlotte said, raising her voice.

Mr. Friedman looked stunned and started to walk away.

"If I win, it could help the store."

He stopped walking but didn't turn around.

Charlotte spoke quickly, afraid to lose his attention. "If I
win, which is a long shot but not an impossibility, then the
name of the store would be on my poster, which millions of
people would see." Charlotte continued to describe the
potential of that attention and the possibility for increased
business for the store. She kept her voice calm, professional,
and hoped her father would see this less as a plea from his
daughter and more as a business conversation.

Mr. Friedman stood silent, his back still turned against Charlotte.

"You will not pursue this any further. I'm going to call this Fontaine woman tomorrow and let her know you're withdrawing."

"You can't do that!" Charlotte shouted. "I'll do it anyway."

Mr. Friedman turned around, a snarl forming on his face. "Do you think they're going to let you after they receive my phone call?"

Charlotte hated to admit it, but he was right. It seemed unthinkable, but she knew a phone call from a girl's father had that power.

"Please don't do this. It might be my only chance."

Mr. Friedman walked toward her on the stairs. Charlotte thought for a moment he had changed his mind, that he was approaching her to apologize, give her a hug, and wish her good luck. But he brushed by her without making eye contact, went to his bedroom, and slammed the door.

Later that night, when Charlotte was certain her parents were asleep, she took the telephone into the closet and called JoJo.

"It was awful, but I have a plan," Charlotte whispered determinedly.

"Charlotte, you sound possessed. I think I like this side of you."

"I need you to do me a favor."

CHAPTER 10

OLIVIA
TUESDAY, MARCH 6, 2018

Olivia stood in Mrs. Glasser's hallway, shaking her head and laughing quietly at the familiar-looking black-and-white rectangular poster in a gold filigree frame. She took her phone out of her purse and texted Priya.

Olivia
I found our Miss Subways July 1949. She's my next-door neighbor.

When she returned to the table, Olivia couldn't resist her urge to stare more closely at Mrs. Glasser. She had typical short white grandmother hair, but it was fashionably styled as if the blue-fingernail-polished girls down at the dry bar had tended to it themselves. And her eyes. Her eyes glowed as brightly as the jewels Olivia always admired in the Crown of the Andes, one of her favorite objects to see at the Met. Mrs. Glasser's skin looked paper-thin but still had a rosiness about the cheeks. Olivia could most definitely see the youth and beauty in Mrs. Glasser's face.

Olivia didn't know if she should blurt out her discovery, which would confirm she had been snooping, or let it simmer for a while. She felt the questions piling up like firewood in her brain. And the splinters were starting to hurt.

"Last time we spoke, Olivia," Mrs. Glasser said, passing her the platter of salmon, "you were in advertising. Are you still, dear?"

Olivia couldn't contain herself. "Yes, um, I am. I'm sorry, Mrs. Glasser, but I couldn't help noticing the Miss Subways poster on the wall in your hallway."

"Yeah, my grandma was quite a beauty in her day. Still is, but you know what I mean," Ben said, taking the salmon platter from Olivia.

"That's incredible," Olivia said.

"That was a lifetime ago," Mrs. Glasser said, smiling and looking like her thoughts were somewhere else for a moment. "How do you know about Miss Subways? It's certainly way before your time."

"My agency is pitching the MTA account, so I've been doing research into historical subway advertising campaigns. I discovered the Miss Subways campaign online last night. And ever since, I've been captivated by it. In fact, when you next check your answering machine, you'll find a message that my associate Priya left for you. We're hoping to talk to some Miss Subways."

"It certainly was quite popular in its day. Just thinking about it now brings back such powerful memories," Mrs. Glasser said, a small smile appearing on her lips.

"Would you mind telling me about it?" Olivia asked.

"I'd be happy to, dear, but not right now. I don't feel up to it. But tomorrow morning. You'll come on my walk with me."

"I'd love to," Olivia said, surprised by the invitation. Or rather, demand. "Thanks."

Olivia looked at Ben, who had a huge smile on his face. He looked at Olivia, then at his grandmother, and then again at Olivia, catching her eye. Olivia smiled back.

The three of them talked about politics, movies, that week's episodes of *Ellen*, and Ben's latest travels, which had been to the Galapagos.

When they had all finished eating (the best home-cooked meal Olivia had eaten in a very long time because it was the only home-cooked meal Olivia had eaten in a very long time), Mrs. Glasser stood up to clear the plates. Olivia and Ben rose to help, but she shooed them away. "You two kids, relax. I'm going to wash the dishes, and then I'll bring out dessert."

Olivia and Ben both protested, but Mrs. Glasser was insistent, so the children did what they were told.

"Have you been to the Galapagos, Olivia?" Ben asked as they both fidgeted with their napkins.

"No, but I'd love to go someday."

"You like to travel?"

"In theory, yes, but I've never been out of the country. I've traveled a bit in the US for work, but I've never traveled for me."

"Where would you go if you could go anywhere?"

"Easy. Paris."

"Ah . . . the Eiffel Tower, the Louvre, Notre Dame."

"No, that's not why actually."

Ben tilted his head with a questioning look.

"It's Paris because, and this is going to sound so stupid to you because you clearly travel quite a bit, but, okay, I can't believe I'm going to admit this to you right now," Olivia said, and hesitated. She looked at Ben searchingly, deciding whether she should continue.

"Go on," he said kindly. "I promise I won't think it sounds stupid, and if I do think it sounds stupid, I promise not to tell you."

Olivia laughed. "Okay," she said, and took a deep breath. "I've always been so envious of people who just casually say, 'Oh, when I was in Paris' or 'Can you believe the light in Paris?' or any other random thing I've been hearing friends and strangers say for years. And I know this must sound so shallow, but I've always wanted to just toss out something like that."

"So you're saying you'd like to use Paris in vain?"

"Absolutely, that's what I'm saying." Olivia laughed. "Stupid, huh?"

"I'm in a bind here because I told you I wouldn't tell you if I thought it was stupid, so you might not believe me even though I'm going to tell you the truth. Not stupid at all."

"Well, I am the queen of the staycation, so if you ever want any tips on which free walking tours in New York City stop at the best restaurants, I'm your gal."

"Okay, good to know."

"I figure I'll travel one day, so I try to save, but somehow my account never seems to be full enough for a trip. Especially one to Paris. But listen to me. I'm going on and on with my problems. Sorry," Olivia said, looking at Ben.

"No problem. It doesn't bother me a bit. I like hearing about you," Ben said sweetly.

"Sounds like you travel a lot."

"I do. Mostly for work, but I'm not complaining. I love what I do."

"What *do* you do?" Olivia asked, taking a sip of her water.

"Have you heard of UseYourWings.com?" Ben asked.

"Of course! My trip portfolio is bursting. You know where you can pin all the trips you want to take and the sights you want to visit at each place?"

"You use it?"

"All the time. It instantly calms me down. I must have, like, thirty-five trips in the process of being planned. And the articles are amazing too. Do you write for them?"

"I do."

"No way!" Olivia said, and banged her hand on the table.

"What happened?" Mrs. Glasser called from the kitchen and appeared in the doorway, holding cupcakes.

"Nothing, Grandma," Ben said.

"Sorry, Mrs. Glasser," Olivia said sheepishly. "I just got a little excited when I heard what Ben does for a living, so I banged the table."

"Oh, he has that effect on all the girls," Mrs. Glasser said, approaching the table now.

"Right. That's exactly right," Ben said, looking at Olivia. "That's why I eat dinner with my grandmother every night."

"Oh, Benjamin. You could have any girl you want. You just don't make an effort."

"I'm busy, Grandma. And I travel all the time. It's hard," Ben said, a blush coming to his cheeks.

"Do you have a special boyfriend, Olivia?" Mrs. Glasser asked Olivia as she put a cupcake on a plate for her.

"Grandma!" Ben said, giving Mrs. Glasser a look.

"Oh, please, Ben," Mrs. Glasser said. "It's a fair question."

"It's fine. I don't mind," Olivia said, looking at Ben and

then at Mrs. Glasser. "And the answer is no. I'm not with anyone special right now."

Olivia took a bite of her cupcake and let the awkward silence pass.

"So tomorrow morning, Olivia. Meet me in the hallway at seven o'clock and we'll go from here."

"Sure. Where do you walk?"

"The High Line. We can enter at Gansevoort and Washington."

"Perfect. But that's an early call time for me, so I'm going to thank you for a truly wonderful evening and get to bed. It was so kind of you to invite me tonight."

"Of course, it was a pleasure having you, dear," Mrs. Glasser said, and stood. She walked toward the kitchen, calling after her, "Don't leave yet. I have something for you."

"Okay," Olivia said, standing to collect her things. "You're a lucky guy, Ben. To have a family like this," Olivia said.

"Funny, because so often I feel like I got cheated out of a family."

They stared at each other for a minute.

"Here you go, dear," Mrs. Glasser said, handing Olivia a heavy plastic bag. "It's leftovers. You'll return the Tupperware when you're done."

"That is so nice of you," Olivia said. "I really appreciate it." She leaned over and gave Mrs. Glasser a kiss on her cheek. "See you in the hallway in the morning."

"Seven o'clock. Don't be late," Mrs. Glasser said, opening the front door.

"I won't. Good night, Ben," Olivia said. He was standing next to his grandma, hands shoved deep into his pockets.

"Good night, Olivia."

Olivia opened her front door at 6:59 A.M. and found Mrs. Glasser at the elevator. The down button was already pushed.

Mrs. Glasser was dressed in black leggings, pink Nikes with white ankle socks, and a fuchsia North Face down jacket. Olivia was similarly dressed, but in all black: black leggings, black Nikes, black no-show socks, and a black Moncler jacket. Jenna's, of course.

They made small talk on the elevator down, Olivia thanking Mrs. Glasser again for the delicious meal, withholding what to her was an embarrassing admission that she hadn't sat at a dining room table with others in years, besides a Thanksgiving here and there at Jenna's.

The doorman looked surprised to see them together. "Mrs. Glasser! Olivia! A little morning exercise?"

"That's right, Nico. Mrs. Glasser is showing me how it's done. I hope I can keep up!"

"Good luck with that!" he called after them as they went outside.

Spring was on deck but winter refused to yield, so Olivia was happy she had her jacket and beanie and gloves. Mrs. Glasser was clearly made of heartier stock, gloveless and hatless and walking quite quickly. Olivia put an extra oomph in her step to catch up.

Once they were on the High Line, Olivia felt warmer and kept pace with Mrs. Glasser. They weren't alone. There was a reassuring representation of New York up early to join them: a woman in head-to-toe Lululemon talking into her mouthpiece and pumping her arms; a tired-looking stroller pusher; business people on their way to work, cross-body bags swaying.

"I Googled you last night, Olivia," Mrs. Glasser said matter-of-factly, staring straight ahead, her pace impressive for an older woman.

"You did?" Olivia asked, looking at Mrs. Glasser. This woman, who she had never really thought about, was continuing to destroy every assumption Olivia had made of her.

"Of course. I like to research my dates before I go out with them." At this, Mrs. Glasser turned to Olivia and winked.

Olivia smiled.

"I see from your LinkedIn profile that you've worked in advertising for your whole career," Mrs. Glasser said.

"I have. I started at Young & Rubicam right out of college and left only a few years ago when my boss, Matthew Osborne, started an agency and I joined him."

"How is that working out?"

"Pretty well. Actually," Olivia reconsidered, "pretty awful right now. We recently lost one of our accounts, and we were counting on winning a piece of business that didn't come through."

"And now you're trying to win the MTA account?"

"Yes, and we're thinking about incorporating Miss Subways into our pitch."

"Would you bring back the contest the way it was?"

"We're not entirely sure what we'd do. Perhaps some sort of juxtaposition with how women's aspirations in the past weren't so different from how today's women approach their careers and their lives. They may be framed differently, and they may appear more quaint in the Miss Subways posters, but women have always dealt with the same struggles in establishing an identity. And tying it into the subway, it would be something like, 'See where the subway can take you. It can take you to this life or that life.' I don't really know yet. I just have to find the right edge and unpack it from there."

Mrs. Glasser didn't say anything, so Olivia turned to her. Mrs. Glasser had a big smile on her face.

"What?" Olivia asked.

"I like how your brain works. You remind me a little of myself when I was younger. So ambitious. Wanting to prove yourself."

"I feel like I have so much to prove. To myself especially. It's a little overwhelming at times, and sometimes I wish I didn't feel that way, but I can't help it."

"It's a good thing. It's what will drive you."

"I hope so."

Mrs. Glasser stopped at a slatted wood bench. They sat down and stared over the railing at the cloudless blue sky. Olivia felt warm from the exercise and from the companionship. It was nice to speak with someone who understood her.

"In my day, it was revolutionary to want what I wanted. Not so much having a job—a lot of girls had jobs and wanted jobs. During the war, many women worked, so it wasn't so unusual. But after the war, the roles seemed to revert back. Most of the women I knew just wanted to get married. They didn't want to build a career."

"But I saw your wedding picture in your hallway, so was it a problem for your husband that you worked?"

"No. Not at all. My husband loved that I was ambitious. I had made it clear from the very beginning that I was a career girl."

"Did you encounter a lot of sexism?" Olivia asked, turning to Mrs. Glasser.

"Oh, sure. And it didn't get better over the years, even as times changed. It may have changed superficially, but there was always an undercurrent. In many ways, I just worked around it. I knew I wasn't going to be able to single-handedly abolish it—it was too ingrained—so I just made tactical decisions at different occasions: sometimes I ignored it and sometimes I addressed it head-on. Essentially, I picked my battles. Ready for more?" Mrs. Glasser asked, standing up.

"Sure," Olivia said, and they resumed their walk. "What was it like to be Miss Subways?"

Mrs. Glasser turned to Olivia and smiled. "To be perfectly honest, it was an exciting time. One of the most memorable experiences of my life. I haven't thought about it in years, but after you left last night, I reminisced. Thank you for that."

"That's fantastic!" Olivia said. "Can you tell me your story?"

They continued walking while Mrs. Glasser told Olivia all about receiving the letter saying she was a finalist, along with her whole experience with the photo shoot and interview and everything that came after. Mrs. Glasser's voice changed, Olivia thought, as she talked about Miss Subways. It was lighter, girlier, as if going back to that time transformed Mrs. Glasser, in a way, to the person she was then.

While Mrs. Glasser told her story, Olivia imagined herself in 1949, going through the same adventure. Olivia had never had something like that happen to her. Something so out of the ordinary from her normal daily life. She could only imagine what it must have been like to have been plucked from the mundane and delivered to a world of glamour and attention, at least for a little bit. "Do you think the experience changed you?"

"Yes," Mrs. Glasser said. "Absolutely. Everything that happened to me after was only possible because of Miss Subways. Let's turn around."

Olivia thought the exercise felt good. She didn't make enough time in her life for exercise. She didn't make enough time in her life for much aside from work. Maybe, she thought, committing to a regular walking schedule was just what she needed. Perhaps with Mrs. Glasser?

"So you said last night you don't have a boyfriend," Mrs. Glasser said.

"Yeah, no boyfriend in sight. There's a man I like, but I have to get it through my dense head that there's no future for us. He doesn't like me how I like him, and however much I try to convince myself that it's for the best, there's part of me that's still holding out for him."

"I've always found in my life that answers become clear at unexpected times. You have to trust that they will and then keep your eyes wide-open for the signs. Sometimes they will be subtle, but they'll always present themselves. And you have to be brave enough to take a risk even if it seems like there are a lot of reasons not to."

Olivia was silent, digesting what Mrs. Glasser had said. It applied to her job and it applied to her life. Olivia just wasn't sure if she'd seen any signs yet. She hoped she hadn't missed them. But she promised herself she'd be more attentive.

CHAPTER 11

"Charlotte Friedman? Mr. Powers will see you now."

The relief Charlotte felt was palpable when Miss Fontaine eventually called her name. Upon her arrival at the office earlier, she fully expected the birds to send her on her way due to the fact that—their notes would clearly say—Miss Fontaine had spoken to Charlotte's father and, well, ta-ta.

And even though that didn't happen, even though the birds directed her to the conference room where the other girls had assembled, waiting for their audience with John Robert Powers, waiting for their chance at becoming Miss Subways, waiting for their lives to be touched by a bit of razzle-dazzle, Charlotte had been wary, expecting the worst. That Miss Fontaine would take one look at her, that a synapse would fire off reminding her of the nasty Mr. Friedman dashing his daughter's dream, and that Charlotte would be back on Park Avenue, left with nothing to remember Miss Subways by, save a crinkled finalist letter and a teacup full of memories not worth having.

But that didn't happen either. Which meant Charlotte's

plan had worked. And that Miss Fontaine believed JoJo when she'd called posing as Charlotte's mother: "I'm so sorry for the inconvenience, Miss Fontaine, but my husband over-reacted when he called you earlier, and he's changed his mind. He has decided to allow Charlotte to participate in Miss Subways after all. It was a terrible misunderstanding, and I hope it won't in any way tarnish Charlotte's chances in the competition."

When Charlotte arrived at John Robert Powers that morning, she'd gone to the ladies' room to put on a fresh coat of lipstick. She told the girl in the mirror that if she didn't want to work at her father's store, she needed to win Miss Subways July 1949. Then she told the girl that there was absolutely no reason why she couldn't.

Hearing her name called, Charlotte stood, took a deep breath, and reminded herself of everything she had to lose. She needed to ensure that the moment she met John Robert Powers, he was convinced he was looking at Miss Subways July 1949.

"Go get 'em," Rose whispered to her.

Charlotte looked around the table, and all the girls who still remained in the room gave her encouraging smiles. Charlotte straightened her dress with her palms—she had borrowed something black, form-fitting, and slightly alluring from JoJo—and followed Miss Fontaine into a large office, outfitted entirely in dark wood, walnut perhaps. Charlotte wasn't sure which had a more commanding presence: the huge desk that sat in the center of the room beneath the floor-to-ceiling windows or the man behind it. Mr. John Robert Powers.

"Mr. Powers, allow me to present Miss Charlotte Fried-man of Brooklyn," Miss Fontaine announced, gently guiding

Charlotte toward Mr. Powers, who stood when she approached.

"Miss Friedman, it's a delight to meet you. Please, sit down," Mr. Powers said, shaking Charlotte's hand and gesturing to one of the leather chairs across the desk from his. "Let's get to know each other a bit."

Charlotte smiled. Her stomach was doing flips. *Breathe,* Charlotte reminded herself.

"Thank you, Mr. Powers," Charlotte said, lifting her chin and giving her hair what she thought was a stylish shimmy. "It's an honor to be here."

"Well, well, the honor is all mine. You're certainly a doll of a girl. How old are you, dear?"

"I'm twenty-one. I'll be twenty-two this November."

"And what sort of job do you have?"

"I'm still in school, Mr. Powers, my final year at Hunter. My ultimate goal is to work in advertising, but for now, as soon as I graduate, I'm going to work in my father's store, which—"

"Isn't that nice? Would you like to be a Powers Girl, Miss Friedman?"

"Oh yes, Mr. Powers. Wouldn't every girl in New York like to be a Powers Girl? But I'll settle for Miss Subways," Charlotte said, smiling. She was starting to feel comfortable with Mr. Powers, who was nothing like she'd imagined he'd be, which was a cross between her high school principal and her father.

"I like this one. She's got pluck." Mr. Powers smiled, directing his comment at Miss Fontaine and the photographer, who was adjusting his camera near a white backdrop in a back corner of the office.

"Why, thank you, Mr. Powers," Charlotte said, recrossing her legs demurely.

"So, tell me, Miss Friedman: Do you have a special beau?"

"Yes, sir. His name is Sam. He's a lawyer at Linden & Linden."

"Oh, a fine Jewish firm."

"Yes, sir."

"Do you have plans to marry?"

"Well, if Sam had his way, we'd already be married, but I would like to establish myself in my career before I settle down."

"And what sorts of things do you like to do in your spare time, Miss Friedman?"

"Oh, all sorts of things, I guess. But I don't have much free time. As I started to say, I work with my father at his store, Friedman's Paint and Wallpaper on Third Avenue in Bay Ridge. I try to be there as much as I can. It's a wonderful store. Every paint color imaginable and books just bursting with wallpaper choices." Charlotte knew that sounded ridiculous, but promoting her father's store was the whole point. At least she refrained from saying it was well lit and there was free coffee on Saturday mornings.

"Fine, fine. Now, tell me, Miss Friedman: Have you ever had your picture taken?"

"Sure, lots of times."

"Fantastic. This will be just like that. Muky here will tell you where to stand and what sorts of expressions to make, and you just need to be yourself. How does that sound?"

"Well, I'll certainly do my best, Mr. Powers."

"Fine, fine. Muky? Miss Friedman is ready for her test

shots. Thank you for your time today, Miss Friedman. It was a delight speaking with you. I think you're a lovely girl and exactly the type we're looking for for Miss Subways."

"Thank you, Mr. Powers," Charlotte said. He began to address papers on his desk, so Charlotte stood and turned to where Muky was finishing his preparations. She wondered if she should make another mention of the store. Or of how badly she wanted to be Miss Subways. She had thought the interview would be longer, that she'd have the opportunity to charm Mr. Powers a bit more, and she feared that she didn't contribute enough during their short exchange to convince him that she was his girl.

"This way," Muky said gruffly.

Charlotte took a final look at Mr. Powers, but he had already picked up his telephone. She smiled at him, though he didn't look up, and set her sights on impressing the photographer. Attempting to sashay the way she saw Rose doing earlier, she felt awkward and laughed to herself.

"Is something funny?" Muky asked.

"No, sir. I just had a thought."

"Care to share it?"

"Um, no, sir. I don't think you'd find it funny," Charlotte said, suddenly nervous around this diminutive man with the indiscernible accent who had not yet smiled.

"Stand on that white paper backdrop," Muky said.

When Charlotte stepped where he directed her to, her heel punctured the paper. A loud pop resonated through the room.

"Oh, I'm terribly sorry, Mr. Muky."

"Just Muky," the photographer said, sneering at her.

Charlotte became flustered, afraid to put more weight on her heels, so she leaned forward onto her toes.

"Now stand in the middle and just smile with your face directed squarely at the camera. No, don't turn your shoulders that way. Just face forward. And stop tilting your head like that—just straight. Lean back. You look like you're going to tip over."

Charlotte felt drops of sweat begin to trail down her back. Muky started snapping photos, and Charlotte tried to look natural as Muky kept yelling at her to do.

Charlotte looked toward Mr. Powers to see why he wasn't stopping this Muky fellow from addressing her in such a nasty way, but Mr. Powers and Miss Fontaine were busy sifting through photographs, probably of other Miss Subway contestants who most certainly had had an easier time with this Muky than Charlotte currently was.

"Look this way. Not over there. There's no camera over there. The camera is right here." Muky gestured grandly, shifting from hip to hip.

Charlotte readjusted herself, her nerves multiplying, and smiled at the camera.

"A natural smile. Not a false smile," Muky demanded.

For the next ten minutes, while Muky barked directions and Charlotte tried to keep up, turning her left shoulder in and then her right, tilting her head just so and then just so in the other direction, serious expressions, joyful expressions, she couldn't help but think this whole thing was going downhill fast. What had started so positively with Mr. Powers was ending miserably with Muky, and she didn't have any idea why this disagreeable man had it out for her.

"That will be all."

Suddenly, it was over. Charlotte smiled at Muky and thanked him, but he had already crossed the room and was deep in conversation with Mr. Powers. Charlotte's shoulders slumped and she felt tears stinging her eyes. She would not cry. Not here.

"Right this way, Miss Friedman," Miss Fontaine said, leading her by the elbow out of the room.

Charlotte looked over her shoulder one last time to try to make eye contact with Mr. Powers. She knew she should say thank you. That he would hear her, smile, and then she would feel better. But he was still talking to Muky, the small man gesturing wildly, angrily.

"That will be all. Thank you for coming, dear. We'll announce the winner next Friday the eighteenth at five thirty sharp. Please return then."

"I will. Thank you, Miss Fontaine."

Miss Fontaine turned back to the conference room to fetch the next girl.

"Miss Fontaine," Charlotte called after her. This undertaking was too important to leave it hanging so tenuously.

"Yes?" She was already halfway down the corridor.

Charlotte approached her and spoke with conviction. "I just wanted to say that I'm so honored to have been chosen as a finalist and, should Mr. Powers decide to choose me for July, I would take the designation quite seriously and live up to the ideals and responsibilities of Miss Subways. I do hope you can pass along that message to him."

Miss Fontaine smiled and told her she would.

Charlotte couldn't leave fast enough. Her cheeks were burning. She smiled politely at the receptionists as she approached their desk, but they were paying as much attention to her as a modeling scout would to a turnip.

Outside on Park Avenue, Charlotte was thankful for the cold air. Yet it seemed to encourage the tears to start

pouring from her eyes. Not one to cry easily, all of Charlotte's fears rushed to the front of her mind. She couldn't go
home just yet. She needed time to collect herself. Seeing a
coffee shop across the street, Charlotte crossed, practically
oblivious to the honking horns.

Charlotte was thankful the coffee shop was bustling and
noisy; she figured no one would notice her distraught state.
She sat in a window-side booth and ordered black coffee and
a slice of chocolate cake. Charlotte had felt something as she
slid into the booth, and now noticed a left-behind copy of
that month's *Cosmopolitan* magazine.

As she started turning the pages, the smiles of the models taunting her, Charlotte chastised herself. How could she
even begin to think she could be Miss Subways? How could
she be so stupid?

Charlotte was halfway through her cake and coffee when
she heard a tap on the window. Startled, she turned and
saw Rose making a funny face. Charlotte smiled and Rose
laughed, and, not being one to wait for an invitation, Rose
whooshed in on the jet stream and plopped right down in
the booth.

"Feel like some company?" Rose asked.

"Sure. Yes. I'm almost done, but you're welcome to
join me."

"I was on my way to the subway but saw you sitting so
forlornly, staring at that chocolate cake as if it were a lover. I
figured you might prefer a live person to commiserate with
rather than some pathetic concoction of flour and sugar."
Rose waved over the waitress and ordered an iced tea.

"Flour, sugar, and chocolate," Charlotte said. "You mustn't
leave out the chocolate."

"Of course, the chocolate. A panacea for all that troubles the modern woman."

"Indeed," Charlotte said, placing another bite of cake into her mouth.

"How'd your interview go?" Rose asked.

"Mr. Powers couldn't have been nicer. But I can't say the same for the photographer. What's with that Muky guy anyway?"

"Oh, don't mind him. He's harmless."

"I sure hope you're right. I couldn't seem to get anything right in his eyes. I tore through his paper with my heel and looked away from the camera. It was stupid with headaches. And as soon as I finished, he stormed right over to Mr. Powers. I'm certain he was saying horrible things about me."

"If it makes you feel any better, mine didn't go so well either."

"I can't imagine that. Just look at you with those violet eyes and glossy hair. You could be Elizabeth Taylor's sister."

"That's kind of you to say, Charlotte. But I had the opposite experience from you. My interview with Mr. Powers crashed like a falling stock market. I think he likes girls he can charm and control. I'm more used to taking control of situations myself. I might have come on a bit too strongly, appeared too confident, perhaps. I probably should have done my damsel-in-distress act. Men like John Powers tend to prefer girls like that."

Charlotte didn't know whether to be offended that Rose was implying she was a damsel-in-distress type or elated that it might mean she had a chance at becoming Miss Subways.

Rose continued, "What did you tell him you do?"

"Exactly what I do do. Well, partly. I'm in my last year at Hunter, and then I'm going to work for my father. I really want to work for an advertising firm, but that's still to be decided. What do you do?"

"I work in a dress shop. This week, at least. I was a cigarette girl at the Stork Club, but that only lasted a month. I've also been a waitress and a babysitter. But I told Mr. Powers that I'm an international airline stewardess and my goal is to receive an Academy Award for Best Actress in a motion picture."

"You lied?" Charlotte's eyes widened.

"The second half is true. But everyone lies on their Miss Subways posters. You think that girl from last summer really wants to be an insurance broker? What girl in this day and age wants to be an insurance broker? What a bore snore. Or that one from a few years ago really thinks—what was it now?—oh right, that 'being a housewife is the greatest career in the world'? Oh, brother, if that isn't a load of patooey. You think all those girls from the Bronx and Brooklyn really love sailing and skiing? I bet they've never seen snow in their lives outside the five boroughs. No, honey, everyone just says what they think will make their lives sound better than they really are."

"I had no idea that's what we were supposed to do," Charlotte said, her voice rising gently in a panic. She unthinkingly wrapped her paper napkin around her fingers and looked down at her mostly eaten cake. Not that she had a choice to make her career sound glamorous—the whole point was to promote Friedman's. But if Mr. Powers was looking for girls with interesting and glamorous jobs, her chances at winning were nil.

"Don't you worry your pretty little head. I'm sure John Powers was quite taken by you with that perfect doll face and sunny-side-up disposition. So advertising, huh?"

"Yes, I hope to get a job in the typing pool. That is if . . ." Charlotte's voice dropped and the tears, those damn tears, started to fill her eyes.

Rose reached her hand across the table to Charlotte's. "What is it, honey? Why are you crying?"

"Oh, it's nothing," Charlotte said, dabbing her eyes with her napkin and trying to regain her composure. She barely knew Rose. Wasn't about to start dumping out her whole life right there on the table next to the pathetic-looking salt and pepper shakers.

"I don't mind. You can tell me. How about if I tell you a secret first?"

"Well, I don't really have a secret," Charlotte said slowly.

"That's all right. I'll still tell you mine. Now let's see: Which one should I tell?"

Charlotte giggled. She couldn't believe this creature, this Rose, sitting across from her. This Rose, who was so many things that Charlotte was not. Supremely confident. Daringly expressive. Unimaginably gorgeous.

"I've been engaged six times."

"Six times!" Charlotte blurted out, and immediately covered her mouth with her hand. "Sorry. I didn't mean to sound so shocked. It's just that . . . How old are you?"

"I'm twenty. How about you?"

"I'm twenty-one."

"I'll be twenty-one on New Year's Eve. How's that for a party? Yes, indeed, six times. I'm still engaged to moron number six, but I'm not sure it'll be for long. He bores me to death and back."

"What's he do?"

"He's an insurance salesman. Now you see?"

Again, Charlotte laughed. She was enchanted.

"So go ahead," Rose said, nudging her chin. "What's your secret?"

Charlotte was feeling more comfortable, so she told Rose all about her father, the store, and that most likely she would be working there full-time.

"I'm sorry to hear that, Charlotte," Rose said sincerely.

"Enough about me. I'm tired of hearing myself talk. What about you, Rose? How does Miss Subways fit into your life?"

"I'm moving to Hollywood in the fall to be in pictures. My cousin has a friend who knows a fellow at Paramount who said he could get me a screen test. But I figured that if I could become Miss Subways or a Powers Girl, or both, it could open doors."

"My goodness, a real-life movie-star-in-the-making just a slice of cake away."

"I'll invite you to my first premiere," Rose said, flipping her hair and batting her long eyelashes.

"Promise?"

"Promise."

Charlotte looked at her watch and was shocked by how late it had gotten. She quickly grabbed some coins from her purse to leave for the bill, collected her coat, and stood to go.

"I'm so sorry, but I have to get home. I have a lot of studying to do."

"Where do you live?"

"Bay Ridge."

"Me too. I'll come with you."

Charlotte and Rose walked to Lexington to catch the subway home.

On the ride back, Charlotte asked Rose how she had become a finalist for Miss Subways.

"I submitted my picture, and then I got the letter."

"You submitted your own?"

"Sure, if you want something in life, you have to go for it. But you know that, going for that advertising career and all."

"I guess."

"Do you have a boyfriend?" Rose asked.

"Yes. Sam. He's a dream."

"You might not know it, considering all my engagements, but I'm never going to get married. And there will be no kids, either."

"Why not?" Charlotte asked, surprised.

"Maybe I'll marry someone out in Hollywood, especially if it will help my career. Sure didn't hurt Lauren Bacall or Vivien Leigh. But babies? Never. There's too much I want to do with my life. I just can't even imagine having kids."

"Why are you waiting until the fall to move to Hollywood?"

"That's when I'll have saved enough to buy a bus ticket and have some money in my pocket to rent a place when I get there."

"How do your parents feel about all of this?" Charlotte asked.

"Well, my father's dead and my mother's a part-time alcoholic, so neither of them really cares that much."

"Oh, I'm so sorry," Charlotte said.

"That's okay. I'm used to it. No point getting sentimental about it. I still live at home so I can take care of my younger brothers and sisters when my mother's, let's just say, not at her best."

"What will they do when you leave?" Charlotte asked.

Rose looked down at her hands.

"Sorry," Charlotte said. "I didn't mean to pry."

"That's okay. Sore subject, I guess. Mother's got a nice neighbor who said she'd help out, and the older ones can care for the younger ones. But I can't hold my life back any longer. I've got to chase my dreams."

Rose nudged Charlotte and pointed up at the Miss Subways poster.

"Hey, guess what?" Rose said to the strangers in the row across from them. "You see my friend here? She's going to be the next Miss Subways!"

The two of them erupted in laughter and made their way back to Bay Ridge.

CHAPTER 12

Olivia was the first to the conference room for the weekly Friday morning meeting. Matt came in next.

"Good morning, sunshine," Matt said, tipping his coffee cup at her.

"Good morning to you," Olivia said.

"Liam Taylor called me. He wanted to know the metrics on the last campaign. I have a follow-up call with him at three o'clock. Can you email me your thoughts so I'm prepared for the call?" Matt asked, looking at his phone.

"Sure. No problem. Those ads did really well. I talked with Monica about it a few days ago and she was pleased, so Liam should be as well," Olivia said, making a note to herself on her laptop.

"Great," Matt said, and put his phone down. He took a breath. "How are you, Liv?"

Well, I'm insanely worried that if I don't come up with something brilliant for this MTA pitch, I'll not only lose your adorable little challenge to Thomas, but I'll also lose my job.

I'm worried that my friend will come home and want her apartment back, which will leave me without a place to live. And I'm madly in love with you.

"Fine, Matt. Just fine."

"Hey, hey," Thomas said, sweeping in, sunglasses and coat still on.

"Hey, great," Matt said. "Let's get started. Olivia, what do you have?"

The three of them discussed all the accounts, some personnel and office management issues, and then Matt turned to the MTA pitch.

"We're a week out," Matt said. "Each of you will give me your presentation this Monday, and I'll decide from there which one to go with. We'll spend next week working on the pitch and finalizing the creative. Friday will be here before we know it. You two ready?"

"Ready as a virgin on her wedding night," Thomas said, smiling at Olivia.

"Really, Matt. Is this who you want representing your agency?" Olivia asked.

"He's just trying to psych you out, Olivia. Don't let him think it's working."

Just then Thomas's assistant, Christina, walked in.

"Thomas, your wife is on the line. She says it's urgent," Christina said. "Oh, and, Matt, I know Thomas said the dinner tonight at Sparks is at seven, but they had to push it to seven thirty."

Olivia saw Thomas look at her quickly and then at Matt, who was staring at his phone and nodding. Something about that moment struck Olivia as strange, but she couldn't figure out what it was.

"Go ahead, Thomas. We're done here," Matt said.

Thomas collected his things and walked out of the conference room.

Matt stood and started to walk out as well.

"You know, Matt," Olivia said. "Ninety-nine percent of Thomas's behavior is completely unacceptable. If we were still at Y&R, I'd report him to HR."

"Liv, you know he's an idiot. He's just a really creative idiot who has a way with clients. Please let it slide off you. Don't pay attention to his nonsense."

"That makes you just as bad," Olivia said, shutting the lid on her laptop.

"Everyone is on edge right now. Let's just get through this MTA pitch and then we can talk about everything."

"That's convenient," Olivia said, nodding. "One of us will probably be fired after the MTA pitch, so essentially you're just delaying this conversation because you know you won't really ever need to have it."

"That's not true," Matt said, smiling at her and giving her the look that always made her feel like there was some chance for them.

"I've got work to do," Olivia said, and walked out of the conference room. As she did, she saw Thomas leaving the office. So she went to Christina's desk.

"Hi, Christina," Olivia said.

"Oh, hi, Olivia."

"I know Thomas had to rush out, so he probably didn't have a chance to tell you to add me to the Sparks reservation for tonight."

"Oh, sure, no problem. Did he fill you in on who's all coming?"

"He gave me a top line but told me to ask you for the full download."

"Sure. So, it's with Edward Freck from the MTA and a couple of men from his office. I guess since you all are late to this pitch, he's agreed to meet in person to review what he discussed with the other agencies at the beginning of the process, but you probably know that already. Sparks Steak House is on Forty-Sixth between Second and Third, and the reservation is at seven thirty. I have a car coming here at seven o'clock to take Thomas and Matt. So I'll let Thomas know to come by your office and grab you before he goes downstairs."

"Oh no, that's okay. I have to do something anyway before the dinner, so I'll just meet them there, but thanks so much."

"My pleasure, Olivia."

Olivia walked to her desk, fuming, and slammed her door behind her. How dare Thomas arrange a dinner like this and not include her. And how dare Matt not tell her about this. There was no way, she decided, that this could be an honest mistake. Olivia would do what had to be done. Take matters into her own hands, control the narrative, and take it from there.

But first, she and Priya needed to decide which angle they were going to take and start crafting their presentation, which they'd have to work on throughout the weekend. Olivia was determined to prevail. If she won the MTA account, this would cement her career not only at The Osborne Agency but also in the industry. This account was huge, and she'd already seen articles about the pitch process and the contenders in *Ad Age* and on advertising blogs. Having her name associated with this win could mean something. Would mean something. For years to come.

The conference room was strewn with the detritus from their lunch delivery: burger wrappers, shake cups, greasy napkins trailing ketchup. Olivia and Priya had been meeting with Pablo, trying to decide which of the three ideas they should go with.

The first idea was having tastemakers decorate subway cars. The second idea was some sort of revamp of or look back at Miss Subways. And the third idea, another that Olivia had come up with, was based on the concept of "The New York Subway Takes You Places."

The concept was that the subway not only literally took you places, from here to there, but it also took you places in your life. A college graduate living in his parents' basement in Queens could get on the subway and arrive at his new paralegal job in Manhattan. A young man who recently immigrated to America could take the subway from his overcrowded apartment in the Bronx to his new vocational school in Brooklyn. A fifteen-year-old girl living on the Lower East Side could take the subway to Bronx Science, the highly competitive public high school. A little kid who wanted to be a zoologist could take the subway to the Bronx or Central Park Zoo.

Olivia explained to Pablo and Priya that the placards would show a photo of one of these New Yorkers, and next to it the copy would read: "I took the subway to_____, and the subway took me to _____." The person in the photo would fill in the answers in his or her own handwriting. So, for instance, the first example would say, "I took the subway to *Fifty-First Street and Lexington Avenue in Manhattan*, and the subway took me to *an exciting and promising career in the law.*"

Pablo and Priya liked the idea and agreed it would make

riders look up because they'd be curious who the latest New York "going places" was, like the original Miss Subways campaign, but it would also show the larger purpose of the subway in that it didn't just transport people, it transported their lives as well.

But when it came time to decide which campaign to go with, they couldn't come to a consensus.

"I think the tastemakers designing cars is going to be a really expensive proposition. My gut says to not go with that idea because we'll have to present budgets, and I'm sure the client will balk at the costs," Pablo said, looking down at the sketches he had been drawing of the "Takes You Places" concept.

"That's true. But I didn't know we had to present budgets for this round," Olivia said.

"I'm not sure we do," Pablo said, "but just in case."

They all thought quietly for a moment.

"I just had an idea," Olivia said. "What if we combine the Miss Subways and 'Takes You Places' concepts? Just thinking out loud here . . . What if we did somewhat of a 'Where Are They Now?' for the Miss Subways winners? The placard could be two panels. The left side could show the original poster, and the right side would show a photograph of the woman today and how being Miss Subways propelled her in her career or her life or meant something to her in some other way. We can re-create the look of the original photo for the current one, and the tone of the new copy could be inspired by the original poster. Not sure how we would do it exactly, but we could riff on it from there."

"Pablo, what do you think?" Priya asked, spinning her pen in her fingers.

"I think it's great," Pablo said, already sketching a two-panel poster based on Olivia's description.

"I do too," Priya said. "I love it." She and Olivia walked behind Pablo to see his sketch.

"Great," Olivia said. "Priya, can you please write up a preliminary brief on the strategy and what we need to do to make it happen? And, Pablo, if you could work on some rough art, that would be great. Let's all meet back here tomorrow morning at nine and we'll go from there. I'll bring breakfast."

"So sorry I'm late," Olivia said, approaching the round table. With a blowout from Drybar and a perfect black dress from Jenna's closet, she felt like Beyoncé and Sheryl Sandberg and Olivia Pope all wrapped up into one pulsating package of female confidence.

"Olivia, what are you doing here?" Thomas asked, looking at her like she was a space alien.

The other four men at the table—the three men from the MTA and Matt—all stood.

"I guess we'll need that extra chair and place setting after all," Matt said to a waiter.

Olivia could tell from Matt's wording that the table had originally been set for six, true to the reservation after Christina had added Olivia to it. She imagined that when the men had all arrived, they'd wondered why there was an extra setting and had had it taken away. She smirked to herself, enjoying the drama of it all. Her insides sizzled at achieving this element of surprise.

"My pleasure, sir. I'll have the table reset right away," the waiter said, smiling at Olivia.

"Olivia, this is Ed Freck from the MTA," Matt said, gesturing to the man to his right. All of the men were still standing except for Thomas, who was sitting, shooting hate daggers from his eyes at Olivia. Ed Freck was very tall and thin, with whispers of white hair tickling the tops of his ears.

"Ed, so nice to meet you," Olivia said, shaking his hand firmly.

"Likewise, Olivia. And these are my associates, Ken Trainor and Evan Greenleaf."

"Nice to meet you," Olivia said, shaking both men's hands.

"You didn't miss much, Olivia," Matt said as they sat. He searched Olivia's face for some answer to the question of why she was there. She gave him nothing but a self-assured smile. "Ed here was just telling us about a hole in one he had last summer at Hudson National."

"But that would be boring to Olivia, so we don't have to talk about that anymore," Ed said graciously, taking a sip of his wine. All of the glasses were filled with red wine, but Olivia's still sat empty. "Olivia, would you like some wine? We're drinking a California Cab," he said, waving over the waiter.

"I'd love some, Ed, thanks," Olivia said. "And please, continue with your story. I'd love to hear about your hole in one." The waiter filled her glass and she took a long sip.

"Are you a golfer now, Olivia?" Thomas asked, his arms folded across his chest.

"Can you believe that outcome at the PGA National a couple of weekends ago?" Olivia asked the men at the table, all except Thomas, whom she ignored.

They continued to speak about golf and then ordered their dinners.

"So you're the Olivia who so impressed Jack Haldon?" Evan asked.

"Olivia and I have worked together since she started in advertising," Matt said proudly, buttering his roll. He looked particularly handsome tonight in a dark suit and lavender tie. Olivia recalled he had been in jeans and a button-down at work that morning, so he must have also gone home to dress more appropriately for these potential clients.

"I can certainly see why Jack spoke so highly of her," Evan said, winking and air-toasting to Olivia across the table with his wineglass.

Olivia smiled tightly and noticed Matt wincing.

Ed changed the subject quickly and began talking about the MTA and their objectives for the new campaign. Olivia asked incisive questions and Thomas was noticeably quiet, still, Olivia assumed, privately fuming over having been had. He seemed especially angry, and Olivia could only presume it was because of the way the MTA men and Matt seemed so deferential to her. She knew they were on their best behavior—even Evan, in his own eyes—because she was female, and Olivia felt particularly conflicted about that. The irony that a woman's gender could be both a liability and an asset in business was not lost on her.

After several bottles of wine and several hours of conversation, they all walked out together. The dinner couldn't have gone better. Olivia better understood what the MTA was trying to accomplish with their marketing strategy, and she was excited to get to work with Priya and Pablo tomorrow to hammer out their approach. But for now, she just wanted, needed, to sleep. She was certainly feeling the effects of all that gorgeous California Cabernet.

"What the hell was that?" Thomas asked Olivia as soon

as the MTA guys left in a cab headed to the West Side. It was past ten and the air was frigid. Olivia wrapped her coat around herself tightly, but her legs were freezing.

"That was me refusing to be excluded from a dinner that I rightfully should have been at. It only shows your weakness and insecurity that you didn't invite me in the first place, Thomas," Olivia said, her hair blowing in the cold wind. She looked down the street and put her arm up for a cab.

"You could have scheduled your own dinner, Olivia. We're on separate teams here. No one was stopping you from calling Ed Freck. You just weren't bright enough to think of it yourself, so you had to bulldoze my dinner."

"I don't have the energy to listen to your childish whining, Thomas," Olivia said, stepping off the curb as a cab slowed in front of her.

"You're on my way. I'll take you home," Matt said, opening the door for Olivia.

"I'll be fine," Olivia said, getting into the cab.

"At least save me the money of having to pay for your expensed cab ride. Think of it as good economics for the agency," Matt said, holding the door.

Olivia looked at him and nodded slightly.

"Good night," Matt said to a stunned Thomas. He followed Olivia into the taxi and shut the door.

They rode for a while in silence. Olivia wanted to confront Matt about why he felt it was okay to exclude Olivia from a dinner she believed she clearly should have been invited to, but she didn't have the energy. And she didn't want to listen to the excuses.

"You're quiet," Matt said, turning in his seat to face her.

"I'm tired," Olivia said.

"You were electric tonight," Matt said, smiling at her.

"What do you mean?" Olivia asked, allowing herself a small smile.

"I mean that you had those clients eating out of your hands. That Evan Greenleaf jackass couldn't take his eyes off you."

Olivia sat silent for a moment and turned to Matt. "I know you mean well, Matt, but it would be so much more satisfying to hear you say that I was electric because of my shrewd questions and intelligent conversation."

"Oh, Liv, you know I didn't mean it like that," Matt said. "You were fantastic in every single way. I thought women enjoyed knowing they were perceived as attractive."

"They do. I do. It's just tricky in a work situation to be feminine but also be taken seriously."

"Well, I take you very seriously," Matt said, smiling.

Olivia's strength to withstand being charmed by Matt was diminishing.

"I've been thinking about this, Olivia, and if we don't win the account, I don't want you to worry about money. If you ever need to borrow anything, I will always lend it to you. You've been nothing but loyal to me, and I would gladly help you out in any way I can."

"Thank you, Matt, but I want to make my own money and not have to depend on anyone else for my needs."

"I completely respect that, Liv. But asking for help doesn't mean you're weaker because of it, and it certainly doesn't mean you're depending on someone else."

Olivia looked out the window. They were getting closer to her apartment. She knew Matt was right, but it was so hard. Thinking about her parents and knowing how her mother felt like she couldn't leave her father because she couldn't survive on her own—financially, emotionally—really struck a chord with Olivia.

Just then the cab stopped short and Olivia rolled into Matt. Her face was right next to his. Before she knew what was happening, he leaned in and kissed her. She could taste the wine, the mint he had taken from Sparks on the way out, and warmth. She heard herself let out a soft moan. But she didn't pull away. She allowed herself to be kissed by Matt. Solely for the reason that it felt good. And she wasn't thinking of anything else. Not tomorrow, not the future, not whether it was a terrible idea for her to be kissing her boss who she was secretly in love with. She just liked the way it felt.

"Do you want to come up?" Olivia asked.

CHAPTER 13

"Ladies, thank you for joining us again." Miss Fontaine stood at the front of the conference room.

Charlotte couldn't believe that Friday at five thirty had finally come. The combination of excitement and dread for this moment was unparalleled in Charlotte's staid life. Her heart was racing. Anabella Duarte looked as if she were going to vomit. Bella London looked as smug and confident as Will Shakespeare at a poetry reading. And Rose. Where was Rose?

"Soon, Mr. Powers will come in to announce the winner. He's been detained on a telephone call. If you'll excuse me, I need to check on an important matter, and I'll be back with Mr. Powers in a few minutes."

Right after Miss Fontaine left, Rose sashayed in, preening as if it weren't the least bit unusual for her to enter a gig once the band had already started to blast.

"Oh, the queen has decided to grace us with her presence," Bella said, snickering as Rose sat next to Charlotte.

"Did you say something, dear?" Rose asked Bella dismissively, raising an eyebrow.

Bella harrumphed and crossed her arms over her chest.

"How are you holding up?" Rose whispered to Charlotte.

"I'm so nervous. I'm not sure I can hold my lunch in any longer. And you?"

"I'm fine. I know I'm not going to win. But I wanted to be here for you in case you did."

Charlotte started to say something to Rose, but the door swung open and Miss Fontaine and Mr. Powers entered.

"Girls, so wonderful to see you all again," Mr. Powers bellowed.

"Thank you, Mr. Powers," they said in unison.

"Every month, I tell you, it gets harder and harder to pick a Miss Subways. You're all lovely girls, and each and every last one of you could be a Miss Subways. So I don't want you to be dismayed if you don't win. We'll keep you in the running for future months." He looked around the room and smiled at each of the girls. "Without further ado, Miss Subways July 1949 is"—he paused and gave the room another pointless study—"Miss Rose Grant!"

Charlotte was stunned, but she did what any dolled-up beauty pageant loser would do: she pasted a fake smile on her face, congratulated Rose, and gave her a heartfelt hug nonpareil.

"I can't believe it!" Rose exclaimed.

Charlotte was pushed to the side by other girls clamoring, most likely spuriously as well, to congratulate and embrace Rose. It gave her a moment to crawl inside her head and consider what had just happened. She lost. There would be no Miss Subways. There would be no increased attention for her father's store. There would be no realization of her grand scheme.

Charlotte looked up just as Bella stormed out of the room, crying. No one chased after her to console her. One of the birds came in with a tray of champagne and they all toasted Rose.

When the excitement had subsided and the girls had packed up their battered prides to leave, Rose turned to Charlotte. "I'm so sorry, Charlotte. I know how much this meant to you."

"Thanks, Rose, I appreciate that. But I know how much it meant to you as well. And I'm happy for you."

Rose hugged Charlotte and thanked her for being so supportive and gracious. Charlotte restrained a guffaw, considering "supportive" and "gracious" were not the two words she'd use to describe how she felt. Bitter and angry, perhaps. Even desperate. But supportive and gracious? Not a bit.

Miss Fontaine approached Rose to tell her what would happen next. Charlotte gave Rose a kiss on the cheek and said good-bye.

"Oh, won't you stay with me a minute, Charlotte? Then we can walk out together."

Listening to what Rose had in store was the last thing Charlotte wanted to do.

"Please," Rose said.

Charlotte gave a small smile, sat down, and prepared for the gross injustice of having to suffer through the winner's briefing.

"The photo shoot will be this Monday at nine o'clock. I know it seems early to do the photo shoot months before the poster will debut, but after your shoot, it takes time for the photo editors to select the best photo and do the retouching. Then the copywriter drafts the poster copy. Then it goes through an approval process with Mr. Powers, J. Walter Thompson, and the New York Subways Advertising Company. Finally, the almost ten thousand posters themselves need to be printed and distributed, and we need additional time for the previous month's posters to be taken down and replaced with the new ones. So you see," Miss Fontaine said, finally taking a breath, "it's quite an endeavor."

Rose grabbed Charlotte's hand. "This is so exciting!"

Charlotte smiled and nodded. And then she returned to the churn of thoughts in her mind.

"Any questions?" Miss Fontaine asked Rose.

Rose shook her head.

"Okay, well then, Miss Grant, I'll see you back here on Monday at nine sharp. Miss Friedman, I'm sorry it didn't work out this month. There's always next."

"Thank you, Miss Fontaine," Charlotte and Rose said.

"I'm still in shock. Pinch me, and tell me that all just happened," Rose said, turning to Charlotte.

"That all just happened," Charlotte said, pinching Rose, perhaps a bit too eagerly.

"Ouch!"

"You said to pinch you."

"Yes, but you didn't have to do it so hard." Rose laughed.

"Your dream came true, Miss Rose," Charlotte said.

"Well, that it did, Miss Charlotte. I hate that you didn't win though."

As Charlotte and Rose stood on the sidewalk, Rose said, "What do you say we go out and celebrate?"

"I'd love to," Charlotte said. "But I'm meeting Sam for dinner near his office."

Charlotte and Sam had made plans to go out to a fancy

restaurant after the announcement. That way, they figured, if she won, they could celebrate. And if she didn't, well, at least there'd be a tasty steak and a glass or three of champagne to soften her spikes.

"Okay, another time," Rose said, leaning in to give Charlotte a kiss on the cheek.

"Why don't you join us? I've told Sam all about you, and I would love for the two of you to meet. How about it?" Charlotte's substantial hesitation to include Rose was clobbered by her nice-girl discomfort in leaving Rose alone on a night like this.

"Are you sure? Don't you want to be alone with him?"

"We can be alone tomorrow night. I insist."

"In that case, sure. I'd love to."

"Do you want to call your fiancé and invite him?" Charlotte asked.

"Oh no. We're over. I couldn't stand one more minute with him."

Sam was already in the handsome dining room when they arrived, and a look of confusion crossed his face when he noticed Charlotte wasn't alone.

"Sam, this is Rose, the divine creature I was telling you about. She's going to join us."

"It's nice to meet you, Rose. Let me get another chair."

Looking searchingly in Charlotte's face to see whether he would be celebrating or consoling with the champagne, Sam asked, "Well?"

Charlotte smiled tightly and shook her head.

"Oh, Charlotte, I'm so sorry," Sam said.

"But Rose won, so we'll celebrate her," Charlotte said, feeling an ounce more supportive and gracious.

"Congratulations, Rose. Whaddaya say we still get that bottle of champagne? Okay with you, Charlotte?" Sam asked kindly.

"That sounds great, though I have to admit, we're one glass ahead of you," Charlotte said as she and Rose exchanged knowing glances.

"Then I better catch up quickly."

While Sam ordered the champagne, Charlotte remembered she needed to phone JoJo.

"Please excuse me," she said, standing. "I promised JoJo I'd tell her what happened with Miss Subways." Sam pulled out Charlotte's chair, and she walked toward the back of the restaurant to inquire about a pay telephone.

"Are you gonna be okay?" JoJo asked once she heard the news.

"Eventually, I guess. But for the time being, I'm not so sure."

"How are things coming with your inquiries at the other agencies?"

"I've heard from all but one. They said their typing pools are filled to capacity. I think it's time for me to accept that I tried my best and sometimes things just don't work out."

"There's gotta be a way," JoJo said wistfully.

"For now, I'm going to return to the table with composure, drink copious amounts of champagne to dull this obscene ache, and we can shred this apple to its core tomorrow."

Charlotte couldn't believe in just two weeks she'd gone from a girl with a bright future ahead of her: an impending graduation from Hunter, a strong likelihood of getting a job offer from J. Walter Thompson, and access to a one-way star-spangled ticket out of Brooklyn. A fresh start on the path to the next phase of her life. But now, facing the reality of giving that all up only to extol the virtues of daffodil-yellow paint versus canary-yellow paint and return to her parents' home in Bay Ridge every night sent a wave of anger through Charlotte. And on top of that, to lose Miss Subways as well. It was too much to process.

Charlotte returned to the table to find Rose gesturing wildly and Sam laughing hysterically. "Sounds like I missed the punch line," Charlotte said when she sat down, taking a sip of freshly poured champagne from the elegantly etched coupe.

"I was just telling your Sam here about how they made the announcement this afternoon, about Mr. Powers, Miss Fontaine, Bella . . ."

Charlotte felt a wave of disappointment that Sam wouldn't hear all that directly from her.

"Sam was laughing because I was imitating Miss Fontaine. Miss Diana Fontaine," she said with a flourish and a regal wrist. "What a phony."

Sam and Rose both started laughing again.

"What do you mean?" Charlotte asked Rose.

"What do *you* mean, what do I mean? There's never been a phonier phony. The way she sashays around and acts all important." Rose moved her hands and shoulders around theatrically, eliciting another wave of laughter from Sam.

"She does have a pretty important job. I actually thought she was nice," Charlotte said, looking at Rose quite seriously and shifting in her chair.

"Well, it's no secret how she keeps that pretty important job," Rose said, winking at Sam and taking a sip of her champagne as the waiter handed them menus encased in black leather.

Charlotte turned to Rose, a puzzled look on her face.

"Oh, Charlotte, dear, you're not that naive, are you?"

Charlotte looked at Sam, who was smiling at Rose.

"Perhaps I am," Charlotte said, agitation creeping into her voice. "Enlighten me, Rose."

"I've heard from trusted sources that she and John Powers work quite—let me choose the precise word—closely. And have worked quite 'closely' since Miss Diana Fontaine got off a sweaty bus in New York City from Waco, Texas, dropped her miserable suitcase in her low-floor single at the Barbizon, and headed straight to 247 Park Avenue to do anything, and I mean anything, she needed to do to become a Powers Girl. I know an Eileen Ford model who made her acquaintance at the Barbizon. This model friend gave up all of Miss Diana Fontaine's secrets, including how she used to be named Annie May Froggat."

"My goodness, I'm just so surprised," Charlotte said.

"Don't be, Charlotte," Rose said. "There are girls like that all over this island, who have everything to lose and would kill their little sisters for the right opportunities."

Charlotte felt taken aback. She looked at Sam, who raised his eyebrows at her and winked. And then the waiter was standing above her, asking her how she took her steak.

Dinner continued, and they all seemed to relax after their champagne glasses were refilled. Sam ordered a second bottle and they devoured their steaks, baked potatoes, and creamed spinach. Rose had them in hysterics with the sagas about each of her fiancés.

As the waiter cleared their plates, Rose said, "So you two seem like a couple of lovebirds."

"She's my girl. The one I'm going to marry," Sam said, reaching for Charlotte's hand.

"Let's drink to that," Rose said, and they all lifted their glasses (were they on their fourth? Their fifth?) to toast. "To your future filled with happiness. And babies! Lots and lots of babies!"

Charlotte and Sam looked at each other, and Charlotte gave Sam a pinched smile.

"I'm a lucky guy," Sam said, leaning over to give Charlotte a kiss.

"Say, when are you two gonna get married?" Rose asked, still holding up her glass.

"As soon as she says yes," Sam said.

"I can't say yes when you haven't officially asked me, now, can I, Sam?" Charlotte asked. Coy as a kitten.

"Well, go on. Ask her," Rose said.

"Maybe I will," Sam said confidently. "Can I borrow that ring you have on there, Rose?"

"I guess I don't really need this anymore," Rose said, sliding off the engagement ring she was still wearing.

Charlotte had had a lot to drink and was watching this theater in slow motion.

"Charlotte Friedman, will you marry me?" Sam asked, pulling Charlotte's left hand toward him and placing Rose's ring on her finger.

"Can we get some quiet, please?" Rose said loudly, turning to the diners around her. "We've got a proposal going on here."

Charlotte was suddenly aware that the whole restaurant had gone church-silent and dozens of sets of attentive eyes were glued to her face. She knew that something was going wrong. Horribly wrong.

"Whaddaya say, doll?" a male voice hurled from the table next to theirs.

"Say yes, honey!" came a female voice from across the room.

"Get on your knee, mac!"

Sam laughed and dropped to one knee before Charlotte. She wanted to bolt. To escape all the laughter and staring and the fact that she was being proposed to with some other woman's rejected engagement ring.

But she didn't. That would have caused a scene.

"Sam, what are you doing?" Charlotte whispered. Patrons started to lose interest and turned back to their steaks and chops.

"He's asking you to marry him," Rose said.

"I'm asking you to marry me," Sam said. "Say yes, sweetheart. I'll make you the happiest girl in New York."

"Say yes!" Rose said. "If he were asking me, I'd sure say yes. What are you waiting for?"

But Charlotte, tired-of-not-making-scenes Charlotte, stood up and ran out. She heard the tittering at her back. Felt her face on fire. The next thing Charlotte knew, she was outside the restaurant and Sam was at her side.

"Charlotte, honey, what is it? What did I do?"

"What did you do?" Charlotte yelled.

"Yeah, what did I do?"

Passersby on the street slowed and stared. The air was frigid, and Charlotte's coat was still inside at the coat check.

"You proposed to me after a hundred glasses of champagne, on a dare, no less, with another woman's tainted ring. Do you not see anything wrong with that?"

"I guess now that you put it that way, I do," Sam said, looking down at the sidewalk.

"Well, it was mean, Sam. And Rose is mean. I thought she was so wonderful. But it turns out, she's just mean. And there you are, laughing with her. At me. And that's just mean." Charlotte was aware she was yelling, aware she was escalating the situation perhaps a little unnecessarily, but she didn't care. This felt marvelous. To say what she meant and not care a lick about what would happen next.

"I was laughing with her because I thought you would want me to. I knew how much you liked her, and I wanted to like her too. And she's funny," Sam said, his hands outstretched, pleading.

"Hmph!" Charlotte huffed, and turned her shoulder to Sam. "You would think she's funny. Like all of the men she's roped into falling in love with her."

"Who said I was falling in love with her?" Sam asked, suddenly seeming angry.

"I'm just saying," Charlotte said.

"What are you saying?"

"I'm saying—" Charlotte tried to figure out what she was saying. Suddenly the alcohol was making that difficult. "I'm saying that I don't appreciate that you made a joke out of proposing to me tonight. I'm saying that I don't appreciate that the very first time you placed a ring on my finger, it had just come off of a woman who has been engaged six times. Six times, Sam! I'm saying that the whole spectacle was just plain revolting."

"And I'm saying I'm sorry," Sam said contritely. "But to tell you the honest truth, Charlotte, I think you're overreacting a bit."

"I'd like to go home," Charlotte said, throwing the ring down on the sidewalk and turning to go back into the restaurant to claim her coat.

There was an unfortunate line for the coat check. When

Rose saw Charlotte reenter the restaurant, she walked right up.

"I'm sorry, Charlotte, honey. I didn't mean to upset you."

"I'm not mad at you, Rose," Charlotte lied. "I'm mad at Sam." But Charlotte *was* mad at Rose. Though she couldn't figure out precisely why. Because she had won Miss Subways and Charlotte had lost? Because she was such a good conversationalist? Because she made Sam laugh like Charlotte had never been able to? Because she charmed Sam and every other person—the men and the women—in that restaurant? Because of her perfect eyes and perfect hair? Because she brought up the topic of babies and could probably have them even though she didn't want any? Because she made Charlotte feel so unworldly with her comments about Miss Fontaine? It seemed Charlotte was upset for all of those reasons. But was that anger? Or envy?

"Don't be mad at him. It was my fault. I egged him on. We've all had too much to drink. I think he was trying to make you laugh."

"I didn't think it was funny."

"He knows that now," Rose said as she and Charlotte looked toward the main dining room where Sam was paying the bill. "It's been a long day. What do you say we go home and sleep it off and everything will be better in the morning? Here's Sam now," Rose said as he approached the coat check.

"I'm so sorry, Charlotte. I didn't mean to upset you. That's the last thing I meant to do," Sam said, his eyes pleading.

"I just want to go home."

They started to walk out of the restaurant.

"Well, aren't you going to offer Rose a ride too?" Charlotte asked Sam. Challenged Sam. "She lives right near us."

Sam looked at Charlotte. She knew he was searching her eyes for what she wanted him to say. What the right answer would be. What wouldn't get him in more trouble with her. She wasn't going to give him anything.

"Of course I was," Sam said tentatively. Then to Rose: "Rose, please, let us give you a ride."

Sam. Always the gentleman.

He hailed a taxi, and the three of them slumped into the backseat, Charlotte listing in the middle. They traveled the Brooklyn Bridge in edgy silence, the impenetrable tension a colorless, odorless gas that permeated their orifices with its virulence.

Based upon where they all lived, Charlotte was dropped off first. Rose was asleep when they pulled up in front of Charlotte's. The cabby waited while Sam walked Charlotte to her door.

"I'm so sorry, Charlotte. Please forgive me. Let me make it up to you tomorrow night. We'll go out, just the two of us."

Charlotte looked Sam in the eye and turned to enter her house without another word.

CHAPTER 14

OLIVIA
SATURDAY, MARCH 10, 2018

"I have bagels and cream cheese, muffins, a couple of egg-and-cheese sandwiches, and lattes," Olivia said, entering the conference room on Saturday morning. Priya and Pablo were already seated, both typing on their laptops.

"Don't you look pretty this morning?" Priya said to Olivia, handing out copies of the strategic brief she had written with execution details for the pitch idea.

"Oh," Olivia murmured. "Bedhead."

They all read quietly while eating breakfast.

"Nice work, Priya," Olivia said, taking a sip of her latte. "This is a great start. Let's take it section by section and hash this thing out. We've got a lot of work to do today."

During one of their breaks, Olivia checked her phone, hoping for a text from Matt. Last night had been magical. She had felt so connected to him emotionally and physically. Their lovemaking had been slow and perfect. It was exactly what she'd needed.

Olivia couldn't help but think this could be the beginning of an opening for them. Especially now that Lily was out of the picture. She knew it was the worst idea to have a relationship with someone in her office, let alone her boss, but she also felt that when you'd found what you were looking for, you couldn't always be too choosy about *where* you'd found it.

Olivia decided to just let it play out and see what happened. It wasn't like she had already started pinning Jenny Packhams and Carolina Herreras onto an "Olivia + Matt" page.

There wasn't a text from Matt, but there was one from a number she didn't recognize:

917.555.8309
Hi, Olivia, it's Ben. I got your number from my grandma. (That sounded so smooth.) Wondering if you'd like to have dinner with me tonight? Hate to ask over text, but I know you're working on your pitch, and I didn't want to call and interrupt your work.

Olivia smiled and shook her head in silence. *Poor Ben,* she thought, *he should not get involved with me.* Olivia wrote back:

Olivia
Hi, Ben. Thanks so much for the invitation. I'm going to be working late tonight, so I'm sorry I can't. Maybe after this presentation is over? See you around the building. :-)

Olivia entered Ben into her contacts. She didn't want to lead him on, but she also didn't want to turn him down completely. There was something charming about the guy. Even though he was absolutely nothing like Matt, and right now everything she wanted in a man could be found in Matthew Osborne.

Ben
No problem. See you around.

The main problem that Olivia and Priya were having was locating the former Miss Subways. And the concept wouldn't work unless they found, in their estimation, at least ten to fifteen of them. They were losing faith that they would be able to pull the Miss Subways idea off within the short time frame they had.

While they waited to hear back from the women, they worked in earnest on the "Take You Places" idea. Pablo was pulling stock photos to use for the different profiles. And Olivia and Priya were drafting copy. They could have had a copywriter work on the creative with them, but they figured it would be faster if they came up with a few ideas themselves, rather than call in a copywriter on a Saturday.

"Who's Thomas working with from creative, Pablo?" Priya asked. It was getting close to five o'clock, and they were all starting to feel exhausted.

"Craig and Chantal. But I'm coming in tomorrow to meet with them and help them finalize their creative."

"Do they have something good?" Priya asked conspiratorially.

Pablo tilted his head. "Priya, you know I'm not going to tell you their idea, just like I'm not going to tell them yours,"

Pablo said seriously. "But if I'm going to be honest, I'd love for you two to win."

"I bet you say that to all your teams," Olivia said.

Matt

Hey, Liv. Free tonight? I have to go out for my brother's birthday dinner but can stop by after.

Olivia

Sure. But you can't keep me up late. I have a mean boss and have to work all day tomorrow.

Matt

I'll have you asleep by midnight. And I'll have a word with this mean boss of yours.

Olivia

See you later.

"Hi!" Olivia said in surprise when Ben opened the door to Mrs. Glasser's apartment.

"Olivia," Ben said, smiling. "You got out of work early."

"Yeah, much earlier than I thought. But," she said, suddenly feeling awkward, "I didn't want to text you because I figured you'd already made other plans." She thought she'd covered that up nicely.

"No big deal," Ben said, flicking his hand in an it's-no-problem gesture. "And you were right. About making other plans," he said, laughing and opening the door widely, inviting her in. "My grandma and I are having a game night.

We're starting with Scrabble, moving on to Rummikub, and if we haven't exhausted ourselves with all that excitement, we might just bust out the Twister mat."

Olivia laughed. "I wanted to ask your grandma something about Miss Subways. But I don't want to interrupt this intense competition."

"Who's there, Ben?" Mrs. Glasser asked, coming to the door. "Olivia, hello. Come in, dear. We were just going to play Scrabble. You'll join us. I made chocolate babka." Mrs. Glasser then turned and headed back toward the kitchen.

Ben looked at Olivia and smiled.

"You're right: she's very hard to say no to," Olivia said, entering the apartment.

"Did you eat dinner, Olivia? I have leftover meatloaf," Mrs. Glasser called from the kitchen.

"Yes, I ate at the office," Olivia called back. "But thank you."

"How are things going at work?" Mrs. Glasser said, coming back to the table, holding a cake plate.

"We have that MTA pitch coming up this week. It's a long story, but I have to give a preliminary presentation on Monday, and if my boss likes my idea, then I'm the one who'll get to pitch the client on Friday."

"Did you decide to use the Miss Subways campaign in your presentation at all?" Mrs. Glasser asked as she sliced the babka.

Admittedly, Olivia hadn't known what a babka was when Mrs. Glasser had first mentioned it, but now she could see it was similar to a soft coffee cake, shaped like a bread loaf with thick veins of chocolate running through it. It looked delicious.

"We really want to," Olivia said, accepting the plate from Mrs. Glasser, "but our creative for it hinges on this concept of 'Where Are They Now?' and besides you, we haven't been able to connect with any other Miss Subways. That's actually why I stopped by. I wanted to see if you'd be interested in participating in the new creative, but I'm realizing it's probably not going to even happen. I'm really sad about it because I thought the history and impact of Miss Subways were so interesting, but ultimately we're probably going to have to go in a different direction."

"That's too bad," Mrs. Glasser said. "But I agree with you. You'll have to tell me all about your other concept while we play. And then maybe after Scrabble, I'll show you the scrapbook from my Miss Subways days."

"I would love that," Olivia said, taking another bite of the heaven that was chocolate babka, her new favorite dessert.

Mrs. Glasser and Ben were both highly skilled Scrabble competitors. Olivia was no slouch when it came to making words, but she didn't know all the twos and Qs, and that was where they killed her.

Olivia's phone buzzed in her pocket. She looked at it while Mrs. Glasser was setting out her tiles.

Matt

I should only be about an hour. I'll let you know when I'm downstairs. Thinking of u.

Olivia

Sounds good.

And why the hell not? It was certainly true:

Olivia

Thinking of u 2.

Olivia put her phone away and looked up to find Ben studying her. She realized she had a stupid grin on her face. She wiped it off and returned to studying and rearranging her tiles.

Later, as they were cleaning up the Scrabble game, Olivia asked Mrs. Glasser if she would be up to showing her the scrapbook.

"Of course," Mrs. Glasser answered. "Leave this. I'll clean it up later. Come."

Olivia and Ben followed her into the living room, where she opened a cabinet below the bookshelf and struggled to remove the heavy book. Ben took it from her and set it down on the coffee table.

Mrs. Glasser sat in the middle of the couch and patted the cushions on either side of her. "Sit."

Olivia and Ben sat on opposite sides of her. Ben lifted the scrapbook onto his grandma's lap.

As soon as Mrs. Glasser opened the large book, Olivia could smell the years it contained. She looked at Mrs. Glasser, whose eyes had gone glossy. Olivia couldn't imagine what it would be like to travel back in time like that. To be ninety and revisit what she looked like, felt like, dreamed of when she was twenty-one.

"This was my best friend, Josephine. JoJo, I called her," Mrs. Glasser said, pointing to a photograph of a girl with wavy brown hair and an exuberance to her smile. Mrs. Glasser took a deep breath.

"Where is . . . Is she . . ." Olivia was hesitant to ask, but she also was so curious to know.

"JoJo died about ten years ago. Breast cancer," Mrs. Glasser said sadly.

"I'm so sorry."

"Aunt JoJo was the best," Ben said. "We were very close to her. She was like a second grandmother to me. And her daughter and grandkids were—still are—like an aunt and cousins. They lived near us when I was growing up, so it was almost as if we had a bigger family."

"Family is so important," Mrs. Glasser said wistfully.

Olivia and Ben looked at each other over Mrs. Glasser's back and smiled sadly.

Mrs. Glasser turned the pages slowly, telling stories to Olivia and Ben about each page. Before the Miss Subways mementos, there were class photos, pictures of her family, pictures of her friends, and the program from her college graduation.

Mrs. Glasser stopped for a while, without saying anything, on a photograph of a young handsome man. She touched the photo with her fingers as if she could somehow bring it to life. Olivia stared at the photo as well, wondering what the significance was, when she saw a tear drop onto the photo from Mrs. Glasser's eye.

Mrs. Glasser reached into her pocket and pulled out a handkerchief.

"This photograph was in a frame in my parents' house on the mantel for years. I used to kiss it every time I walked by it. This is my brother. Harry. He died in the war."

Olivia put her arm around Mrs. Glasser's shoulders.

What must it be like to lose all the people you love? Olivia realized at that moment that besides James and Jenna, she didn't love anyone. She was an only child, so besides her parents—and finding any love for them was difficult— she had no family who she was even remotely close to. A huge wave of sadness washed over her, and she felt like she was gasping for air. She didn't realize she had made a sound until she felt Ben touching her shoulder. She looked at him over Mrs. Glasser's back.

Are you okay? he mouthed to her.

Olivia nodded and looked back down at the scrapbook.

Mrs. Glasser's mood changed noticeably when she got to the Miss Subways mementos.

There was a photograph of Mrs. Glasser sitting on the subway, smiling and pointing above her to her own Miss Subways poster, and a few posed ones of her from what she said was her launch event. She mentioned that most of the Miss Subways had had launch event photos taken of themselves with their families, but there were none like that of Mrs. Glasser. The only other photo from the event was a candid of Mrs. Glasser and a gorgeous young woman who looked like Elizabeth Taylor with a fuller face. In the photo they were talking to each other with serious looks on their faces.

"Was that a friend of yours?" Olivia asked.

"That was Rose Grant," Mrs. Glasser said in a clipped voice, and turned the page quickly.

Mrs. Glasser had included a bunch of newspaper clippings, some that mentioned her and some that mentioned Miss Subways winners who had come after her.

She said there used to be a club of sorts of the Miss Subways winners, and they would go on outings and to dinners. She pointed to an article from *Collier's* that featured her and a bunch of other girls playing around at the beach.

"I saw that spread while I was doing research," Olivia said.

"What a glorious day that was! I haven't looked at

this scrapbook in ages. I've forgotten what's all in here," Mrs. Glasser said.

Suddenly she closed the scrapbook and lifted it with some effort back onto the table.

"Are you okay, Grandma?" Ben asked, concerned.

"Just tired. All of those ghosts can do that to an old lady. You kids don't leave on my account. I'm just going to bed." She got up from the couch and started to walk to her bedroom. "Stay, stay," Mrs. Glasser said when she saw Ben getting up to walk with her. "I'm fine."

Ben and Olivia honored her wishes and silently watched her walk toward her bedroom. They heard her shut the door.

"She must really be tired, because she never goes to bed without cleaning up the kitchen."

"I can do that," Olivia said.

"That's fine. I don't mind," Ben said, pulling the scrapbook back off the table and opening it on his lap. "This book is amazing. She's never shown it to me before. I feel like I've seen every photo album in this apartment a hundred times but never this scrapbook."

Olivia moved a little closer so she could see. Ben flipped it open to the middle, and it was the page of photos from Mrs. Glasser's launch event. There was something about the way that Mrs. Glasser seemed to be reacting to whatever that Rose Grant was telling her that seemed strange to Olivia. She bent over to have a closer look.

"You noticed that too?" Ben asked.

"Yeah, your grandma looks agitated, doesn't she?"

"She does. But she turned that page so fast, I just figured she didn't want to talk about it. I never heard that name Rose Grant growing up. I guess she was someone my grandma wanted to leave in the past."

Ben turned the pages, and they looked again at all the newspaper clippings. As they turned the last page, some letters slipped out onto the floor.

Olivia bent over to pick them up and then handed them to Ben. He turned them over and looked at the return address. There were about ten envelopes, all sealed but one. All from the same return address: Rose Grant, 140 Westbury Road, Beverly Hills, CA 90210.

Olivia felt her phone buzz and looked at the screen.

Matt
I'm downstairs.

Olivia
Tell Nico to send you up. I'm just next door. I'll meet you in hallway in minute.

"I've gotta go, Ben," Olivia said, standing up.

"'Go confidently in the direction of your dreams,' Olivia," Ben said in a professor voice, and smiled at her.

Olivia looked at him, her eyes opened wide. "No way. You didn't just say that."

"'Live the life you have imagined,'" Ben continued, his voice booming.

"That's my favorite quote," Olivia said, bewildered.

"Mine too," he said, continuing to smile. "It's wrong, you know."

"What's wrong?"

"The quote."

"What do you mean?" Olivia asked.

"Thoreau actually said," Ben said, clearing his throat dramatically, "and I quote, 'I learned this, at least, by my experiment: that if one advances confidently in the direction of his dreams, and endeavors to live the life which he has imagined, he will meet with a success unexpected in common hours.'"

"Well, I'll be . . ." Olivia said, surprised.

"I was a philosophy major."

"I have that quote on my bulletin board in my office. The fake one, I guess," she said, laughing.

"It's a good one. Too bad all the quote memes have bastardized it so that it's more digestible by today's standards. I liked it the way he originally wrote it."

Ben closed the scrapbook and set it down on the coffee table. He grabbed the letters and walked with Olivia toward the dining room, where she had left her purse.

"Oh, let me help you clean up," Olivia said, starting to put Scrabble tiles back into the burgundy velveteen pouch.

"Don't worry about that. You go. I've got it," Ben said.

"Thanks. And thanks for letting me crash your game night."

Ben started walking with Olivia toward the door. He was still holding the letters.

"I'm fine. Thanks, Ben. I'll see myself out." Olivia really did not want Ben and Matt to cross paths.

"No problem," Ben said. "I was raised to show a lady to her door."

Olivia smiled nervously and opened the door.

Just then the elevator dinged.

"I'm fine, Ben, but thanks," Olivia said, thinking if he closed the door now, he would be inside before Matt walked out of the elevator.

But Ben just stood there in the threshold of his grandmother's apartment, watching Olivia make her way four paces to her own apartment door.

Olivia was fumbling with her keys, trying to get the right one. She finally had the key in the lock and had turned toward Ben to give him a telepathic message to shut his door when she saw Matt come out of the elevator.

"Hey, Liv," Matt said, smiling.

Ben turned to look, and Olivia felt her stomach drop.

"Hey, man," Matt said kindly when he saw Ben standing there.

"Ben, this is Matt Osborne. Matt, this is Ben." She cringed, but she felt like Ben and Matt wouldn't see her as anything but calm.

Ben moved the envelopes from his right hand to his left and put his right hand out to shake Matt's.

"Hey. Nice to meet you," Ben said.

"Yeah, man," Matt said. "Nice to meet you too." He turned toward Olivia. "I thought you lived next to an old lady."

Olivia winced. "An older lady," she said, emphasizing the "er." "And Ben is her grandson. We just had a little game night," Olivia added, smiling warmly at Ben.

"Nice," Matt said.

Ben was looking at Olivia quizzically, but she just continued to smile as if it were normal to have good-looking men come to her apartment late at night. She didn't owe Ben an explanation. So why was there part of her that felt like she did?

Matt walked toward Olivia's apartment and turned back to Ben. "Hey, it was nice meeting you, Ben. See you around."

Ben nodded, and Matt went into Olivia's apartment.

Olivia was about to follow him inside but turned toward Ben, who was about to go back into his grandma's.

"Hey, Ben," Olivia called.

"Yeah?" He turned around, a dejected look on his face.

"Are you going to read those letters?"

"Not sure."

"Okay," Olivia said gently. "Good night. Thanks again."

Ben nodded and turned away again. Olivia felt a pang of something she couldn't quite interpret. And then she followed Matt inside.

CHAPTER 15

CHARLOTTE
MONDAY, MARCH 21, 1949

Charlotte flew down the stairs. The telephone had rung several times, and she wanted to answer it before the caller gave up, since she was anticipating a response from one final agency. She would most likely hear via letter, but, Charlotte thought, it wouldn't be completely out of the ordinary if they decided to phone her instead.

The plan was that if it was another no, she'd put on her most comfortable shoes and her most confident expression and walk up one side of Madison Avenue and down the other until she found a suitable placement. At this point, even unsuitable would do. She'd actually considered canvassing the engagement notices to see if any of the girls were in advertising, their impending nuptials most likely indicating their present employer would soon need to fill a seat.

"Is this Charlotte Friedman?" a familiar voice asked. Charlotte sensed a bit of urgency in the voice, like a drop of grapefruit juice in a morning glass of OJ.

"It is."

"This is Diana Fontaine from the John Robert Powers Modeling Agency. Rose Grant, our first selection for July's Miss Subways, is unable to fulfill her responsibilities. Since you were Mr. Powers's next choice, would you be able to come to our offices right now to do the photo shoot?"

"Right now?"

"Yes. Right now."

"What happened to Rose?"

"I'm not at liberty to say."

"Does that mean—"

"It means you, dear, are officially Miss Subways for July. Are you able to come?"

"It'll take me about an hour on the train, but I'll be there as soon as I can."

Charlotte hung up the phone and froze. So many questions ran through her mind. What on this great green earth had happened to Rose? *Unable to fulfill her responsibilities*? What could that even mean? But Charlotte knew she had no time for fruitless reverie.

Thankfully, she was fully dressed, as she was planning on going to Manhattan anyway for a class. She'd call Professor Finley's secretary later to claim illness, though Professor Finley was well known for not excusing any absence unless it was due to the student's own untimely death.

Once she was on the train, and had offered a prayer of thanks to the Miss Subways goddesses via Thelma Porter's poster overhead, Charlotte was able to think about what this could mean. A second chance at her plan had to be some sort of sign, right?

She couldn't wait to tell JoJo. Sam was a different story. After their proposal fiasco on Friday night, Charlotte had woken up late the next morning. The sour taste in her mouth no match for the dull thud in her head and the sharp ache in her heart. Memories of the night before had come rushing back, and Charlotte tried to parse out her confused and conflicted feelings for Sam and Rose. Was her anger justified? Or was she overreacting to something that was just a joke? A lame joke, perhaps. But a joke, nonetheless.

The more Charlotte scrutinized the previous night, the clearer the lens through which she viewed everyone's actions. And while Charlotte wasn't madly in love with how the whole night unfolded, she was certain that Sam and Rose were just having fun. And perhaps that wasn't such a bad thing. She had been confident that when Sam showed up later that day—which he most certainly would—with a bouquet of flowers and an apology as fragrant, she'd forgive him.

But Sam hadn't shown up with a bouquet, an apology, or otherwise on Saturday afternoon. Or the entire weekend, for that matter. Charlotte's speculations as to why that was ranged from the morbid—*he must have been hit by a crosstown bus and is in a coma on the top floor of a Midtown hospital*—to the unlikely—*he was so drunk that he woke up the next morning having no memory of the fight the night before*—to the self-flagellating—*he finally realized that after all those proposals, she would never say yes, so he packed up his hopes with his overtures and set out to find a less difficult woman.*

Charlotte enlisted JoJo to pick apart every last moment from Friday night, but JoJo, in commensurate best-friend form, couldn't find a fault with Charlotte's behavior. She did say that there were always two sides to a story, but considering Sam didn't have the gizzard to show his face, she was unable to take his deposition and would have to rely on Charlotte's account in full.

Still, Charlotte was unsettled. And sad. And confused as to why Sam had gone quiet. She supposed that it was possible he was consumed with work; that wouldn't be such an unlikely scenario, as he often had to work weekends, sometimes on short notice. But eventually, she settled on believing that he was angry at her for making a spectacle of what he thought was a fine proposal—perhaps a bit unorthodox, but still a proposal—on an equally fine night.

But for now, on to the next, Charlotte thought as she exited the subway station on her way to John Robert Powers for the photo shoot.

Charlotte couldn't believe what Miss Fontaine was telling her. "She just didn't show up?"

"That's correct. And she didn't write her telephone number on the form we gave all of you girls. We only had her address, and we're not in the business of dispatching couriers to Brooklyn to hunt down Miss Subways contestants."

"I'm sure she'll come eventually, Miss Fontaine. Couldn't you wait just a bit longer?" Charlotte asked, peering toward the front door, certain Rose would blow in on a perfumed breeze any second, looking like she was right on time. Charlotte was surprised she was campaigning for Rose, but it didn't feel right to be opportunistic. To have such a windfall at the expense of someone else's misfortune.

"Unfortunately," Miss Fontaine said in an exasperated tone, "I've given her all the time I can for now."

"There must be a perfectly reasonable explanation," Charlotte said.

"I'm sure there is," Miss Fontaine agreed. "But we've got work to do. Are you ready, Miss Subways?"

Charlotte had never had her makeup professionally done. She'd been to the beauty parlor; what girl hadn't? But sitting in the glamorous, spacious, and well-lit hair-and-makeup studio at the offices of John Robert Powers was a different experience altogether.

First they asked Charlotte if she'd like something to drink. *Coffee, Miss Friedman? Tea, perhaps? Or champagne, if you'd prefer?* Charlotte decided on tea, thinking that would be the best choice to settle her stomach. But then considered champagne, as that would be the best choice to settle her mind. In the end, she asked for, and received, both.

Charlotte felt regal and giddy, perched upon the pink vinyl salon chair, her arms folded in her lap and her toes tapping the footrest below. She stared at her reflection in the lightbulb-framed mirror that took up most of the wall across from her, excited to see the transformation that would happen before her eyes. She'd never taken a turn at this particular type of ball.

Professionals bustled about her, their industry creating a bee-like hum as they debated curls and cheek colors, lip shapes and eyebrow arches, and Charlotte, poor Charlotte, kept getting reprimanded for looking over her shoulder for Rose.

Miss Fontaine popped her head in once or twice to give approving nods or ask for updates. *Her hair's so thick, Miss Fontaine. What long eyelashes she has, Miss Fontaine. What do you think of this lip color, Miss Fontaine?* Charlotte felt like a show animal competing for the blue ribbon at a county fair, and she didn't mind one bit. It was helping take her mind off the rest of her life. At least a little.

Miss Fontaine didn't care for the sweater Charlotte was wearing, so, when Charlotte's hair and makeup were complete, Miss Fontaine whisked her into another room and sorted through a rack of clothing. She selected two tops for Charlotte to choose from—a navy jewel-necked sweater with pearl buttons at the shoulders and a white short-sleeved blouse with a wide collar—but while Charlotte was contemplating the choices, apparently too slowly for Miss Fontaine's taste, Miss Fontaine returned the blouse to the rack, held the sweater up under Charlotte's chin, and thrust it at her.

"This one will be perfect."

"Still no word from Rose?" Charlotte asked Miss Fontaine as she changed behind a screen.

Charlotte imagined the worst: that Rose had been hit by the same crosstown bus as Sam. Or that something awful had happened to someone in her family. Why else wouldn't she be there? This opportunity was everything to Rose.

"I'm afraid not, dear," Miss Fontaine replied as Charlotte came from behind the screen. "But don't look too glum," Miss Fontaine added, lifting Charlotte's chin with her long, manicured finger. "Assuming she has a reasonable explanation, I can put her back in the running for next month. But you, Miss Charlotte Friedman, make a captivating Miss Subways for July!"

Charlotte managed a small smile, but her concern for Rose overshadowed every molecule of joy she should have felt. Soon, though, after the reality of the situation had gained a foothold between her jewel-bedecked ears, and after Charlotte realized she would be a fool to forfeit this final-lap opportunity on behalf of a girl she'd known for a mere two weeks, she asked for a second glass of champagne to raise a toast to victory and to Miss Fontaine, to the pretty birds at reception, to all the paint cans in Friedman's storeroom, and to Mr. John Robert Powers and Muky.

Speaking of, Charlotte was petrified to face the small

man again as she made her way with Miss Fontaine to the photography studio, down another long hallway lined with picture frames full of the gorgeous. But she needn't have worried, because Muky was a love.

"Miss Friedman, welcome back. So lovely to have you here, dear," he said, holding her right hand in his and kissing it repeatedly. And audibly.

"Thank you, Muky. I'm delighted to be back."

Charlotte wasn't sure what had turned Muky's sour side to sweet, but she didn't much care. This new Muky suited her just fine.

Charlotte adored the photo shoot. The flashing lights and persistent instructions kept her mind engaged. Miss Fontaine monitored her charge protectively. And Charlotte, though careful not to look away from the camera even a millimeter while Muky was shooting, noticed Mr. Powers himself peeking in while Muky was changing the film. Charlotte was amazed it took all this buzzy effort to end up with the one perfect photo that would grace her Miss Subways poster.

Once the lens cap had been replaced, Miss Fontaine walked Charlotte back to reception. She thought she'd have another opportunity to speak with Mr. Powers, hopefully to give an additional plug to Friedman's Paints and Wallpapers, where she could be found should any Miss Subways fans care for a photo, but Miss Fontaine told her that he'd gotten all the information he needed during their initial conversation and he would pass that along to the copywriter. Charlotte pressed on, but Miss Fontaine told her that would be all, thank you very much, dear.

Charlotte was back on the street in front of 247 Park Avenue before she knew it, and if it weren't for the thick layer of makeup on her face and the stylish curls in her hair, she wouldn't have believed any of it had ever happened.

"Hello, Sam," Charlotte said curtly when Sam picked up his line. She was still angry—and confused—that he hadn't been in touch since Friday night.

"Charlotte. I've been meaning to call you all weekend. I got pulled into—"

"We can talk later. I'm calling from a pay phone," Charlotte interrupted. "I need Rose's address. I figured since you dropped her off on Friday night, you'd know where she lived." All business.

"What do you need that for?"

"She didn't show up to the Miss Subways photo shoot today, and I want to go by and see what happened."

"She probably forgot about it or something."

"Forgot? That's ridiculous. Just please give me her address."

"Aw, just leave well enough alone, Charlotte."

"I'll decide that for myself, Sam."

Once Sam told her where Rose lived, Charlotte got off the phone quickly. She didn't like how he sounded, nor how he tried to dissuade her from checking on Rose. The whole conversation felt as off as month-old milk.

Rose's neighborhood, though not a far distance from Charlotte's, was the moon to the sun. A neighborhood whose inhabitants and architecture had decided it was no longer worth the trouble and had finally given up trying to be like the ones a few streets over.

The main door to Rose's building was unlocked, and Charlotte opened it slowly. The vestibule was dark, and Charlotte waited a moment to let her eyes adjust. She noticed GRANT on a mailbox that said 4B, so Charlotte began the climb. Every few steps presented another obstacle: a missing tread, a forgotten jack from that morning's game, abandoned garbage taking a sojourn on its way to the incinerator. And each landing, with its open doors, provided a glimpse into the bowels of Brooklyn itself.

Charlotte reached the fourth floor and knocked gently on 4B. A little boy opened the door.

"Who are you?" he asked, all spunk and six or seven.

"I'm Charlotte. Who are you?"

"Paddy."

"Hi, Paddy. Does Rose Grant live here?"

"She's my sister," he said, gesturing to the open door behind him. Charlotte could see movement, could smell something unidentifiable. "Wanna talk to her?"

"I do. Could you please let her know that I'm here?"

Paddy turned back and disappeared from sight. Charlotte felt it rude to stare into the apartment, so she pretended to have dirt underneath her nails and busied herself extricating it.

"Charlotte."

Charlotte looked up. "Rose?"

"In the flesh," Rose said, her palms up in surrender.

Charlotte wouldn't have recognized her if she'd been going down the steps while Charlotte clamored up. She'd only seen Rose twice, but each time the makeup and hair and clothes seemed effortless. Charlotte realized now that a great deal had gone into that facade. "I came to see if you were okay."

"I'm standing here, aren't I?"

"Why didn't you go to the photo shoot today?" Charlotte asked, concerned. This Rose was a complete one-eighty from the Rose that Charlotte was expecting. Clearly, something was not right.

"How did you find out?"

Charlotte hesitated. "Miss Fontaine called. She asked me to do the photo shoot in your place."

"And did you?" Rose asked, narrowing her eyes.

"I did. I'm so sorry. I just thought—" Charlotte began to plead.

"I changed my mind."

"You don't want to be Miss Subways anymore?"

"That's what changing your mind meant last time I looked it up."

"You don't have to be so rude. I was worried about you."

Rose laughed sarcastically. "I'm the last person you should be worried about, Charlotte."

"Is your mother okay?"

"Yes. She's okay. I'm okay. We're all okay. Can't you just accept that I don't want anything to do with Miss Subways? It's a dumb beauty contest. I have more important things to focus on."

Charlotte felt like a bully had just hurled a rock at her eye. Almost felt a physical jolt. "What's gotten into you, Rose?"

"Nothing, Charlotte. Now be on your way, and don't think you can always put on your Pollyanna smile and your best coat and your clean gloves and your apple pie and make everything okay."

"I really don't know what you're talking about," Charlotte said indignantly.

"You wouldn't, honey. I've gotta go." And she shut the door.

Charlotte stood there. Disbelief and confusion spread through her like warm cream in coffee. And she had no idea what she'd done to make Rose react to her that way.

"Charlotte, is that you?" Charlotte's mother called from the kitchen as soon as Charlotte opened the front door.

"It's me."

"What is all over your face? And your hair!" her mother said, walking toward her.

Charlotte was confused by the question and then remembered the makeup and the curls. She had planned to stop somewhere on the way home to erase the glamour, but in the midst of all the Rose drama, she'd forgotten.

"JoJo decided to do a makeover on me," Charlotte lied. "Do you like it?"

"Not one bit. Now go take care of it all before your father sees you. And then come back down because it's almost time for dinner."

As she was walking upstairs, Charlotte heard the telephone ring. Her mother answered it.

"Charlotte! Sam's on the telephone for you."

Charlotte picked the handset up from the table where her mother had left it resting to tend to the soup. "Hello, Sam." Charlotte was still perplexed by Sam's weekend disappearance and had decided to let him drive the boat.

"I hate that we haven't spoken since I dropped you off Friday night. I'm so sorry again for what a dope I was with that whole marriage proposal fiasco. Now that I think back on it, I can't believe I even did that. What was I thinking? Will you forgive me, Charlotte?"

Charlotte held a quick debate in her mind. The side in favor of forgiving Sam argued that Charlotte, quite dismayed from losing Miss Subways to Rose and a tad affected by multiple glasses of champagne, may have overreacted a little to Sam's unorthodox proposal and thus, she should forgive him. The side opposed argued that not only was Sam a boor for attempting the whole thing, but he didn't even bother to call and apologize all weekend long. Yes, but the side in favor argued—though each side was allowed only one turn at the podium—it's *Sam*: kind, loving, considerate Sam. He messed up. Get over it and move on. And the winner of the golden debate trophy is . . .

"I'll forgive you, Sam. I know you didn't mean anything by it. But it was just a combination of the champagne and Rose's forsaken ring and Rose's gleaming charm and everything else, and it just made me so angry. Don't do that again, okay?"

"Never. Well, I can't promise I won't propose again, but I can promise that when I do, it will be nothing like the last time."

"Deal. By the way, I got quite a shock when I went to Rose's this afternoon."

"What do you mean?"

"She was all disheveled and mean. Something seemed really peculiar. And she didn't forget about the shoot. She said she had changed her mind, whatever that's supposed to mean."

"Strange. So, what will they do about the Miss Subways for July?"

"It's me. I actually did the photo shoot today. They called me in when Rose didn't show up."

"That's wonderful, Charlotte. Congratulations!"

"Thanks. Part of me hates the way I won it, but if the whole goal, as I told you the other day, is to bring attention to my father's store so I don't have to work there, then I guess it doesn't matter how I won. As long as I did."

"That's my girl. Say, can I see you Saturday night?"

Once they'd arranged their date and Charlotte had cleaned up for dinner, she came back downstairs to find her mother rinsing lettuce in the sink.

"I owe you an apology," Mrs. Friedman said without turning around. Her voice, Charlotte thought, sounded tinged with regret.

"For what?" Charlotte asked.

"For not pushing your father to find another solution to his problem of running the store. You should start your job, Charlotte. I apologize for not letting you pursue your dreams."

Charlotte was shocked to hear her mother say that. She hadn't known what her mother could possibly feel she needed to apologize for, but it wasn't that.

"My goodness. I didn't know you felt that way. I'd always believed you thought it was silly for me to work in advertising. To be honest, Ma, you've never really encouraged my career."

"I don't think it's silly, Charlotte, and that's what I'm trying to tell you," she said, turning around to face Charlotte, a fervor in her eyes. She wiped her hands on her apron and continued. "You need to do what makes you happy. You're young and you have your whole life ahead of you. Not following your dreams will make you angry and resentful."

"So are you saying that if I get a job, I can start after graduation like I was supposed to?"

"I'm not saying that, because I don't think your father will go for the idea no matter how hard I try to convince him. But I want you to know that as soon as the store is doing better, you have to do your advertising, Charlotte. You just have to." The words rolled out emphatically and urgently.

"Okay, Ma. I will," Charlotte said, reaching for her mother's hand. It was a rare moment of connection between the two of them, something Charlotte hadn't felt from her mother since Harry died, but Charlotte welcomed it. She hadn't realized how much she missed her mother.

Mrs. Friedman looked toward the door that separated the kitchen from the hall and lowered her voice, saying, "You know, I don't always agree that what your father thinks is the best decision really is. He's made mistakes in the past."

"Like what?"

Mrs. Friedman looked at Charlotte seriously and seemed to be deciding how much to say.

"Like when we were first married," Charlotte's mother said, looking out the window again. "He told me I had to stop my career."

"You had a career?"

"I did."

"Doing what? Why didn't you ever tell me?"

"I buried that part of me a long time ago, Charlotte. Plus, you never asked."

Charlotte was simultaneously nervous and calm about this intimacy with her mother. She had caught glimpses of her mother sharing tender moments with Harry, always Harry, but she had never really experienced them herself. She remembered one time, trudging into the kitchen after school. Harry had gotten home before her and was in the kitchen, eating cookies and drinking lemonade with their mother. Charlotte remembered sensing, even though she was so young, that they were sharing a secret. And she had felt the air, their expressions, their voices change as soon as she entered. Remembering that moment when she was older, after she had lost Harry and every semblance of security and happiness she had ever known in her family, Charlotte realized that while she didn't doubt her mother loved her, she understood that it was different, less substantial, than the love her mother had for her brother. Charlotte had accepted that to be true and had never imagined there was ample room for her.

"Is it too late? Can I ask now?"

Her mother turned back to Charlotte and smiled. "Sure you can. I was training to be an opera singer." She put her hand over her mouth and opened her eyes wide.

Charlotte's jaw dropped and her mother laughed.

"Why do you look so surprised, Charlotte?"

"I had no idea. That just seems so, I don't know, incongruous with how I know you."

"You mean because I'm always so quiet and absorbed in my puzzles?"

"Yes."

"Aha, but you don't know what's going on in my mind. Verdi. Puccini. Mozart. It may look like I'm solving puzzles, Charlotte, but I'm also singing arias."

"Why have you never sung out loud?"

"I did. You don't remember, but I would sing to Harry and you all the time when you were little."

Charlotte felt a pang and a sharp memory of hearing her mother sing.

"Your father heard me one day and told me he never wanted to hear me sing again. He said it was a silly dream of mine and the sooner I gave it up, the sooner I would realize my place was in the home with the children."

"Anger and resentment."

"Still. And I don't want you to feel this way. Don't get me wrong; I loved raising you and Harry. But I know I could have pursued my singing as well. And that would have made my life even more joyful," Mrs. Friedman said, smiling tightly at Charlotte. "I know Sam's not the type of man who would ever hold you back from your dreams."

Charlotte thought about what her mother had said. Anger and resentment. Not high up on Charlotte's wish list of things to feel as she got older. For now, all she could do was wait for July first, when her Miss Subways posters would be plastered across the five boroughs, and then wait for the Miss Subways admirers to swarm Friedman's Paint and Wallpaper.

CHAPTER 16

OLIVIA
MONDAY, MARCH 12, 2018

Presenting first, Thomas was already seated at the head of the table, Pablo to his right. And Ty, his account executive, to his left. The three of them were in their best suits and conferring quietly. Behind them were two easels, both obscured by black cloth.

Priya rushed in and joined Olivia in the back corner. Olivia was so curious about what Thomas had come up with. And, if she was honest with herself, Olivia felt strange seeing Pablo so tied into Thomas right now. She had perfected her presentation with Priya, but because this wasn't an actual rehearsal of the presentation that would be given Friday, she hadn't thought to get Pablo involved in the pitch. So she gave a point to Thomas for enlisting Pablo in his presentation, and she also wondered if Pablo felt slighted that Olivia hadn't included him in hers. But she didn't have time to entertain those concerns further, because Matt walked into the room.

He sat at the opposite end of the table from Thomas, directly in front of Olivia and Priya. "Whenever you're ready,

Thomas," Matt said, placing his phone facedown on the table.

Thomas launched into a review of the stated needs of the MTA and the way his team had approached their method of achieving those goals. It was essentially a rehash of what was in the initial brief and also some of what had come out at the dinner with Ed Freck and the other MTA guys on Friday night. Olivia had a similar opening to her presentation, which she decided to condense into one sentence and start instead with the creative approach.

"We ultimately decided," Thomas continued, "to refocus the typical subway rider's attitude toward his or her daily commute. We wanted to transcend the physical construct of the subway in their mind. To have them stop seeing their commute as going from point A to point B in a metal box, and rather have them reimagine and elevate the process.

"In the past, through various other MTA programs, art has been brought into the subway. Our concept 'Subway Star Cars' makes the subway"—Thomas paused and looked directly at Olivia—"into art itself.

"This concept, which I'll explain in a moment with some gorgeous visuals imagined by Pablo, will create a tremendous amount of buzz in the city. It has the potential to be rolled out over the course of a month or the course of a year, in whatever time frame works for the MTA. Commuters will be flocking to actually ride on the subways to see the Subway Star Cars for themselves. There's tremendous opportunity for collateral material and an app to bring in additional revenue for the MTA or a charity it designates. Finally, the project has legs, as the cars themselves can go on as an art installation at the Transit Museum, Vanderbilt Hall at Grand Central, or in some other venue."

At first, while Olivia was listening to Thomas's pitch, she thought how uncanny it was that his idea was similar to her original one. But clearly, as he continued and her blood pressure began to rise, Olivia realized it wasn't just similar—it *was* her original idea.

Priya and Olivia were looking at each other in disbelief.

Olivia couldn't believe it. Could Pablo have given her idea to Thomas? The only other person was Priya. There was the possibility that Thomas could have somehow spied on their conversations or stolen papers out of Olivia's office, but she had a hard time believing that, either.

It was taking all of Olivia's dwindling willpower to not stand up and say something, but she decided to let Thomas finish, see if he had completely stolen her idea, and deal with the issue from there.

"So, the creative," Thomas said. "Pablo?"

Pablo stood next to the first easel and held the corner of the black cloth.

"As Thomas mentioned, our idea is to have the subway cars themselves reimagined as art. The plan is to invite influential New York City tastemakers, like artists, actors, sports figures, models, and members of the media elite, to design an individual subway car in his or her own creative way."

"You stole my idea!" Olivia shouted. She was standing up. She had tried to keep her cool, tried to wait until the presentation was over, but this was just too egregious and she couldn't hold it in any longer.

"Olivia, please," Matt said. "Remember our agreement that the waiting team wouldn't say anything during the presenting team's pitch?"

Olivia looked at Thomas. He was glaring at her, the

corners of his mouth turned up in such a way that he looked like a cross between Jack Nicholson's Joker and a smirk emoji.

Pablo looked incredibly uncomfortable and even took his jacket off, draping it across the chair in front of him. The sweat circles under his armpits were spreading like batter pouring into a brownie pan.

"I do remember, Matt," Olivia said with a sting in her voice. "But that was before I knew that they were going to steal my idea and present it as their own. This is unacceptable."

"I'm sure they didn't steal your idea, Olivia. Let's just be courteous and let them finish," Matt said, his voice edging on condescension.

Olivia stayed standing and made a sarcastic gesture with her hand to Thomas to continue. She was incensed.

"For instance," Pablo continued, and pulled the black cloth off the easel with a flourish. "We would offer Anna Wintour, the editor in chief of *Vogue*—"

"This is ridiculous," Olivia said, shaking her head.

Pablo continued with the idea of Anna Wintour taking over a car on the E line. And then he discussed Beyoncé taking over a car. He essentially repeated verbatim the initial concept description Olivia had presented to him a week earlier. Olivia was astonished by the flagrant audacity of Thomas and Pablo. It was unthinkable to her that they could be so brazen. And she realized that not only did *they* not care, but clearly they didn't think *Matt* would care either. Or even worse, that he wouldn't believe Olivia's side of the story.

Priya gently tugged on Olivia's arm and encouraged her to sit down. "Let them finish this sham and then we'll get our turn. You can speak to Matt in private and clear the whole thing up," Priya whispered.

Olivia sat down and listened to Thomas and Pablo wrap up their presentation. Matt, clearly impressed, asked questions and gave small suggestions, but held back from commenting fully. Olivia assumed he wanted to hear her presentation and would then give them both his full appraisal once he'd decided whose idea to move forward with. Though, Olivia realized, whether he picked Thomas or Olivia, he would be moving forward with her idea.

Olivia tried to take deep breaths. She didn't want to let that mockery she had just witnessed affect her. She and Priya took their positions at the head of the table to begin their presentation. They had settled on the original "Takes You Places" campaign after they were unable to locate any Miss Subways alumnae besides Mrs. Glasser. Olivia had been disappointed at first, but she was happy with how their creative had come out.

As she was talking, Olivia knew that while the concept she was suggesting was strategically more in line with the MTA's vision and was significantly cheaper and easier to implement, it wasn't nearly as sexy, in advertising speak, as the idea Thomas had presented. Olivia could see it in Matt's eyes, could imagine what he was thinking: *Yes, Liv, good execution. Smart idea, but a little boring, no? A little predictable?*

Olivia finished her presentation and tried not to look at Thomas. The one time during her presentation that she had, he was actually laughing. She had looked away quickly, but he had successfully distracted her and she fumbled her words.

Once she had finished, Matt asked the requisite questions and gave a small amount of input, clearly trying to be consistent and show parity in his approach to both her and Thomas.

"Thank you to everyone in this room," Matt said, standing, "for what is clearly an enormous amount of hard work and creative thinking. I'm incredibly impressed. It's almost eleven o'clock. Let's meet back here in an hour, and I'll let you know which direction I've chosen." Matt quickly walked out of the conference room.

"I don't get it," Olivia said, directing her anger at Thomas and Pablo, who were on the other side of the room from her. "How could you just blatantly steal my idea and pass it off as your own?" Her face was starting to turn red no matter how much she was trying to keep her cool.

"Liv, come on. Let's not do this," Priya said quietly to her.

"Answer me," Olivia said, ignoring Priya.

Thomas and Pablo were silent. Thomas had a smug and unyielding expression on his face. Pablo's face, on the other hand, was difficult to read.

"You're not going to get away with it," Olivia eventually said, storming out of the conference room. She slammed the door behind her and walked purposefully to Matt's office. His door was shut.

"I need to speak with him, Layne," Olivia said firmly.

"He's on the phone," Layne said kindly.

"Business or pleasure? This is really urgent."

"Um, Olivia, I really shouldn't say," Layne said.

Olivia took that to mean it was a personal call and opened Matt's door. Layne jumped up and walked in behind her to let Matt know Olivia had stormed the castle.

Matt was reclining in his chair, his feet up on the table, but gathered himself when he saw what was going on.

Olivia heard the person, the woman, on speakerphone say, "So tonight, Matt?"

"Lily, I have to go. Sorry. I'll call you back," Matt said, clearly shaken by the sight of an enraged Olivia in his office.

"But, Matt—" Olivia heard before Matt hung up the phone.

"Great." Olivia sad-laughed to herself. Lily.

"Sorry, Matt, she just walked in," Layne explained.

"It's okay, Layne, not a problem," Matt said.

Matt stood and walked Layne to the door and shut it behind her. Olivia was pacing, but Matt took a seat on his couch.

"Liv?" he asked. She was annoyed at how amused he seemed to be.

"Thomas completely stole my idea. I have notes, Matt. I can show you I'd been working on that idea since the beginning. Priya can vouch for me. And, well, Pablo could have also, except he's the one who took the idea to Thomas, so of course he'll deny it," Olivia said, speaking quickly and angrily.

"How do you know he didn't also come up with the idea?" Matt said, speaking calmly.

"Oh, please, Matt. Don't be so fucking naive."

"It was a good idea," he said, nodding.

"I know it's a good idea," Olivia said, softening a little. In that split second, though, she remembered Matt had been in what was clearly a flirty conversation with Lily and that her idea had been stolen, and her outrage doubled. "But it's too expensive to pitch to the MTA and you know that. And, wait a minute, are you really going to let them get away with this? This is a cardinal sin in our industry, Matt."

Matt was silent, clearly contemplating his next move.

"I'll tell you what . . . ," he began. "Let me have till noon as I initially requested, and I'll let my thoughts be known then. But I need to get some things done, so if you'll please excuse me."

Olivia stood there, shocked. Shocked that he wasn't outraged, at least discernibly, at what Pablo and Thomas had done. Shocked that he was speaking to her as if she were five. Shocked that he had just dismissed her so rudely. She knew that she shouldn't get, and she didn't want, special treatment just because she and Matt had spent the last three nights together. But it was hard to reconcile this Matt with the one in her bedroom.

Olivia walked purposefully out of Matt's office and back to her own. She slammed the door behind her and plopped down into her chair. Staring into space, she rewound what had happened. It wasn't any easier to comprehend the second time around. She looked at her bulletin board, where she'd pinned her original notes so she could start collecting evidence against Thomas. Her eyes landed on a small poster. She read her favorite quote aloud: "Go confidently in the direction of your dreams. Live the life you have imagined."

At that moment, Olivia realized that working at an agency where Thomas's brand of unethical behavior could be tolerated was not the life she had imagined. And the direction of her dreams? Olivia asked herself that as she plotted her next move.

CHAPTER 17

"Meet Miss Subways Charlotte Friedman. Ambitious Charlotte is in her final year at Hunter College and targets a career in advertising. When she's not spending time with her lawyer-on-the-rise boyfriend, Charlotte's an art enthusiast and enjoys visiting museums with her parents."

Charlotte's posters had just gone up on the subways that morning, so it was during her trip into Manhattan that day for the launch event at the Times Square subway station that she saw her poster for the first time.

Charlotte almost burst into tears when she saw that the poster didn't mention her father's store. She had heard that the copywriters took liberty with the descriptions, but this was over the line. An art enthusiast! Museums with her parents! Charlotte couldn't recall ever having gone to a museum with her parents. She knew it sounded more refined than a mention of a paint and wallpaper store, but still. Charlotte stared at her feet, thinking about her future and the disastrous turn of events.

When she looked back up to read the poster again, just to

confirm what she already knew, Charlotte looked more closely at the photograph. She almost didn't recognize herself. The girl in the photo looked like her, Charlotte thought, but a softer, more angelic version. She knew the photographers had a way of retouching the photos to eliminate blemishes and the sort. But it was an entirely different thing altogether to see that practice applied to one's own face.

"Is that you up there, honey?" asked the man sitting across from Charlotte, pointing at another of the placards, this one directly above Charlotte's head.

"It is," Charlotte said timidly. At first she considered telling the man no, not wanting to draw too much attention to herself. But what the heck? Charlotte decided to suck all the sugary juice out of this experience as long as it lasted. Perhaps that was the reason why she decided to sit directly under her poster in the first place.

Charlotte wore a light blue sleeveless satin dress with a jeweled belt cinching her waist and a matching brooch at her right shoulder. She had gone with Miss Fontaine two weeks ago to Lord & Taylor to pick it out. As soon as they had walked into the dress department, a saleswoman named Rosalie had come to greet them. Apparently, Miss Fontaine was not only well known to Rosalie, as evidenced from the double-cheeked kisses they exchanged, but had made an appointment, because as soon as Rosalie looked at Charlotte, she said, "And this must be Charlotte, Miss Subways for July." Then Charlotte received her first double-cheeked kiss.

The shopping expedition surpassed every one of Charlotte's expectations. Rosalie deposited Charlotte and Miss Fontaine in what must have been the bridal dressing room. It was massive, with two white silk-covered benches for guests and a two-step platform in front of a gleaming three-way mirror. Another girl brought them champagne. And then Rosalie began appearing with the most dazzling array of colorful dress confections. There was the rose-colored one that Charlotte dismissed simply because of the name of the color itself. The emerald green with the pale green embroidery overlay went onto the maybe rack. The red with the black bow on the back was, they all agreed, a bit overwrought. The black polka-dotted suit, though elegant in its fit, seemed too businesslike. As soon as Charlotte tried on the light blue satin, well, they all agreed, that was the one. It was formal yet appropriate, sophisticated yet demure, special but not too precious. Charlotte had never worn something so exquisite. She twirled around and peacocked in the mirror, much to the delight of Rosalie and Miss Fontaine.

It was a little fancy for the subway, which might have been what drew that man's attention to her, but it made Charlotte feel as special as a little girl in the front row of the dignitary bleachers at the Macy's Thanksgiving Day Parade.

Charlotte played nervously with her fingers, ensconced in their lovely white cotton gloves embroidered with seed pearls, another gem from her shopping expedition with Miss Fontaine.

Miss Fontaine hadn't told Charlotte much about the launch. Only that there would be photographers and an unveiling of a large version of her poster. It would be symbolic, of course, because the posters would already be in all the subway cars. Miss Fontaine had told her which platform to meet at, and when Charlotte arrived, she was delighted to find that quite a crowd had gathered. She spotted Miss Fontaine near the dais.

"Miss Fontaine," Charlotte said over the din, tapping her on the shoulder.

"Charlotte! How lovely you look, dear. Come sit right over here on this chair. We'll start in about fifteen minutes."

There was a row of five chairs directly behind the dais, each marked with a name and title. Charlotte's said *Miss Charlotte Friedman, Miss Subways July 1949.* She wondered if she could take the sign home with her as a souvenir. Another chair was marked for Mr. Powers, and the other three were for representatives of the New York Subways Advertising Company. Charlotte was disappointed that no one from J. Walter Thompson would be there. She thought it would have been a valuable opportunity to introduce herself.

While she waited, Charlotte considered the implications of her poster. She felt a deep thrill that this day had finally come. But the possibility of Miss Subways solving her immediate problem had been obliterated. All the Miss Subways followers she hoped would seek her out at Friedman's would now be hanging around the Impressionists gallery at the Met instead.

The camel's back was officially broken. And deep down, where the truth mattered, Charlotte knew that working in her father's store would feel like a gold-medal failure. That it would be living the life her father had imagined for her brother. The life that neither Harry nor Charlotte wanted. She had wanted more for herself than to just be another girl who couldn't support herself outside of the nest prepared for her by her parents. A tidy, safe nest protected from the big scary world outside Bay Ridge. No, Charlotte ached for a life unprescribed. Where she could feel independent and important. She had believed completely and thoroughly that she would have that.

But now that she had graduated and none of the other job prospects had come to fruition, Charlotte realized that she had to just resign herself to the new reality that she would be living at home, working in her father's store, and that was that. Not every girl's dreams came true. Not every girl was destined to feel like she had sidestepped expectations. Not every girl could be significant.

For the time being, though, Charlotte took a deep breath and tried to enjoy the experience swirling around her. Photographers were setting up their tripods. Journalists milled around, writing in their notebooks. Passersby stopped to ask what was happening. Charlotte was stunned that this was all for her. Nothing had ever been *all for her* in her entire life. Such a lovely fuss.

When it was time for the ceremony to begin, the gentlemen took their seats next to her, and Miss Fontaine stood off to the side. The CEO of the New York Subways Advertising Company spoke first about the program, how it had been so successful, how they envisioned it continuing for years to come.

Charlotte looked out at the crowd with bright eyes. She had to willfully hold her hands in her lap; her excitement and nerves felt like they were going to blast out of her, most likely starting at the tips of her fingers. Photographers took candids of her. But Charlotte pretended not to notice; she didn't want to spoil the shots. Onlookers pointed at her, and she caught the tail ends of their whispered, "She must be the next Miss Subways." Like they were in on a secret. Charlotte thought she had seen a familiar face in the back of the crowd but figured she must have imagined it as it slipped away.

Mr. Powers spoke next. First he gave a brief explanation of his agency's involvement in the program. And then he spoke about a young woman, about her ambitions, about her interest in the fine arts. It took Charlotte a second to realize he was talking about her. Miss Fontaine hadn't told Charlotte she was going to have to speak, but the next thing she knew, Mr. Powers was calling her up to the dais and the photographers' flashes were bursting like the sky over the Hudson on the Fourth of July.

"Go on, dear," Miss Fontaine whispered to Charlotte, who felt glued to her seat. Though public speaking would be important for her future career, it hadn't been something she'd ever done effortlessly in school.

Thankful for her gloves, which were most definitely preventing showers of sweat from spraying out of her palms, Charlotte gingerly approached the dais. Mr. Powers kissed her on the cheek and presented her to the crowd of anticipatory journalists and photographers.

"Well, I'm, um, I'm so happy to be here," Charlotte said, suddenly blinded and distracted by the flashes. "And, well, I never would have imagined for one second I'd ever be Miss Subways." She was starting to feel more comfortable, but decided to keep it brief lest she faint and end up as a blue satin puddle sprawled across the filthy platform. "I ride the subway all the time, and I'm so excited to be part of this program. It's a true honor. Thank you very much."

It was only when she sat down that she realized she had missed the opportunity to mention the store. Her heart sank. But there was no time to sulk, because the photographers were directing her to pose with the various dignitaries, including Mr. Powers.

"Where's your family?" one of the photographers shouted. From another: "Yeah, let's get a shot with the family." And still another: "Or the boyfriend."

"I'm so sorry. My, um, my family was unable to come

today," Charlotte said, smiling widely and hoping that would suffice. Her stomach tightened in panic at the thought of her parents finding out. It was a good thing her parents never rode the subway, the necessities of their lives squarely within walking distance. There was no way they—her father, especially—would forgive her for blatantly disobeying them. Though, Charlotte realized, that was a distressing thought (disobeying her parents wasn't something she was proud of), she also felt elated, liberated. Proud was *exactly* how she felt. Proud of winning (by default, but still), proud of doing something for herself, and proud of how strategic she was being in her effort to save her advertising career and her father's store.

"Okay, dear, just look this way and smile," the first photographer said. The flashes resumed.

The whole event must not have taken more than ten minutes, and after answering questions from a few of the journalists who waited in line impatiently to speak with her, it was over. Charlotte did say, innumerable times, that when she wasn't visiting museums with her parents, she could be found at Friedman's Paint and Wallpaper on Third Avenue in Brooklyn and that she hoped people would come and visit her there. She noticed the journalists kept writing while she said that; now she could only hope they'd be able to make out the shorthand when they returned to their unkempt desks downtown.

Charlotte thanked Miss Fontaine and Mr. Powers for the experience. They wished her well and told her they'd be in touch if there were ever any opportunities that would suit her. And then she was free to go. Though Charlotte wasn't really expecting one, she couldn't deny a twinge of disappointment that Miss Fontaine hadn't presented her with a contract to be a Powers Girl. But she decided not to dwell on that, choosing to indulge the giddiness she felt instead. There had been such an emotional lead-up to this event over the past several months. Never one to relish having the spotlight directed at her, Charlotte was surprised to find how much she enjoyed the attention that being Miss Subways brought with it. A sense of confidence swept through her, and she felt herself straightening her back and lifting her chin. She wondered if this feeling would stay for a while. She hoped it would. Perhaps she only needed to have the sun shine on her a first time to realize how warm it felt.

As she walked away, Charlotte saw that familiar face again in the back of the crowd. But this time, it didn't slip away. It walked right toward her.

Rose.

"Charlotte, congratulations. Your poster is beautiful. I'm really happy for you," Rose said.

Charlotte, shocked to see Rose, a pleasant Rose at that, just stood there, unable to formulate a response. She had thought about Rose often these last several months. Perplexed as to why Rose had been so dismissive when Charlotte had gone to visit her after the Miss Subways photo shoot, Charlotte had written her a letter. Rose hadn't responded. Charlotte had worried about Rose, but realized, after some time, that if Rose didn't want to reciprocate the friendship, for whatever reason, Charlotte would have to accept that.

"Can I buy you a cup of coffee?" Rose asked. "There's a place just outside the station."

Charlotte thought Rose seemed exceedingly nervous, and what was it about her that looked different?

"I'm not sure that's such a good idea," Charlotte said, looking Rose straight in the eye, angry that Rose would be so Rose enough to assume that Charlotte would just act as if nothing had transpired between them.

"I can understand why you might feel that way, but please, just have a cup of coffee with me and hear me out."

Charlotte was curious to hear what Rose would have to say. Plus, Charlotte thought, she had such a pretty dress on and nowhere else to go that day. She might as well get more use from it. So she agreed.

They walked in silence side by side up the stairs from the subway station to the sidewalk above. Rose gestured to the right and they turned and walked toward the coffee shop. A couple was leaving as Rose and Charlotte approached, so the man held the door for them. Rose walked in first and Charlotte, walking behind her, gasped.

When they got into the restaurant, Charlotte couldn't help herself and she looked straight into Rose's eyes and then straight down to her midsection. Just then, the hostess asked them to follow her to their table.

Charlotte didn't say a word, just followed the hostess, and sat across from Rose in a booth by the window. A waitress came right over and they both ordered coffee and a slice of cake.

"It's true," Rose said as soon as the waitress walked away.

"What's true?" Charlotte asked.

"I'm pregnant."

"Congratulations," Charlotte said, and then looked at Rose's ring finger. It was empty.

"Yep, no ring," Rose said, holding up her left hand and wiggling the finger that gave most girls of their generation an identity. "And no fiancé number seven in sight." She'd said it sarcastically. She wasn't smiling.

"How far along are you?" Charlotte asked.

"Almost four months. I'm due in December."

"Why didn't you tell me? I would have been there for you, Rose," Charlotte said, extending her hand to Rose's across the table.

Rose pulled away and buried her head in her hands.

Charlotte was not an unfeeling person. In fact, she was just the opposite. But while she felt awful for this pregnant woman sitting across from her who was clearly alone and scared, she was finding it progressively difficult to feel awful for Rose.

"Charlotte, I have to ask you something," Rose said. Her hands were shaking as she pulled them away from her face.

Charlotte looked at her expectantly.

Rose continued slowly, "Will you raise my baby?"

"What?" Charlotte shouted. Other patrons looked at them, so Charlotte lowered her voice. "Are you out of your mind? Why would I possibly do that?"

"Because Sam is the father."

CHAPTER 18

OLIVIA
MONDAY, MARCH 12, 2018

Olivia
Are you free for lunch?

Ben
Not sure that's such a good idea.

Olivia
Sorry about Saturday night. That was so uncool
of me.

Ben
It's fine. I get it. Gotta work. Have a great day.

Olivia took out her phone and did a quick search on Safari.
Then she left the office without telling anyone and walked
down the block to the L train at Fourteenth and Eighth.

Olivia was trying not to concentrate on what she was
doing. And she certainly was trying not to concentrate on

how she was feeling, which, at the moment, comprised a toxic mess of nausea, excitement, anger, and several other subtle, unrecognizable, and not entirely pleasant sensations.

Though the day had become quite warm, a welcome change from the cold snap they had been experiencing, Olivia gathered her coat around her. She bounded down the steps into the subway station and swiped her MetroCard. The train was just arriving, and Olivia was happy she didn't have to wait. She wasn't sure her resolve was strong enough right now, and she didn't want to change her mind and back out.

She got on the train and found a seat on the cold molded plastic. Looking around, Olivia saw her fellow passengers wearing masks of disinterest. But Olivia knew that very few of those masks reflected what was going on in the brains of their owners. Everyone was entertaining their own parties of inner turmoil. No one had it easy.

As passengers both disembarked from and joined her car, at Sixth Avenue, at Union Square, at Third Avenue, at First, and then for the ride under the East River (which she always tried to not think too hard about lest she feel claustrophobic), Olivia felt a little panic at what she had just done.

After her conversation with Matt, she had decided she had to get out of there. She knew Thomas was going to win—she'd seen it in Matt's eyes. And she could also tell he didn't much care that Thomas had stolen her idea. Perhaps Matt felt it was all part of the game, and that if Thomas was brazen enough to do it (perhaps to get back at Olivia for crashing his MTA dinner), and it could land them the account, then all good by him.

But could Matt really feel that way? Wouldn't the fair thing be to let *her* present whichever idea Matt liked best? For some reason, Olivia didn't think Matt would do that.

Olivia chided herself for being too impulsive, for not waiting to hear what Matt would decide, for just running out rather than facing the firing squad head-on and making her voice heard.

On the other hand, her message was loud and clear. She wouldn't stand for an agency that would condone, even encourage, such behavior. And she no longer would stand for Matt. Sure, she had taken him to her bed on her terms, but she couldn't entirely take the emotions out of the situation, couldn't make it entirely transactional. And with Lily back in the picture and Matt clearly not wanting this to be anything but extracurricular, Olivia realized she had been sacrificing her self-respect. She *wanted* to be one of those women who could just have sex without getting attached, and she *had,* with men she didn't care for, but it was different with Matt. Different for her, at least.

The train pulled into the Bedford Avenue station, and as soon as Olivia surfaced to street level, the Brooklyn air rushing about with its urgency and the sunlight stinging her eyes, her phone buzzed with incoming texts.

Priya
Liv, where the hell r u? Been looking for u everywhere. Time to go to conf room.

Priya
Liv???????

Priya
Did u really bail?? Starting to worry abt u bec I know u wouldn't do that.

Priya
Going in. Will let u know what happens if u don't show. V worried!

Olivia typed out a quick apology to Priya:

Olivia
Sorry. There's something I have to do. Thanks for covering for me. I'll call you in a little while.

Then she silenced her phone, turned around on the corner to get her bearings, and headed west on North Seventh Street for three blocks. She turned right on Kent Avenue, her uncertainty increasing with the ascending street numbers.

North Eighth Street. *This is crazy, Liv.* North Ninth Street. *What are you thinking?* North Tenth Street. *Maybe this isn't such a good idea.* North Eleventh Street. *Just turn back. Don't make a complete fool of yourself.* North Twelfth Street. *Don't lead him on, Liv. That's unfair.* And then she was there. She looked up at the building number and then at her phone screen to the search result to make sure the numbers matched, and then she had one last thought. *Well, you're here. You might as well go for it. You've never been one to back down from a challenge, so why start now?*

Olivia looked at the building directory and then headed for the elevator. She touched the button for the fourteenth floor and stared above her head as the numbers lit up one by one. The elevator stopped, and Olivia took a deep breath. The doors opened into one of the most arresting reception areas she'd ever seen.

The walls were made completely of brick, and there was

a palpable energy emanating from the employees in the open-plan office space. A bright orange kayak hung from the ceiling between the elevators and the reception desk. Behind the reception desk was what appeared to be an actual wing of an airplane emblazoned with the UseYourWings logo.

"Can I help you?" a twentysomething guy with long hair asked Olivia.

"Hi. Yes. I'm looking for Ben—" Olivia realized she didn't know his last name. She didn't know if it was his mother or father who was Mrs. Glasser's child.

"Glasser or Montgomery?" the receptionist asked.

"Glasser," Olivia said, smiling. Her stomach was still roiling.

"And your name?"

"Olivia Harrison."

"Please have a seat, Olivia, and I'll let him know you're here." He gestured to a seating area just off to the side. Olivia almost ran right into a woman riding a hoverboard down the hall.

"Sorry!" she called to Olivia.

Olivia sat down and noticed there were several iPads on the coffee table. She picked one up and unlocked the dark screen. It went straight to the UseYourWings home page, and she began clicking around the familiar site. It was a surreal feeling to be in the headquarters of a site she had spent so much time on.

"Olivia!"

Olivia looked up. Ben was standing in front of her, his hands stuffed deeply into his pockets. He was wearing dark jeans and a checked navy button-down. He looked adorable. Olivia felt a flutter in her chest, and she knew she had made the right decision.

She hadn't quite been able to make sense of her feelings, but ever since Saturday night, when she let Matt into her apartment and said good night to Ben in the hallway, something had been nagging at her, a voice telling her that she was focusing on the wrong man. It was confusing for Olivia because she was so attracted to Matt in so many ways, while Ben seemed so nice, maybe too nice, and, even worse, predictable. But the more she thought about it, the more Olivia realized that those were actually *good* things for a man to be. That she deserved to be with a man who would be kind to her and whose motivations were clear and rational. She'd been surprised to find herself thinking of Ben ever since.

"What are you doing here?" Ben asked. Olivia couldn't read his tone. She realized he liked her and she had paraded Matt right in front of him. Hopefully that little display didn't erase all the feelings he had for her. Because she was definitely starting to feel them too.

"I'm sorry to drop in unannounced," Olivia said suddenly, and uncharacteristically, nervous. She felt her cheeks flush like a sixth grader staging a fake run-in with her crush at the lockers. "And I'm sorry I didn't respect your text that you had to work—"

"Come with me," Ben said, and gently grabbed her hand.

They walked through the main floor of the office. Olivia had worked for a big company when she was at Y&R, but it was nothing like what she was seeing now at UseYourWings. This was hipster heaven. Each desk area had bumper stickers and postcards from different foreign cities. Olivia saw meetings going on in little annexes filled with comfy couches. And in the center of the space, mounted on a board, was a huge map of the world with pins and colorful strings and all sorts of decor.

Ben noticed Olivia looking at the map.

"Every time an employee travels somewhere, he or she gets to put a pin on the map. So far, we've collectively traveled to a hundred and two countries and almost two thousand cities."

"Wow!" Olivia said, staring more closely at the map as they passed by it. She leaned in to see Paris covered with dozens of pins.

Olivia followed Ben to the back corner of the space, and they entered an office with floor-to-ceiling windows overlooking the East River. He stood by the door as she walked into the office, her jaw dropping as she got closer to the windows to see the spectacular view. She was shocked at what a nice office he had, and the thought crossed her mind that perhaps her next job should be at an internet company because they seem to be flush with money. Ben closed the door behind her.

Olivia stood close to the window, looking at the Manhattan skyline, and when she turned around and started to talk, he was standing directly in front of her. She startled, and he gently put his hands on the sides of her face. And then he kissed her. Slowly, softly. And when he stopped, he smiled at her. Olivia was stunned. Heart racing, palms sweaty, permasmile stunned.

"You were saying?" Ben asked, clearly amused. He sat down in his office chair and gestured for her to sit in one of the ivory-colored Knoll leather chairs across the desk.

Olivia smiled and cocked her head, a bit surprised, and certainly intrigued, at the confidence Ben showed. Perhaps he wasn't as predictable as she had thought. "I was saying," she continued, "that I'm sorry to come when you clearly didn't want me to."

"Ah, young Olivia. Clearly, you were mistaken." He smiled.

"Clearly," Olivia said.

"So why did you come?" Ben asked.

"Because something happened at work and for some peculiar reason, you were the person I wanted to talk to about it," Olivia said, tilting her head and raising her eyebrows.

"Peculiar, indeed."

"Indeed."

"What happened?" Ben asked.

Olivia told him about the pitches, about how Pablo and Thomas stole her idea, and about how Matt seemed not to care.

"Matt? The same debonair Matt I met making his way into your apartment Saturday night?" Ben asked.

"Same one," Olivia said, nodding.

"Seems our Olivia is involved in an office romance."

"Not exactly. But Matt is old news."

"I see," Ben said, hardly containing the glee painted on his face.

"Part of me is appalled by my impulsive decision to run out of there. And the other part of me is giddy. I just don't know what I'm going to do next."

"Feel like taking a trip to California?" Ben asked. "Ticket's on me. I have loads of miles. Company perk." He winked. "Even enough to get you your own hotel room."

"That sounds amazing. I don't even know what to say."

"Say yes."

"There's no way I can go. I have to go back to my office. It's ridiculous that I even left. Are you going for business?"

"Remember those letters from Saturday night? The ones that fell out of my grandmother's scrapbook? Well, I read them. And now I want to go to California."

"Quite cryptic, Ben," Olivia said, raising her eyebrows. "You must have a nice boss to let you just take off to California like this."

"Yeah, something like that," Ben said.

Olivia felt her phone buzz. She pulled it out of her pocket and saw a text from Priya.

Priya
We lost. Not sure if it's bec ur not here or bec Matt chose Thomas. Where the f r u, Liv????

"From the sound of the text I just got," Olivia continued, "it appears I may be out of a job, so perhaps I could take a little journey to the left coast with you. Might be good for my soul right about now."

"The flight's at seven thirty tonight. I'm leaving here"—Ben gestured to his wheelie bag—"at five. Can you make it?"

"Yeah," Olivia said, standing. "I have to take care of a few things, but, sure, I can make it." Olivia felt aflutter. She liked to think of herself as spontaneous, but she'd never really had an opportunity to test out the theory.

"Birthday?"

"What?" Olivia asked.

"When's your birthday? For the ticket."

"August eighth, nineteen eighty-six."

"Leo," Ben said, nodding with a smirk.

"Yep," Olivia said, smiling. "Through and through."

"Keller," Ben said, pressing a button on his phone system but holding Olivia's gaze with a penetrating stare. Olivia felt like confetti bombs were going off in her stomach. "Please book a ticket with my miles for the JetBlue flight I'm on tonight at seven thirty to LAX for Olivia Harrison, date of birth eight, eight, eighty-six. And see if there's another seat in Mint. If not, move me back to coach so we can sit next to each other."

Ben hung up and came around his desk to where Olivia was sitting. He took her hands in his, and she stood up.

"Do you remember when my grandma asked you if you had a boyfriend?" Ben asked.

Olivia nodded. She couldn't stop smiling.

"I put her up to that."

"You did? But you got mad at her for asking."

"I know. That was good, right? Threw you off the trail. That was our little act. We practiced that," Ben said, laughing.

"Wow. You two should really take your act on the road. I think there's a market out there for that kind of show."

"I find you incredible, Olivia. And I am still trying to understand how it is that you aren't in a relationship."

"Priorities, I guess," Olivia said. "And I guess the right guy hasn't ever come along."

Ben looked into Olivia's eyes and squeezed her hands. He kissed her again. Longer this time. When they pulled apart, their faces were right up to each other. They were both smiling.

"Do you want to meet me here and go to the airport together?" Ben asked.

"No, I think that will just take longer for me. I'll grab a cab and meet you there."

They kissed once more and when Olivia was able to pull herself away, she walked out of Ben's office, beaming. Had he really just invited her to California? And taken care of all the arrangements? No one had ever done anything like this for her. Took care of her. She had to admit, though she was staunchly in favor of taking care of herself, that it felt kind of nice.

CHAPTER 19

"Sam is the *what*?" Charlotte asked. Her hands had reflexively hardened to fists at her sides.

"He's the father," Rose said quietly.

"How could you say such a thing?"

"Because it's true. I'm so sorry, Charlotte. I'm sorry I ever got involved with him. He doesn't care about me. He loves you, and I know that. I honestly do, and I'm so sorry."

"Does he know?" Charlotte asked. She was so in shock, she was having trouble figuring out which of the questions swirling in her mind she should ask first.

"Yes."

"Have you been having an affair?"

"No."

"When were you together?"

Rose looked down at her hands.

"For heaven's sake," Charlotte said. "Just tell me what I need to know and get it over with already."

"The Saturday night after the three of us had gone out

for steaks. The next day I was so disgusted with myself, I just couldn't do the Miss Subways photo shoot that Monday. And when you showed up at my apartment that afternoon, I panicked. That's why I was so rude to you."

"How do you know the father isn't your last fiancé or some other guy?"

"Because I'd never been with my fiancé that way, and there's been no one since that night with Sam."

"I can't believe this," Charlotte said, kneading her fingers. Her heart felt like it had been squeezed through a meat grinder. Extruded raw and decimated on the other side.

"I'm so sorry, Charlotte."

"I don't care that you're sorry, Rose," Charlotte said, enjoying the sting that hit Rose's face. "I don't care about you one bit. I care about Sam. And if what you're saying is true, then he not only was intimate with you but he's been lying to me for months."

"He loves you. I think he's just trying to figure out how to handle this."

"Don't you tell me what *you* think Sam is doing. You don't know Sam. You don't know anything about him," Charlotte said, the anger rising in her voice.

"You're right," Rose said, her palms up in surrender. "You're absolutely right. I don't."

They were silent while the waitress brought their coffees and cake.

"So let me get this straight," Charlotte said, visibly appalled. "You're intimate with my boyfriend, become pregnant with his baby, and now you want me to raise this baby? On my own? Without a husband, because it's very clear Sam will never be my husband, and I can't imagine what man would want to marry me if I'm raising the child of my ex-boyfriend and ex-friend if you ever even were a friend. This is ludicrous!"

"That's what Sam said you'd say. He begged me not to even ask you, and I told him I wouldn't."

"You told Sam this ridiculous idea? My goodness, this just keeps getting better," Charlotte said, laughing in disbelief and then taking a sip of her coffee.

"He told me to have it taken care of, but I just couldn't do that."

"Why don't you raise your own baby and do the honorable thing and get Sam to marry you?"

"I can't, Charlotte. First of all, Sam would never marry me. He won't even look at me. He's disgusted with me. I seduced him."

"Takes two to tango, Rose," Charlotte said.

"I know, but let's just say he wasn't a willing dance partner, and I loaded him with alcohol."

"That's beside the point."

"I can't raise this baby. I don't want to be a mother, Charlotte. I would be a terrible mother. I've had the worst mother for a role model, and I don't want to mess up this innocent baby. I have things I want to do. I want to go to Hollywood. I still want to be a star."

"And I have things I want to do. I want to have a career. I can't do that *and* take care of a baby. A baby that's not even mine!"

"Sam told me you can't have children."

"Oh yeah, what else did Sam tell you about me?" Charlotte said, her eyes challenging Rose.

"That he didn't care about that. That he wanted to marry you anyway. And that you two would eventually adopt a baby. That's why I thought this wasn't such a bad idea." Rose was calm.

"When Sam and I talked about adopting, it was going to be when we were married. And it certainly wasn't going to be a baby that he had conceived in an illicit affair. So, no. A big fat NO."

"Please, Charlotte. I'm begging you."

"Why can't you just put the baby up for adoption like normal girls do in your situation?"

"I could, but I wanted to give you the opportunity first. You and Sam. I know this is awful for you to hear, but this is his baby after all."

"Stop saying that, Rose!"

"Maybe you can just think about it, Charlotte. Maybe you can talk to Sam and see if there's any way the two of you could find a way to reconcile and raise this baby. I realize how absurd it all sounds when I hear it coming out of my mouth, but I also know that you and Sam are meant for each other. The day after the three of us had dinner, I looked up his number and called him to ask him to go to a movie. He didn't want to. But I convinced him it would take his mind off you and how upset he was. He was angry because he didn't know why you had made such a big deal out of his proposal. I think he just did what men do when they're mad and acting stupid. I brought a flask and encouraged him to drink it during the movie. It's all my fault, Charlotte. I know that's hard to make sense of because he was there too. But I take full responsibility. Please, just think about it."

Charlotte stood up. She had nothing left to say. Rose scribbled her telephone number on a piece of paper and pushed it across the table to Charlotte. Charlotte grabbed the paper, crumpled it up, dropped it back onto the table, and walked out.

Back on the sidewalk in the fresh air, Charlotte felt like someone had just shot her out of a cannon. She was disoriented and hot. She didn't know where to go next. And then she did.

"Welcome to Linden & Linden," a sturdy receptionist said to Charlotte when she approached the imposing desk. Charlotte had never visited Sam at work. She was surprised by how luxurious the waiting area was. She knew Linden & Linden was a prestigious firm, but she hadn't expected this.

"Hello, I'm Charlotte Friedman. I'm here to see—"

"Charlotte!"

Charlotte was surprised to see Sam walking through the waiting area. "Sam."

"What are you doing here?" Sam asked, a smile developing on his face. He leaned in to hug Charlotte and she stood stony. He looked into her eyes searchingly. "I was just on my way to talk to an associate. Will you come to my office with me? We can talk privately in there."

When they arrived at Sam's office (How large it was! With a window! And a view!), he stood at the door and ushered her in. He closed the door gently and pulled a curtain across the window that faced the rest of the office.

He gestured to her to take a seat in one of the plush chairs across from his desk and he sat next to her in the other. He turned the chair to face her. She remained facing forward.

"Charlotte, you look beautiful. That dress! How did

the event go? I'm sorry I couldn't get away from here. I really tried."

"I had a visitor there. A pregnant visitor who then asked me for coffee so she could propose the most preposterous idea I think I've ever heard in my whole entire life. Would you like to know who my visitor was and what she said?" Charlotte formed a tight smile with her lips and stared directly at Sam.

"I think I know," Sam said, staring at the floor.

"You lied to me, Sam. And how could you do something so awful and then act like everything was normal these past few months? I feel like such a fool!"

Sam looked up at Charlotte and his eyes were filled with tears.

"Oh no, you don't. Don't you cry and think I'm going to feel all sad. You wipe your eyes right now and tell me what you have to say for yourself, or I'm going to walk right out of this office and never speak to you again. The only reason I'm here is because I want to hear directly from you how you could have lied to me like that. And Rose? Sam, Rose?"

Sam wiped his eyes with his shirtsleeve and took a deep breath.

"Charlotte, the first thing I want you to know is that I love you. I've never been sorrier about anything I've ever done in my whole life, and I love you. You deserve an explanation; you deserve way more than that. So thank you for coming here today so I can tell you what happened."

Sam proceeded to tell Charlotte a similar story to what Rose said. How he was so distraught that Charlotte was angry with him. How Rose seduced him with alcohol and wiles. How that doesn't excuse his behavior. And how the next morning he was so disgusted with himself, so ashamed, and so distressed about jeopardizing their relationship.

And then he told her that the reason he didn't tell her, which he felt might even be worse than what he did with Rose, is because he thought if Charlotte knew what he had done, she would never take him back. He had decided to never tell her and that the guilt he would feel for his entire life would be just punishment. And that he would spend that life making it up to her by treating her like she deserved.

"I know now that lying to you was wrong. I know it's made this whole thing worse. And I regret that and my behavior more than you could ever know."

Charlotte was silent. She felt numb. Like her brain was so overloaded with virulent stimuli that it wasn't allowing her to process any of it. She took a deep breath and tried to make sense of it all.

"Did you consider Rose's idea of adopting the baby?" Charlotte asked in a cold voice.

"To be honest, at first I thought she was out of her mind. I even asked her to take care of it. I was angry and confused and have heard guys talking about that sort of thing. But the more I thought about it, the more I thought that *I* would take the baby. Rose doesn't want to be a mother. And I don't think anyone should become a mother who doesn't want to. What kind of life does that make for the child?"

"*You* would take the baby?"

"Yes, I would. I think that's the right thing to do. Ideally, when I think about having a baby, I would like to raise it with you as my wife. But I understand I may have just done absolutely everything in the world to prevent that from ever happening."

"Oh, Sam, this is all too much."

"I know, Charlotte. It is all too much. So let me say what I know to be true and clear. I love you. I am going to be a father. I want nothing else in this world than to be married to you when I become a father, to be a parent with you. I know that's so much to ask, too much to ask, Charlotte. Way, way, way too much to ask. But please, if you can, please just consider it."

Charlotte looked into Sam's eyes. It was her Sam, staring at her imploringly.

"Let's just say I do consider it, which I'd be crazy to even do, but what about my future? There's so much I want to do. I'm not ready to stay home with a baby."

"I've thought about that. And we could either have my mother watch the baby, or maybe your mother would want to help. And if neither of them does, we could hire a nanny. I've been saving my salary, and we have enough money to move into an apartment. It would be small, but it would be ours."

"I have to go, Sam. My head feels as if it's about to burst," Charlotte said, standing up and turning toward the door.

"I understand, Charlotte. Can I see you tomorrow once you've had some time to think about it?"

"Sure," she said, then reconsidered. "No, no. I don't think that's a good idea. I'm not sure I'm going to even give it a passing thought. And if I do, the chances of accepting such a ludicrous proposal is altogether unlikely. If the world turns upside down and somehow this seems like a reasonable idea, I'll be in touch."

And with that, Charlotte opened the door and saw herself out.

Before going home, Charlotte stopped at JoJo's to change out of her Miss Subways clothes. She couldn't waltz into her own house in that number.

When Charlotte entered her bedroom, JoJo was sitting up in her bed, drinking tea, and reading a magazine.

"I'm so sorry I couldn't be there today to support you, Charlotte! This flu is a real pain in the neck. Tell me everything!" JoJo said, blowing her nose and tossing the tissue into an overflowing trash can. She patted the bed next to her, but Charlotte shrewdly, in light of the attendant germs, chose JoJo's vanity chair on the opposite side of the room.

"I don't even know where to begin," Charlotte said, shaking her head. "There's way too much to tell."

"That's wonderful!" JoJo said.

"Hold your wonderfuls until the end of the story." Then Charlotte told JoJo everything that had happened, starting with the Miss Subways launch and ending with Rose and Sam.

"He's the what?" JoJo had shouted when Charlotte told her that particular nugget.

"I don't know whether to laugh at the absolute absurdity of this mess or to cry at how awful it all is," Charlotte said.

"Sam said he would raise the baby on his own?"

"Yes, JoJo, but don't be getting all sentimental about that *poor* man raising a baby all by himself."

"Sorry. It's all just so unthinkable. And the nerve of that Rose. If I ever meet her, I don't know what I'd say. Or do. So what are you going to *do,* Charlotte?"

"Are you even suggesting I should do something?"

"Well, maybe," JoJo said, tilting her head at Charlotte and raising her eyebrows. "Let's just go there for a minute, and let's start with Sam. Pretend this Rose and the baby situation doesn't even exist. I can't believe I just uttered those words. But let's just go with Sam for a minute. Are you with me?"

"I'm with you," Charlotte said tentatively.

"Sam did something awful. We all know it was awful. Sam admits—"

"*Now* he admits. Now that he's been caught."

"Yes, true. But he still admitted it, and better late than never, Charlotte. He is a man, after all."

"Don't let him off the hook for doing something atrocious just because he's a man."

"I'm not letting him off the hook. I'm just saying that he wouldn't be the first man in the world to do something utterly asinine and then realize how utterly asinine it was. And you wouldn't be the first woman in the world to take back said man and forgive him because said man loves you more than I've ever seen a man love a woman."

"You've barely seen any couples in love, JoJo. Your reasoning is faulty."

"I've seen plenty in the pictures, Charlotte," JoJo said, raising her hands in the air.

"Oh, great. That's a terrific basis for comparison." Charlotte laughed despite herself.

"So back to starting with Sam. Is there any possible way you would consider getting back with him?"

"Why would you even want me to be with a man like that?" Charlotte asked.

"Because I don't think he's a man like that. And I don't think you think he is either."

"Ah, but he is. He showed us he is. He *is* a man like that, JoJo."

"Come on, Charlotte. You know what I mean. There are

men like that and there are men who might do that but aren't like that. And you know with every bone and blood vessel and nerve and whatever else is in your body that Sam's the latter and that's the plain and honest truth."

Charlotte just stared out the window.

"Right, Charlotte?" JoJo demanded.

"Right, JoJo," Charlotte whispered.

"Okay, we're getting somewhere. So there is this tiny hope that someday, with enough groveling on his part, you might consider getting back with Sam," JoJo said, taking a deep breath, as if this whole exercise was exhausting her, which in her state, it probably was. "Now, do you want children one day? Don't think too hard about it—just answer the question."

"Yes, Judge JoJo. Yes, I believe I want children one day."

"Great. Thank you for your direct answer and for not trying to evade the line of questioning."

"You're welcome." Charlotte was smiling. She was so lucky to have a friend like JoJo, who would overthink this whole situation so Charlotte didn't have to do it alone.

"Sadly enough, due to your endometriosis, you won't be able to conceive a baby. Is that true?"

"Yes."

"Sorry, Charlotte," JoJo said, dropping the Justice of the Supreme Court act for a moment.

"I know, JoJo. It's okay. I'm used to the idea by now."

"And you would have had to adopt a baby, correct?"

"Correct."

"And now you have an opportunity, a really sicko opportunity but one just the same, to adopt a baby that is biologically half Sam's."

"Yes, and biologically half Racy Rose's."

"True. But still biologically half Sam's. And available."

"But my career, JoJo. And our future agency. A baby would hold me back."

"I hate to say it, Charlotte, and please forgive me, but your career right now is looking like it might be based on understanding the finer points of a paintbrush. Perhaps this is one way of avoiding that fate."

"Don't think I hadn't thought of that."

"But let's say you do find a way to work in advertising; there are mothers who work, Charlotte. You wouldn't be the first to hire a nanny. I know it's completely outside the strictures of our chauvinistic society, and we'll probably be shunned for it by most of our friends, never mind our mothers' friends, for doing something so unwomanly and something that defies all proper and conventional maternal instincts, but we don't really care about all that, do we? I'm planning on doing it someday too, although first I need a boy to just ask me out for a milk shake."

Both girls stared at each other in silence.

"How did you just do that?" Charlotte finally asked.

"Do what?" JoJo said, and sniffled.

"Get me to even consider all of this?"

"Because believe it or not, Charlotte, I don't think it's the worst idea I've ever heard. At first I did. And I think the whole thing is appalling and awful and downright crazy, but when you break it down into its parts and consider that the two parents would be you and Sam, I think it's got potential."

"You're insane. Just like the rest of them," Charlotte said, starting to unzip her dress. She took her street clothes out of the closet and began changing into them.

"Perhaps I am. Perhaps it's this awful flu that's making

me think funny because normally we would be reversed in situations like this. You would be the sentimental one trying to convince me that something is a good idea, and I would be the one turning it into Swiss cheese and telling you you're out of your mind."

Charlotte laughed and hung the blue dress on a hanger.

"Mind if I leave this here for a while?"

"Be my guest," JoJo said, gesturing to her closet. "But I charge rent."

"What are you talking about?"

"The rent payment is you have to think about Sam's suggestion and my reasoning. Just think about it, Charlotte. Sam is the man for you. And there's a baby! I know it's early. I know you're young. You're so young. But sometimes life presents opportunities at inopportune times. And sometimes you have to ignore all the reasons to say no even if there are a lot of them, and go with the reasons to say yes."

CHAPTER 20

OLIVIA
MONDAY, MARCH 12, 2018

When Olivia emerged from the subway, back in Manhattan, she called Priya.

"Where have you been? I've actually been worried," Priya said, a distressed tone in her voice.

"Sorry, Priya. I lost it. I had to get out of there."

"It was a shit show, Liv."

"What happened?" Olivia decided at that point to walk toward her apartment and not back to the office.

"Matt said that, though he liked both ideas, the 'Star Car' was more out-of-the-box and he thought it would make for a better presentation. He thought our 'Take You Places' idea was good to keep in the back pocket in case the client balked at the budget of the 'Star Car,' but he was going to go with that. He thought ours was a little safe. Anyway, since you weren't there, I brought up to Matt that they had stolen our idea, and Pablo and Thomas unequivocally denied that and said you were just jealous because their idea was better. Matt decided that since you weren't there to state your case, he was just going to go with them. He seemed annoyed that you weren't there. I told him you were having a family emergency and you needed to go home."

"Thanks for covering for me. I'll be honest with you, I'm not sure if I want to work with Matt anymore. I didn't realize I was done until I walked out, and now I'm not so eager to ever step foot back in there."

"What are you going to do?"

"Not sure, but I'll start by calling HR at Y&R to beg for my old job back. Just last week I thought that if I lost my job at The Osborne Agency, it would be a disastrous, end-of-the-world situation, but now I realize I was afraid of losing something else, something I honestly don't care about anymore."

"Well, keep me posted, Liv. What do you think will happen to me?"

"You'll be fine. I'll call Matt tomorrow and tell him that I promised you a huge severance package if you left so he better not let you go if the MTA account doesn't come through."

"Olivia, there you are!"

Olivia exited the elevator on her floor and found Mrs. Glasser sitting in a chair in the hallway, her apartment door closed.

Olivia's first thought was that Mrs. Glasser was locked out of her apartment, but then why the chair? And that noise? Why was the television on so loudly in her apartment?

"Here I am."

"I called you at your office, but they said you weren't there."

"Why didn't you call my cell phone?"

"I didn't want to bother you."

Olivia didn't understand the logic but just went with it.

"Why aren't you at work?" Mrs. Glasser asked.

"Worst long story ever. But I don't think I work there anymore."

"For crying out loud, what are you talking about?"

Olivia briefly explained what had happened with the pitch.

"Some things never change. Come in for some tea and we'll talk about it."

"Thank you, Mrs. Glasser. I would love to. But I actually am going to visit a friend, and I have to pack and get to the airport." Olivia didn't want to tell Mrs. Glasser she was going with Ben. Too soon to get the whole family involved.

"Olivia, come inside," Mrs. Glasser said firmly, standing up and opening her door. When she did, the noise stopped.

Olivia looked over Mrs. Glasser's shoulder and saw that her apartment was filled with elderly women.

Mrs. Glasser held the door open, and all of the women stared at Olivia.

"Is that her, Charlotte?" one of the women asked.

Mrs. Glasser nodded. "Olivia," she said, "here are your Miss Subways."

Olivia was shocked. She looked at the faces. All smiling. All looking at her expectantly. A half shudder/half laugh escaped her, and she felt her eyes tearing up.

Mrs. Glasser nudged Olivia and she took a step forward into the apartment. Then Mrs. Glasser started the introductions. She gave each woman's name, and the woman in turn announced her Miss Subway month and year. Many of the women even had their posters in their laps. There were thirteen of them. And they all seemed to be glowing like warm honey in an old-fashioned cut-glass honeypot.

"It's wonderful to relive our Miss Subways memories, dear. I haven't stopped smiling since Charlotte called me," one of the women sitting up front said to Olivia.

"We heard you were going to tell our story," a woman in the back said clearly.

"Is that true, Olivia?" another woman on the couch asked.

Olivia turned to Mrs. Glasser. "What have you done?" she asked, shaking her head, a delighted expression on her face.

"I brought your campaign to life. It took me longer than I thought it would to get in touch with everyone. I hope it's not too late."

Olivia embraced Mrs. Glasser and found tears dropping from her eyes. Two acts of generosity in the same day. And from two people of the same family. Olivia was stunned.

Even though, at this point, there was no professional reason to do so, Olivia spent the next two hours asking the women all the questions she had about what it was like to be a Miss Subways. Her curiosity was insatiable. Did it change the trajectories of their lives? Did it make them feel differently about themselves? Was it a memory they cherished and embraced or did they feel scorn toward it in any way? And so on.

The women were only too eager to tell her their thoughts, their stories, their memories. They all had different answers, but the themes were similar.

Miss Subways, most seemed to say, was a unique punctuation mark in an, up until then, otherwise unremarkable life as a young woman in the Bronx, Brooklyn, Manhattan.

After winning the contest, they came to think of themselves as special, some for the very first time in their lives. People treated them differently, if only for a short while, but it was a poignant discovery of self-worth. Many of the women re-called being represented incorrectly—but never unfavor-ably—in the copy on their posters, but that it was almost like playing a role. It had propelled some to modeling careers.

What the women all agreed on, looking back on it now, was how sexist the whole thing was. It was a beauty contest dreamed up by and executed by men, with men writing what they thought other men wanted to read on a poster with a photo of a pretty woman. Many resented the fact that of the two or three sentences of their description, one sentence was devoted entirely to whether or not they had a man in their life. But it seemed normal to them then, they explained. It was just the way of the times.

Many of them recalled that their employers had insisted on getting the approval of their husbands before they could continue their jobs after getting married. And many gave up their careers entirely, choosing instead to do what soci-ety expected them to do: keep a house and have a family. Not that they resented that, either, but they didn't feel as if they had much of a choice.

And one woman was quite weepy-eyed as she talked about how much opportunity young women today have.

"Ah, but don't we owe that to all of you?" Olivia asked. She had been hypnotized by what the women shared. By how honest they were. By how forthcoming they were with memo-ries that seemed so fresh.

"A lot of it, sure," Mrs. Glasser said. "But you girls have a bravery we didn't have. I know that's because times have changed and the expectations placed upon you are different, but we didn't see as many outspoken girls in our day."

"What's interesting to me," Olivia said, "is that people today talk incessantly about work-life balance and making choices and sacrifices and blah, blah, blah, as if it's something new that women have to deal with. But listening to all of you, I realize that's just about being a woman. The times may have changed, but the identity crises we all go through don't. The societal structures may have a new coat of paint, but they're still the same impenetrable walls and ceilings underneath that modern gloss. And we're still expected to do much more than any of us is capable of doing."

A silence fell over the room, and the woman sitting next to Olivia put her hand on Olivia's leg and asked, "So are you going to bring Miss Subways back to New York? Are you really going to do that for us, Olivia?"

Olivia didn't have the heart to tell them the truth, so she told them the next best thing. "Well, I'm certainly going to try."

Once Olivia finished talking with the women, she went back to her apartment and quickly packed for the trip to California. She didn't know where she was going or what she was going to do there, but, she reminded herself, she didn't really care. She would be with Ben. And she was deliciously curious to see what that would be like.

Luckily the traffic wasn't bad and Olivia made it to JFK in good time. Ben was standing against the terminal building, typing on his phone when she approached him.

"I'm here," she said.

"Let's do this," he said, smiling at her and taking her hand in his.

Olivia had been on a plane a few times, but the closest she had ever gotten to first class was when all the bathrooms had been clogged in coach and she'd gotten to use the one up front. She was excited that on this flight, she'd get to enjoy more than just the lavatory.

Ben explained that JetBlue's Mint was a little different from a normal first class, which was typically more staid. Mint was all purple uplighting and innovative gourmet food and chichi amenity kits and more channels on the television than Olivia had in her apartment. Plus, free movies and a seat that went all the way back. Olivia didn't know what to do first, and wished that the flight were longer than six hours.

Once they'd settled in and were on their second special minty lemonade, Ben began telling Olivia why he needed to go to California.

He had read the one unsealed letter first. It was from Rose Grant, the woman his grandmother had gotten upset about. In it, she had written something about having kept her promise for so long and now she wanted to connect. That she had respected Mrs. Glasser's choice to not be in touch all these years, but now that they were old ladies (her words, Ben explained), couldn't they just drop it all and get together to reminisce?

Ben couldn't think of anything more exciting than reuniting his grandmother with her old friend.

"Not to put a damper on these activities, and trust me, that's the last thing I want to do, but didn't you think your grandma seemed pretty agitated when I asked her about the woman in the picture who turned out to be Rose Grant? And in the letter she said she had kept her promise to stay away. What do you think that's all about?"

"My grandma's a reasonable woman. I'm sure she's over whatever it was that complicated their relationship. And if I'm making a huge mistake, that's a risk I'm willing to take."

"Does Rose Grant know you're coming?"

"She does. She included her number in the letter to my grandma, so I just called it and she picked up on the first ring. I told her I was Charlotte Friedman's grandson and that I had found a letter she had written my grandmother and I wondered if I could come meet her. She was silent for a moment, and then she told me to come. So I'm—so *we're*—coming."

"I hope it's okay I'll be there too. I could always wait back in the hotel while you meet her," Olivia said.

"Don't be silly," Ben said.

"I do have one request for this trip."

"What's that?"

"That we don't talk about work at all. I hope you don't think that's selfish, considering I know so little about what you do, but I just need to not think of anything having to do with work for a few days."

"That's good with me. I could use a bit of a break from work myself."

"Thank you."

Ben turned to look out the window and when he turned back around, Olivia thought his face looked harder, his features more pronounced.

"I hope it's not too aggressive to say that it seems like we might be starting to develop something here."

Olivia smiled and nodded.

"I feel like I need to warn you about my past, a weakness I have, so you can make the decision at the beginning whether you want to be involved with someone like me."

Olivia took his hand. "Go ahead," she whispered. This was clearly important to him, whatever it was, and she wanted him to feel safe and comfortable revealing his truth. Her mind began racing about all the different things he could possibly be referring to, but before she was able to settle on any one assumption, Ben started to talk.

"When my parents died, I was so young. I processed it like a child. My grandparents were so on top of it, bringing me to therapists, buying me a dog. They did everything they could to make me feel like I was loved. And it worked. I adapted to the new normal and went on with my life. I remember feeling like I had to be the perfect child so I wouldn't upset my grandparents. I know now that I was terrified of them leaving me as well. I got good grades and went to a good college; people always were so complimentary of how well I had dealt with my parents' deaths. I wrapped myself in that identity. I became the kid who was so strong. I wore it like a badge of honor.

"But soon after I graduated from college, the girl I had been dating for a couple of years, the girl I thought I was going to marry, broke up with me, and something in me snapped. All the therapy I've been through since then taught me that it was a whole abandonment issue I had never fully dealt with from my parents. But I spiraled after she broke up with me. I started drinking heavily, I lost my job, and—"

He stopped and turned abruptly to look out the window. Olivia squeezed his hand and whispered, "It's okay." She ached for how painful this seemed to be for Ben. But she knew she needed to let him get it out. On his terms.

Ben turned back, his eyes wet. He laughed with a disgusted tone, took a deep breath, and stared straight ahead. "I actually tried to kill myself one night. Jesus, this is so embarrassing. I don't know what I was thinking. I think part of me wanted it to work and part of me wanted my grandmother to find me so I could get some help. She found me puking and . . . it was a mess. She called 911 and I ended up going into rehab.

"A lot has happened since then. It shocks me sometimes when I realize how lucky I got and how lucky I am to be doing well in recovery. I'm almost eight years sober," he said, looking at her and raising his eyebrows.

"That's amazing," Olivia said quietly, smiling at him and nodding.

"Anyway, I know it's probably a little too early to dump all that on you, but I didn't want this to come out later and then have you feel like I was hiding something."

"I'm so sorry you went through all that," she said, and squeezed his hand again, placing it in her lap. "But that doesn't scare me off, Ben. It actually makes me want to be with you even more. And it's a little hilarious, to be honest."

"Hilarious?" Ben asked, pulling his hand away and giving her a strange look.

"No, no, no," Olivia said, reaching for his hand again. "Bad word choice. So not hilarious. Definitely not hilarious. What I meant to say, but botched so horribly, is that it's interesting, yes, 'interesting' is a much better word, because when I started getting to know you, you seemed like such a straightlaced, predictable guy."

"Ouch," Ben said, shaking his head and laughing.

"It's just, you were this really nice, seemingly conservative guy who played Scrabble and ate babka with his grandma. It never occurred to me that to get *there,* you had to go through all *that.*"

"Yes, luckily, I am not put into temptation mode when I'm at my grandma's. I had been feeling really badly lately, so I began spending more time with her. She knows how to get me back on track. And the bonus was that I started seeing you. So I made it a regular thing. Don't tell my grandma you had something to do with my hanging around her place more often."

"Secret's safe."

They both laughed.

"What a mess."

"Actually not at all, Ben. It means a lot to me that you would feel comfortable enough to open up to me like that. Thank you."

"I can't imagine you have any deep, dark secrets. You seem so strong and well adjusted."

"Hardly," Olivia said, suppressing an anguished laugh. She stared straight ahead at the seat-back screen and took another sip of her lemonade.

"Anything you'd care to share?" Ben asked, turning his head to look at her profile.

Olivia sighed. Her mother had called her over the weekend, unpacking a new load of baggage and expecting Olivia to drop everything and fix it all. Olivia tried to have empathy for her mother, but she found it difficult, not only because

she was entrenched in work mode, but also because she felt
like she had reached the end of that particular rope. Olivia
had dealt with the infected dynamic between her parents for
her entire life. Had witnessed and endured horrible things.
At what point could she just give herself permission to turn
away for good? That was what her mother's phone call had
stirred in her.

Olivia turned to face Ben. "It's all a mask. A hardened
shell," she said soberly, pursing her lips.

"What is?" he asked gently.

"My strong and well-adjusted demeanor."

"In what way?"

"In the way of having a truly messed-up childhood with
lots of fun trauma to pick apart for the rest of your life."

"Talk to me, Olivia."

Olivia took a deep breath, the pain and exhaustion and
frustration of it all exhaling into the intimate and heavy
space between them. She had discussed her parents with
James, but their relationship was admittedly superficial, filled
with sarcastic banter and patterns carried over from college.
So she had never truly gotten to the heart of it with him.
And Jenna had been gone for so long, had missed so much
of what had happened recently. Olivia realized that she'd
only dealt with her pain through extensive online research
and imagined conversations she had with her father while
she was in the shower. Furious and vehement speeches filled
with shameful accusations and sheer contempt, all the hatred pouring out to combine with the torrent of water she
made hotter and hotter until she couldn't stand the temper-
ature or the vitriol any longer.

She turned to Ben and told him everything. The words
and stories and memories and pain spilling out of her as if

they had been desperately searching for a home forever. He held her hand and let her speak. Let her tell him how she felt and how she just couldn't do it anymore. How she couldn't enable her father, how she couldn't rescue her mother, how she couldn't keep putting herself last in a trio of dysfunction. How she realized that the only way to heal was to extricate herself entirely from the one relationship that was supposed to be the most pure and protective. But it wasn't.

And when she had relieved herself of the burden, she put her head on Ben's shoulder and he wrapped his arms around her.

"Thank you for sharing that with me. I'm so sorry you've had to deal with all of this. Now I know why you're so strong."

"It's a mask, remember?" Olivia said. She felt drained.

"It's everything but, Olivia."

Ben asked her questions, kind yet pointed, and got to the heart of the issue for Olivia. She realized after they'd been discussing her family for a while that being able to share herself with someone might have been what she needed all along to absolve her of her guilt, her shame, and her uncertainty about whether she was making the right decisions.

And when they were done, Ben turned his body toward her and lifted her chin with his finger. He kissed her, and it was the most loving kiss Olivia could ever remember receiving. The difference, she realized at that moment, between Ben's kiss and all the kisses she had ever had with Matt, was overwhelming.

The next morning, after a great night's sleep in their separate rooms at Shutters in Santa Monica, they headed to

Rose's house in Beverly Hills in their swanky rental convertible. Turned out Ben had points at Hertz as well.

Olivia felt like she was getting whiplash. She didn't know where to look first. Ben drove east on Pico toward Beverly Hills. He was going to take surface streets the whole way, but when Olivia saw signs for the 405, she said she'd always wanted to say she'd been on the 405 (it wasn't Paris, but it would have to do), so Ben got on the 405 north and took it a few exits to Wilshire. When they got closer to Beverly Hills, and the palm trees seemed denser, Olivia's eyes grew wider. She saw the Beverly Wilshire Hotel on her right (*Pretty Woman*!), and then they turned left onto Rodeo Drive. Olivia knew Ben was a good guy because he didn't make fun of her pure delight in seeing Los Angeles. In fact, he was a decidedly generous tour guide.

Ben wound through the side streets until they stopped at a smallish Spanish-style house with beautiful, lush landscaping.

"This is it," Ben said.

They pulled up to the intercom at the gate and Ben pushed the button.

When a young woman's voice answered, Ben said, "I'm here to see Rose Grant. It's Ben Glasser."

They heard a beep, and the gate slid open. Ben and Olivia looked at each other, and then Ben drove in and parked in the middle of the driveway, just outside the front door.

They got out of the car and walked up to the door. Ben rang the bell and they heard footsteps.

"Hello," a young Hispanic woman said to them. She was smiling and holding back a small yapping dog.

"Hi," Ben said. "We're here to see Rose Grant."

"Yes, Señora Grant said she was expecting you. She is in

the backyard, playing tennis. Por favor," she said, and turned, leading them across the foyer.

Tennis? Ben mouthed to Olivia, and nodded, impressed.

They walked through the living room. When they passed the fireplace, Olivia punched Ben on the arm and pointed to the mantel. To the three Oscars displayed there. She opened her eyes wide.

"You can go there," the woman said, pointing out the French doors to the tennis court.

Rose was on the far side of the court, moving slowly but purposefully, hitting ball after ball consistently back to the young man in tennis whites feeding them to her from the near side of the court.

He noticed Ben and Olivia and shouted to Rose, "Rose, you have visitors!"

"Who is it now?" Ben and Olivia heard Rose say. The sun was in her eyes, so it would have been difficult for her to see them.

"You can tell her it's Ben Glasser, Charlotte Friedman's grandson," Ben said.

The tennis pro repeated that to Rose. She stopped, dropped her racket, and walked across the court.

When she got to where they were standing, she looked at Ben and then grabbed him in a huge embrace.

They were both laughing, and eventually she pulled away.

"Let me look at you," she said. "My God, you're gorgeous. Is this your wife?"

"No, just a friend, Ms. Grant. This is Olivia," Ben said.

"Call me Rose, please," she said to Ben, and then she looked at Olivia and held her hands. "Olivia. You're lovely. It's wonderful to meet you." Then she gave Olivia a hug.

"Come. Come inside. Flor has made us some snacks and

iced tea. I wasn't sure what time to expect you, but I've had enough tennis for today, so this is perfect."

She linked arms with Ben and Olivia, one on each side of her, and they walked to the house.

"Actually, it's beautiful out. Let's sit outside." Rose poked her head into the house, and Ben and Olivia heard her say, "Flor, we'll take the refreshments outside, please."

They all sat down at a round table, and Olivia was able to get a good look at Rose. She had only seen that one photo of Rose from Mrs. Glasser's scrapbook, but Olivia could see the resemblance to Elizabeth Taylor. Her hair was gray but full, and she had a youthful energy to her. Her cheeks were flushed from the tennis, and she hadn't stopped smiling since they had met. She was gorgeous.

"So you knew my grandma?" Ben asked.

"Yes. Such a long time ago. But I want to hear about you, Ben. You too, Olivia. Tell me all about yourselves."

Flor brought out the snacks and iced tea, and Ben told Rose all about his life. When he mentioned that his parents had died when he was young, Rose grew noticeably upset.

"I'm so sorry to hear that. That must have been terrible for you and your grandparents."

"It was. Did you know my parents?"

"No," Rose said. "I never knew them."

When Ben and Olivia had told Rose all about themselves, Ben made his proposal. "Would you consider coming back to New York with us to see my grandmother?"

"Oh my. Does Charlotte know you're inviting me?"

"No. I know from the letter of yours I read that you two had some complications, but so much time has passed. I thought I'd surprise her."

"That would be quite a surprise."

"So what do you say? I took the liberty of reserving a plane ticket in your name that leaves tomorrow morning. I would just need to call to confirm it and add your birth date. It would be our honor to escort you to New York. I've even booked a hotel for you near my grandmother's apartment. Please come."

Rose was silent and looked from Ben to Olivia.

"What the hell?" Rose said. "You only live once." Then she stood up, poked her head into the house, and shouted, "Flor, pack my suitcase. I'm going to New York!"

CHAPTER 21

CHARLOTTE
SATURDAY, JULY 2, 1949

"Charlotte!"

Charlotte was in her room and heard her father calling for her. She was about to answer when she heard his shouting escalate.

"Charlotte! Come down here right this minute!"

Charlotte ran down the stairs. Her father was screaming so loudly, she thought he was having a heart attack. Or being murdered.

"Teddy! Are you all right?" Mrs. Friedman ran into the hall, where the entire family had now convened.

Mr. Friedman was neither having a heart attack nor being murdered. But he was hanging up the telephone.

"Charlotte, I've just received quite a surprising phone call from Irv Mann. Is it the truth?" he asked sternly.

"What did he tell you?" Charlotte's panicked mind immediately went to Rose and the baby, though she couldn't imagine how her father's friend Irv from down the block would know that Rose had asked Charlotte to adopt her baby.

"Calm down, Teddy," Charlotte's mother said. "You're going to get your blood pressure too high. Come, let's go into the kitchen and I'll make some tea. Dinner's almost ready."

"I will stay right here, Sarah," he said firmly to his wife. "Now, Charlotte, what is this I hear about you being Miss Subways?"

"What?" Charlotte's mother asked, a shocked look on her face.

"Irv tells me that he was on the subway today and he looked up and there was Charlotte on posters all throughout the car."

"Is it true, Charlotte?" her mother asked.

"Yes, but—"

"But what?" her father asked impatiently.

"But I was going to tell you and I'm so sorry that I didn't, but I knew you'd be angry and—" Charlotte stopped and looked from her mother to her father. "Anyway, I did it for you and the store. But it all got messed up," Charlotte said, enraged.

She caught her mother giving her father an angry look and nudging her chin toward Charlotte. Her father stayed silent.

Charlotte took a deep breath and continued, "I just thought if I could use Miss Subways to bring attention to the store, I'd be able to fix everything for you."

"And for yourself."

"Yes."

"You're a disgrace," Mr. Friedman said under his breath, and walked out the front door.

Charlotte felt the words like a slap across the face. It was moments like these when she missed her brother most.

"Oh, Charlotte. I'm sorry, honey. That was dreadful of him." Mrs. Friedman gathered Charlotte up and hugged her.

"He's awful," Charlotte said, sobbing.

"Come, let's have some tea."

Charlotte followed her mother into the kitchen and collected herself. "I know I shouldn't have disobeyed you and Papa to do Miss Subways, but I'm twenty-one years old! I'm not a child anymore, and I shouldn't have to do whatever my mommy and daddy tell me to do!"

"You're right. That's why I called."

"Called? What do you mean?"

"I listened to your father call that Miss Fontaine from the Miss Subways and tell her he forbade you to be considered. I thought that was horrible, so as soon as he left for the store that day, I called her back. I told her to please ignore my husband's call, that he had changed his mind, that he was embarrassed to call back personally, and to allow you to continue with the competition."

"You did that?" Charlotte was stunned.

"I think she must think your parents are lunatics." Mrs. Friedman laughed. "But yes, I did that."

"Thank you."

"You're welcome."

"But why didn't you tell me so I could go back there? As far as you knew, I wasn't going to disobey Papa's decision."

"I knew you'd go. At least I hoped it. And when you came back that day saying JoJo had given you a makeover, I knew for sure you had. But why did *you* think they would let you participate? Were you planning on going in there to plead your case?"

"You sure you want to hear this?" Charlotte asked, smiling and covering her face with her hands.

Mrs. Friedman smiled tentatively and nodded.

"I had JoJo call Miss Fontaine, pretend she was you, and rattle off a similar script to the one you used."

"But that would mean Miss Fontaine received two calls from your mother that day."

"That's right," Charlotte said, confused. "I'll have to ask JoJo about that."

"Well, I'm glad it all worked out. And congratulations on winning. That's marvelous."

"None of it matters, though. I'm still where I was when I started. My plan failed. I had wanted them to mention the store on my poster, but instead they said I like going to art museums with my parents."

Mrs. Friedman laughed.

"Ma, it's not funny!" Charlotte protested, and managed a giggle herself before turning serious again. "And even if I wanted to stand up to Papa and tell him I wouldn't be working in his store, it's not like I have any other job prospects. There isn't a job in advertising to be had out there."

"Oh dear. I can't believe I forgot!"

"What?"

"Two letters came for you today."

Charlotte and her mother walked to the hall table together. Charlotte picked up the letters and was surprised by both return addresses. She was about to rip open the more unexpected one when she heard a knock on the door.

Sam.

"Hello, Mrs. Friedman. Charlotte, I need to talk to you," he said, looking distraught. He glanced from Charlotte to her mother.

"Whatever you have to say to me, you can say in front of my mother."

"I'm not so sure that's a good idea," Sam said, an indecipherable expression on his face.

"That's fine. You kids talk," Mrs. Friedman said kindly, turning to walk away.

"No, Ma. You can stay right here. Sam, what do you have to say?"

Sam looked at Charlotte, clearly making a decision that there was no time to waste, and then said urgently, "Charlotte, it's Rose. She's had an accident. She called me from the hospital. Will you please go with me? The baby—"

"You want me to go with you, Sam? Well, I'll be—" Charlotte was shaking her head in disbelief.

"Who's Rose? What baby?" Mrs. Friedman asked.

"Please, Charlotte. I completely understand why you think this is outrageous and that I have no right to ask you, but I'm begging you. Please come with me. I need you."

"Charlotte, go with him," her mother said angrily.

"Ma, you don't understand!" Charlotte said, turning to her mother.

"What's there to understand? Sam clearly needs you, so you go."

"Fine," Charlotte said, stomping her foot. "I'll come with you, Sam, but I don't like this one bit."

"There's no time, Charlotte. We'll talk about it once we're there." Sam grabbed Charlotte's hand, said good night to Mrs. Friedman, and then headed with Charlotte to the hospital.

Rose was sleeping when Charlotte and Sam arrived at her room. The doctor was standing at the door, writing on her chart.

"How is she?" Sam asked.

"Are you a family member?" the doctor asked.

"No. Yes. Well, kind of," Sam sputtered. He looked at Charlotte and took a deep breath. "I'm the father of the baby."

"Oh, so you're the husband?" the doctor asked.

"No."

"I see," the doctor said, looking hard at Sam. And then looking at Charlotte.

"Are you a family member, dear?" the doctor asked Charlotte.

"No, I'm—"

"She's my girlfriend."

"Well, this is highly unusual. But since you're the father of the baby, I can let you know that everything is going to be fine."

"Thank goodness," Sam said, relieved. "What happened?"

"She told us she fell down the stairs. She has a number of lacerations, but she'll be okay."

"And the baby?" Charlotte was surprised to hear the question come out of her mouth.

"The baby will be just fine also. I've done an examination and everything looks stable. Nothing to worry about. Miss Grant needs to rest, but she'll be like new before you know it."

"Thank you, Doctor," Sam said.

Sam and Charlotte sat on the little couch in Rose's room.

Sam turned to Charlotte and tentatively took her hands in his. She didn't pull them away. "Thank you for coming with me, Charlotte. I'm sorry I had to ask. But thank you."

"You're welcome," Charlotte said, her voice devoid of emotion.

They sat there for quite some time, neither of them talking, both of them absorbing the situation. Not sure what they were supposed to do or say next.

Rose stirred and opened her eyes. She looked over and saw Charlotte and Sam.

"Hi," she said softly, her voice raspy.

"Hi," Sam said, standing.

Charlotte felt like an intruder.

"Thank you both for coming," Rose said.

"What happened?" Sam asked.

"It was my mother. She said she was disgusted by the sight of me and pushed me down the stairs in our building," Rose said. Her eyes were hard. "My little brother saw what happened and called an ambulance. I heard my mother tell the ambulance man that I had gotten dizzy and fallen."

"Oh, Rose. That's awful. I'm so sorry," Sam said softly. Kindly. "How are you feeling now?"

"I feel really tired. And sad. They gave me painkillers that they said would make me sleep. But the baby's okay."

Sam smiled at her and squeezed her hand. Charlotte was unconvinced that Rose was entirely happy about the baby being okay. And she was disgusted by the intimacy she was being subjected to, so she stood to walk out of the room, muttering under her breath that she was going to get some coffee. Her actual plan was to get the heck out of there, but she wasn't interested in starting a conversation about it.

"Sam, do you mind getting the coffee? I'd like to talk to Charlotte alone," Rose said.

"Sure, sure," Sam said. And then, turning to Charlotte, he said in a whisper, "Is that okay with you, Charlotte?"

She rolled her eyes but nodded in a resigned manner.

Sam looked searchingly at Charlotte and walked out of the room.

"I can't imagine what's going through your mind right now," Rose said sadly.

"It's mostly not good, to tell you the truth," Charlotte said snidely, sitting on the sofa and crossing her legs.

"I realize that you're in an unimaginable position, Charlotte. If you choose to go back with Sam, then you're also choosing to be in this baby's life, since Sam has agreed to raise it. But if you decide that raising this baby would be impossible, then you have to give up Sam."

"What an insightful analysis, Rose," Charlotte said cynically.

"It's nuts that we've ended up here," Rose said. "When I met you, I was so enthralled by you, and now look what I've done to you."

"You were enthralled by me?" Charlotte asked, shocked. "Why?"

"You're everything I've always wanted to be. You're so intelligent and ladylike and kind and polite. You have this marvelous boyfriend who loves you like crazy. You know exactly what you want to do with your life. And it's pretty obvious, now that I've gotten to know you a little, that you're going to accomplish all that and more."

Charlotte was stunned. "When I met you, I thought *you* were everything I wanted to be. You were so glamorous and outspoken and confident and brave. Those are things I've never been."

"You don't want to be anything like me, Charlotte. All of those things are just a mask I put on because I'm so scared," Rose said, starting to cry. "My whole life, I've been so scared. First of my father, who was so violent to my mother and me. Then she started drinking and I was always afraid of her. Afraid of making her upset. Afraid of her blaming me for my father's violence. I was always walking on egg-shells. That's why I had to put on that bold identity. It protected me. Or else I would have been completely broken."

"I had no idea about your father," Charlotte said softly. The last thing she wanted was to be sympathetic to Rose, but how couldn't she be?

"I know I did the worst possible thing I could have done to you, Charlotte. And to think all I really wanted was to be your friend." Rose shook her head. "I made a mess of everything. I always have. And now look at me." She waved her hands over her midsection. "The best thing for this baby would be for it to not have me anywhere close." Rose laughed sadly.

"I haven't made a decision yet about Sam or the baby," Charlotte said, beginning, against her better judgment, to feel a tinge sorry for Rose. She couldn't imagine what her childhood had been like. Would Charlotte be just another person to reject Rose?

"I know you're someone who's played by the rules all her life. And I don't mean that as a bad thing. You're smart and reasonable. But, and forgive me if I'm overstepping, it seems to me that part of your struggle with this decision is that if you say yes to Sam and the baby, you'll convince yourself that you didn't do what was right for *you*. That you will have done what's right for Sam. And me." Rose winced. "But that's not what this would be, Charlotte. Taking this risk, on Sam, on being a mother right now, to someone else's baby, would be showing yourself what a brave modern woman you are."

Charlotte was quiet. She looked at Rose and then out the window. She was annoyed that Rose, who had so terribly disrupted her life, was acting so familiar.

"No offense, Rose, but I see what you're doing."

"What do you mean?" Rose looked confused.

"I know you've had a bad life, and I'm sorry about that. And I'm sorry that your mother has been so horrible to you, but this, this"—Charlotte waved her arms around Rose and the hospital room—"this is all just part of the same routine. You're saying what you think I want to hear so that you can ease your mind of the guilt, so that you can give your baby to people who you know would do a tremendous job of raising it, so that you can run away to Hollywood and escape your responsibilities." Charlotte was pacing now, her voice rising.

"No, Charlotte. That's not it at all," Rose said, trying to sit up in her bed, but the pain got the better of her.

"Why should I believe you?" Charlotte said, getting up close to Rose's face.

"Girls, girls, what's going on?" Sam asked, alarmed, re-entering the room with coffee cups.

"Absolutely nothing," Charlotte said disgustedly. "I'm going home."

Charlotte walked out, fully expecting Sam to stay to console the mother of his baby.

"Charlotte, wait!" Sam yelled after her.

"No, Sam." Charlotte turned.

A nurse shushed them.

Charlotte lowered her voice, saying, "You made your choice back in March. Now you have to live with the consequences."

She walked quickly down the corridor. Sam caught up with her and they took the elevator down in silence.

"Stop following me!" Charlotte cried to Sam as he walked next to her down the street back toward her house.

"No. I'm never going to stop following you, Charlotte," Sam said, stopping and holding her gently by the shoulders.

Charlotte stopped and turned to him. "She's awful."

"I know she's awful. This whole thing is awful. But this is where we are."

"So you think I'm just supposed to capitulate and enter enemy territory, willing to do your and Rose's bidding?"

"I only want you to do this if it's what you want."

"How would I not think of Rose every single time I look at that baby? How could I possibly raise that baby as my own?"

"It would be a one-day-at-a-time deal. And each day, I imagine your hatred for Rose would disappear a little and the love for the baby would replace it until you loved that baby so much, you wouldn't even identify him or her with Rose."

"Do you honestly think that's even possible, Sam?" Charlotte asked skeptically.

"I think I do."

They started to walk again, slowly and silently down the street.

"Let me ask you this, Charlotte. If there were no baby, would you consider getting back together with me?"

Charlotte didn't hesitate. "Yes." She was a bit surprised by her answer, but it had been something she had been thinking about ever since she had spoken to JoJo. She knew Sam. She loved Sam. She was sick about what had happened but thought that she could get over it. She gave herself a million excuses to justify what he had done: They weren't married yet. Sam was a man and men had other needs. He had been drinking. He had never in the past done anything to jeopardize their relationship. Charlotte hated that she was sticking up for him, when deep down she didn't think any of those excuses were valid enough for hurting her as much as he had, but she also didn't want to let Rose be the critical factor defining her relationship. She didn't want to give Rose—sad, pathetic Rose—that power.

Sam turned to her. "Charlotte, I'm so happy to hear you say that," he said, his voice cracking. "Losing you, losing us, can't be an option. I don't know what I'd do without you in my life. You're the most incredible person I've ever met. You're so different from other girls, Charlotte. You're so ambitious, and I love that about you."

"What would it all look like, Sam? Play this out for me."

"I've thought about this a lot. If you decide to raise this baby with me, we'll get engaged as soon as possible. The right way. We'll tell our parents and figure out who's going to watch the baby while we're at work. I would never expect you to not pursue your career, and I need to know that you know that."

"I know that," Charlotte said, allowing a small part of her to play along with the scenario Sam was laying out.

"You wouldn't have to have anything to do with Rose during her pregnancy or the delivery. I would never leave that to you. There's a lawyer in my office who handles adoptions. I've already spoken to him and he said it would be watertight. You and I would be the parents, and we could design it so that Rose would have as much or as little—"

"Or as nothing."

"Or as nothing to do with the baby as we want. I've discussed that with her, and she is fully prepared to have nothing to do with the baby. She feels that the baby is better off without her being involved. When the baby is born, he or she would immediately be ours. We would have a separate room in the hospital from Rose, and we would take care of the baby there until he or she is ready to go home. Then Rose would go on her way and we would go on ours. To our new apartment with a perfect nursery to raise our child. I will never think of Rose as the baby's mother, Charlotte. You will be the mother. It will always be our baby."

Charlotte was silent, absorbing all of this information.

"I know this isn't ideal," Sam continued. "But I want to marry you and I want to have a family with you, and if this is the way it's meant to be for us, then let's just go for it. I can only imagine how difficult this is for you, Charlotte. But please trust me. Trust that I'm the same man you've always loved. You know I will be there for you. And I will never, for the rest of our lives, ever do anything to hurt you."

They had arrived at Charlotte's house. Charlotte realized she was exhausted.

"Can I come in for a Coke?" Sam asked gently.

"I don't think that's a good idea, Sam," Charlotte said. "I'm just so tired of thinking and talking about all of this. Give me tonight. Let me sleep on it, and I'll tell you my decision tomorrow."

Charlotte was glad it was dark in her house when she got home. She didn't know if her father was still out and she didn't care. Then she remembered the letters. She had been so caught up in Sam arriving at her house and whisking her off to the hospital and all its attendant drama, she had stuffed the letters into her purse and completely forgotten them.

Ripping open the envelopes, one after the other, Charlotte read each letter carefully. And then she read the first one again just to be sure.

CHAPTER 22

OLIVIA
WEDNESDAY, MARCH 14, 2018

When Olivia woke up, her bed was empty, but there was a note on the pillow next to hers from Ben. *Good morning, beautiful . . .* , it began. And then Ben had written that he had to make a few work calls from his room and reminded her what time they needed to meet in the lobby to leave for their flight.

It was still early and Olivia felt energized, so she went for a run on the beach. She picked up an egg burrito and a latte on the way back and thought that she could get used to this LA lifestyle. She was supposed to meet Ben in the lobby in an hour, so she got ready and packed up.

After they had left Rose the afternoon before, Olivia and Ben had returned to their own rooms in the hotel to rest and get ready for dinner. After dinner—a romantic and delicious affair at 1 Pico, the hotel restaurant—there was an awkward moment when they got off the elevator. Ben's room was to the right and Olivia's to the left, but true to his way, he walked Olivia to her hotel room door. They kissed at her door, and decided to take it inside when a room service cart almost ran them down. They shared a fun night complete with laughter, the Travel Channel, kissing, and other lovely bits until they both fell asleep in Olivia's bed.

Olivia had left her phone turned off since she'd arrived in LA. She'd been avoiding it, but, realizing she needed to face reality, she turned on her phone just before she headed down to the lobby. Immediately, the notifications started loading on her screen, alerting her to several urgent texts and voicemails from both Matt and Priya. And an email from Jenna.

Olivia opened that one first, and her stomach dropped when she read that Jenna and Chris had gotten engaged and would be moving in together. That Jenna felt just awful, her words, for leaving Olivia in a bind, but that they were going to need the apartment back at the end of April.

"Damn it," Olivia said. That gave her less than six weeks to find a new place and move out. Without a job or any savings to her name, she couldn't even imagine how she could make that happen.

Just then her phone rang. It was Priya, so Olivia picked up.

"Olivia. Finally. You can't just drop off the face of the earth like that," Priya said.

"Why not? It feels really good," Olivia said.

"Seriously, Liv, listen. Something's happened. Where are you?" Priya asked in a serious tone.

"In LA. Why? What's up?" Olivia knew Priya wasn't one to be dramatic, so she was concerned.

"LA? Jesus. Why are you in LA?"

"Long story, but I'll be back tonight. What's going on?"

"You're not going to believe this. Sit down."

"Okay, sitting."

"Well, we all went home Monday night assuming you were gone and Thomas was going to present the 'Star Car' idea on Friday to the client. But when I got to work yesterday morning, Matt asked me to come into his office. Unusual. He said he had just gotten off the phone with Thomas, who was crying—"

"Crying? Why?"

"His wife left him. She found sexts on his phone and accused him of having an affair."

"Bastard."

"The reason he told Matt this was because he said he needed to go away to clear his mind, and he wanted Matt to hold his job and keep paying him while he was away. Like a medical leave thing. And then he admitted that he was having an affair with Pablo—"

"Our Pablo? No way!"

"Yes, and he admitted to stealing your idea and he was sorry. It's like God found Thomas or Thomas found God yesterday and he was absolving all his sins. Matt had called Pablo in, before he called me in, and Pablo admitted it was all true and offered his resignation. On top of all this, your neighbor—"

"Mrs. Glasser?"

"Yep, Mrs. Glasser stormed in here yesterday on a rampage, demanding to speak to the young man in charge. Matt and Mrs. Glasser were behind closed doors for over an hour, and when they came out, they hugged like they had served in the same platoon. Apparently, Mrs. Glasser told Matt about your idea to pitch Miss Subways to the MTA and that she had located thirteen former Miss Subways winners. Matt was absolutely floored by the concept. Remember, Liv, we never presented Miss Subways to him. He loves it, and he wants you to present it to the client on Friday."

"That's in two days, Priya!"

"I know. It's almost the middle of the day here. So I've already done a lot of the prep work. I wanted to see if you were on board before I emailed it to you. So, say you're on board."

"I don't know."

"Of course you know, Liv. This is your agency. You helped build it as much as Matt did. And Thomas is gone. It's your moment to shine. To go into that MTA pitch and knock their subway socks off."

"I really thought I was done with that place, but you're stirring my creative juices with that enticing spoon of yours. Mrs. Glasser did that?"

"Yes. Do this for her, Liv."

Olivia hung up and called Matt.

"I'm an asshole, Liv, and I'm sorry. I knew there was some aspect of truth in what you were saying about Thomas and Pablo stealing your idea, but I didn't want to believe those guys could do something like that. I threw you under the bus, and I'm sorry."

"Why did you do that?"

"Mostly because I was being hyperconscious of not showing you any special attention. Please come back. I love this Miss Subways concept. Mrs. Glasser, who is amazing, by the way, and so smart, pitched the whole concept to me. She's even coming in today to work with Priya on the idea. I figured if you didn't come back, we would still present it to the MTA on Friday. But it's your pitch, Liv. Please do it. It's a winning concept and you deserve the glory."

"I don't want to work for you anymore, Matt," Olivia said sadly. "If I'm being totally honest with myself, I still have feelings for you, even though I have every reason not to. It's just all too complicated, and I think I'm better off keeping my distance from you personally and professionally."

"Oh, Liv. Don't you realize I have feelings for you too? But the reason I don't act on them, well, at least in a mature way, is because I don't want you to be stuck with me. Please don't have feelings for me, Liv. I don't deserve them."

Olivia took a breath and tried to digest what Matt was saying. And it made sense. Not that it was possible to just fall out of love with someone, but the past few days had shown her that there were better guys than Matt out there.

"Fine, I'll do the pitch," Olivia said, not entirely convinced that she wanted to, but something was pulling her toward it. Perhaps her dire need for a salary. And she felt she owed it to Mrs. Glasser.

"Thank you, Liv! Thank you. You're going to be sensational. And if you win this for us, I'm going to give you a big raise and a bonus when we sign. Deal?"

"Priya *and* me."

"Deal."

Rose wasn't at the ticketing counter when Olivia and Ben arrived at LAX. They waited fifteen minutes, and then Ben started to get concerned that she'd changed her mind. He called her house, and Flor said she had left forty-five minutes ago. Ben was just looking up the number for the car service when they saw Rose, decked out, approaching them.

"You're here," Ben said, giving her a kiss.

"Where else would I be?" Rose asked.

Ben took her suitcase, and they got in the bag-check line.

While they waited for the flight, Rose told them about her childhood in Brooklyn and how she was excited to go to New York because one of her sisters lived in Manhattan and she'd get to see her.

Rose said she moved to Hollywood when she was twenty-one and had a screen test with Paramount; they signed her to a contract on the spot. She said she made a number of pictures, some had even had critical success, but she never found stardom.

Olivia asked her about the Oscars.

"Those were my husband's, dear. He was a famous director. We lived quite a glamorous life in Hollywood. So many wonderful memories."

Rose told them story after story about the famous actors and actresses who were their friends, the parties they went to, the exotic places they traveled to.

"Did you have children?" Olivia asked.

"I never wanted to be a mother," Rose said wistfully. "I thought that because I *had* a terrible mother, I would *be* a terrible mother."

"That's how I feel," Olivia said.

"Don't make the same decision I made. I actually think the opposite can be true, meaning that if you had a terrible mother, you are that much more conscious of being a wonderful mother yourself."

"Do you regret it?" Olivia asked.

"I don't regret making the decision to not be a mother when it was my decision to make. I think it was the right decision for me. But I regret now that I don't have children.

Most of my friends have died, and I'm very lonely. I keep myself busy, but I think it would be nice. I know for sure that I would have liked to have had a relationship with grandchildren."

It was late when they arrived back in New York. Ben and Olivia helped Rose check in to her hotel, and then Ben dropped Olivia back at her apartment.

"I'll call you tomorrow morning once I've gotten Rose and my grandma settled," Ben said.

"I'm so disappointed I won't be there to see it in person, but we only have one day before the pitch."

"Completely understand. I'm just so excited for my grandma to see that I've brought Rose Grant for a visit. I can't wait to see the look on her face."

CHAPTER 23

CHARLOTTE
WEDNESDAY, JULY 6, 1949

Prompted by Saturday's two unexpected letters and her conversation with Sam, the subsequent days became a time of reckoning for Charlotte. Time to contemplate her future. To lay all the moving parts onto a table, analyze them, and make decisions on their behalf.

The letter from J. Walter Thompson had been entirely unexpected. A spot in the typing pool had opened up and would Charlotte be available to fill it beginning on Monday, July 18? Mr. Hertford wrote that Charlotte's tenacity a few months back had impressed him, and she was the first girl who had come to mind.

Charlotte was stunned. She would have the opportunity to work in advertising after all! And even if Professor Oldham was right and she came as close to a real-life advertisement as a teenage boy to a pinup girl, it didn't matter. She was on her way to being a career woman, to supporting herself, to actualizing her dreams. As soon as nine o'clock rolled around on Monday morning, and without thinking too hard about it, Charlotte telephoned Mr. Hertford and accepted with gratitude and enthusiasm his very kind offer.

The only problem was convincing her father. She had been working at the store full-time the last couple of weeks since her graduation, and she knew her father relied on her. He had to be out of the store quite a bit, and there were long stretches when she was the only one there. The store was still struggling financially, so Charlotte was left with the awful realization that if she started the JWT job on the eighteenth, less than two weeks away, she'd be abandoning her father and leaving him in a precarious position.

She wondered if doing the right thing meant putting her father's needs before her own or the other way around. She finally decided, after a few days of strenuous thinking, that though it seemed ridiculous, considering her father had been so awful to her, she couldn't put the store in jeopardy. Doing so would hurt them all, and she wouldn't be able to live with herself if she were the reason he had to shut down.

But Charlotte had dreaded having to phone Mr. Hertford at J. Walter Thompson again, so she'd been putting the atrocious act off. She could only imagine the god-awful impression he'd have of her, and she knew she could kiss any hope of future employment good-bye after that particular call.

With all that on her mind, Charlotte called Sam and told him that she needed more time to think. He was upset and frustrated, as Charlotte knew he would be, but she didn't care one bit. She was starting to get tired of putting others' needs first. And it felt good not to.

It was the second letter she received on Saturday, though, that allowed Charlotte to take her mind off everything that worried her. At least for a while. And that turned out to be all she needed.

Charlotte had read all about past Miss Subways outings in the papers, so she was over the moon to receive the letter from Miss Fontaine inviting her to participate in one the coming Wednesday. *Collier's* wanted to do a fluff piece on Miss Subways and photograph the girls at Jones Beach on Long Island. A lovely fuss.

Charlotte couldn't think of anything more exciting and even bought a new swimsuit for the occasion: a darling, all-white getup with a halter neckline and a matching white ribbon at the waist that she formed into a peppy bow. She told her father it was JoJo's birthday, so she couldn't work that day. Surprisingly, and more due to his lack of out-of-store appointments than an act of kindness toward Charlotte, he let her go.

When Charlotte arrived at the beach that day, she was surprised to find she was the last one there. The girls had all gathered off to one side and were sitting in chairs, having their hair and makeup tended to. Miss Fontaine spotted Charlotte, led her over to the other girls, and made introductions.

"You're even prettier in real life, honey, if that's even possible," Dorothea Mate, Miss Subways June 1942, said, shaking her hand.

"It's nice to meet you. I feel like I already know you, since I stared at your face on the subway the whole way here," said Enid Berkowitz, Miss Subways July 1946, laughing.

One by one, each of the women introduced herself to Charlotte. There was Ruth Lippman, January 1945, and the Clawson triplets of May 1944, each one prettier than the next. Charlotte was most excited to meet Marie Theresa Thomas, March 1946. She had become a Powers Girl and had been on television and in a Coca-Cola ad. But she was as sweet as a kitten and Charlotte was charmed.

Charlotte felt like she was staring at celebrities. Considering she was such a fan of Walter Winchell's columns about Miss Subways in the *Daily Mirror,* she felt like she personally knew some of these women. They seemed so comfortable with each other, which brought on a wave of shyness in Charlotte, but then she remembered they were pros at all of this. It was she who was the neophyte.

There were eight of them altogether, and they gathered in folding chairs to be primped while the photographer set up. Charlotte could barely contain her excitement as her hair and makeup were finished. She felt beautiful, even though there were no mirrors. There was something to be said about an inner glow.

The photographer's assistant called them over and had the girls jump rope, make pyramids, do a tug-of-war, and otherwise frolic around. They certainly were a boisterous and lively group! Charlotte was having the time of her life. The other girls couldn't have been nicer, and they included her as if they'd known her as long as they'd known each other. The photographer snapped away, and Charlotte barely noticed him because she was so engaged.

Charlotte admired how confident the other girls seemed. She wondered if she appeared that way to them too.

"I'll have to get your telephone number from Miss Fontaine," Dorothea said to Charlotte as they stood next to each other, having a drink of water after the egg-rolling race. "We have a Miss Subways club, and I'd love for you to be part of it."

"I'd love that," Charlotte said. "Thank you."

"Don't think twice. We usually meet in Manhattan. Where do you live?"

"I'm in Brooklyn now with my parents, but I'm moving to Manhattan soon."

"That's right. Your poster said you have a special guy. Are you two getting married?"

"Not exactly," Charlotte said, looking away.

"Oh, I'm sorry, honey. I didn't mean to pry."

"That's okay. We just had a bit of a falling-out." And then, before she knew what she was saying, she blurted out, "He knocked up another girl, and now he's adopting the baby and wants me to be the mother."

"Well, I'll be," Dorothea said. "That's one for the ages."

"Tell me about it. My goodness, I barely know you. I can't believe I just told you that."

The other girls were milling about, drinking water. The photographer had to change his film so he had given the girls a break.

"That's okay. Your secret's safe with me. So what are you going to do? Do you love him?"

"I did. And then I didn't. But to be perfectly honest, I can't stop thinking about him, the him I used to think he was. So I guess I still do love him."

"Then do it. I'm married, and it's the best thing. Men you can fall in love with don't come around very often, honey, regardless of how many proposals from strangers you'll get as Miss Subways. If you've found a good man and he loves you, forgive his faults and move on. I know a girl whose husband strayed once before they were married. It bothered her for a bit, but I will tell you the honest truth: she's completely gotten over it. It's like they have to get that out of their systems before they get married. Maybe it's the ones who don't stray before they're married who you have to worry about."

Charlotte had never thought about it like that before.

"And adopting a baby is one of the noblest things you can do," she said. "It sounds like that baby was meant to be yours. I don't know you very well, but you sound like a reasonable girl. If you think there's a shred of possibility that this could turn out okay, I say go for it. Sounds like that fellow, despite what he did, has a good head on his shoulders if he's offering to adopt that baby and raise it himself."

The photographer called the girls back and asked them to hold hands and run toward the water. Which they did about fifty-seven times until he got his shot. But it gave Charlotte a chance to think.

When they were breaking up, Miss Fontaine pulled her aside. "Charlotte, dear, you did great! I knew it would be a good idea to include you in this. And now that I know what a good fit you are with the other girls and how easygoing you are with photographers, I'll be sure to invite you to other press events."

At that very moment, Charlotte realized exactly what she needed to do in order to ensure she was in front of that typewriter on the eighteenth. And after conferring for a few more moments with Miss Fontaine, Charlotte knew her instincts had been correct.

Luckily, it was slow at the agency for Miss Fontaine, and she had time to help Charlotte make all the arrangements. Time was literally running out for Charlotte. She had to turn around the fortunes at her father's store or she could forget all about her dreams of backlit skyscrapers, cigarettes in the break room, memos in triplicate, and a shared apartment on a low floor in Manhattan.

Charlotte hadn't notified her father about the plan, knowing that he would give her an unequivocal no. So she arranged it all behind his back.

On Friday morning, the first newspaperman turned up just before 10:00 a.m. Mr. Friedman typically stayed in his office until ten thirty, so Charlotte and Miss Fontaine were able to set up without him knowing. They hung bunting, inflated balloons, and unfolded the sign they had printed for the occasion. Miss Fontaine even brought one of Charlotte's actual Miss Subways posters, which they hung on the wall behind the cash register. They stood back and admired the effect.

"You're Charlotte Friedman!" the first newspaperman said.

"I am. Welcome to Friedman's Paint and Wallpaper. My father founded this store, and we've been serving the needs of Brooklynites for almost two decades."

Additional photographers and journalists began to enter the store. They took a look around, grabbed a pastry and a cup of coffee from the table in the back corner, and assembled around the chairs in front of the small platform Charlotte and Miss Fontaine had set up.

Charlotte knocked on her father's office door.

"Come in!"

"I'm holding a press conference downstairs in five minutes. A large number of photographers and journalists have already arrived, because they like doing articles featuring Miss Subways winners in their daily lives. There's a fantastic turnout, and I'm hoping it will result in favorable coverage in the local papers. As you know, my goal is to increase business for the store, so at the end of the presentation I'm going to announce a special promotion. Please come down if you'd like to join us."

Charlotte took a second to enjoy the look on her father's face, then she turned around, shut his office door behind her, and walked down the stairs with an ear-to-ear smile plastered across her face.

"You should have seen it, JoJo," Charlotte said later that night as she and JoJo walked toward a back table at Thompson's.

On their way to sit down, Charlotte noticed people pointing at her and heard someone whisper, "She's Miss Subways." It had happened several times, at different places, since her poster had gone up. When people recognized her, she felt a little thrill. The lovely fuss.

Once they were seated, JoJo opened her eyes wide and asked, "What did he say?"

"Wait, before I tell you, I have a question. When you called Miss Fontaine at John Robert Powers to pretend you were my mother, what did she say?"

"Didn't I tell you? I didn't actually speak with her. I left a message with her secretary."

"Oh, that explains it. Because you'll never believe this one. My mother went behind my father's back and also called Miss Fontaine to tell her I could participate in Miss Subways. Miss Fontaine must think my mother is crazy!"

"Or persistent."

"Anyway, back to my father. He came down the stairs right after me, but he couldn't say a word because Miss Fontaine had begun her introduction. So he just stood there. I was petrified he was going to kick everyone out."

"So how'd it go?"

"We had a great turnout, the journalists asked me buckets of questions, and the photographers must have used up all their film. It all depends on whether the newspapers print the story, though. We'll just have to wait and see."

"What did your father say when it was over?"

"He went back to his office and stayed up there all day. I closed the store at five o'clock and haven't seen him since."

"My goodness, Charlotte."

"I've given it all I've got. This has to work."

"I got a call from Sam today," JoJo said tentatively.

"What did he want?" Charlotte asked, trying to keep her voice level.

"He said you haven't been returning his calls and he wanted to know if I had any idea what you were going to do."

"I've been avoiding him."

"Why, Charlotte?" JoJo asked pleadingly.

"Because I'm struggling with how I go about telling him that I'm not going to choose him."

Charlotte and JoJo were both silent. Until she'd spoken those words, Charlotte hadn't been certain that was what she really wanted.

"Why does it seem, Charlotte, that you think you'd be weak or giving in if you marry Sam and raise the baby?"

"Because it would be."

"I thought that might be how you're feeling. I actually think it would be the opposite."

"How so?"

"I don't think we need to get too deep into this ancient and well-played conversation again, but I will say one thing. I will admire you greatly if you marry Sam and adopt the baby. I think it is the strongest possible thing you could do at this point in your life."

"And give up on everything I want so I can give Sam and Rose everything they want?"

"I know this is an awful situation. But don't think that in order to pursue your dreams in advertising, you have to push everything else out of your life."

Charlotte just stared.

JoJo continued. "I think you should go for it. Take a risk."

"Do you really think that?"

"You know very well that I always say what I mean."

"But it accelerates my life so much. This isn't how I thought my future would look."

"Very few things in life unfold the way we thought they would. In fact, you should be suspect when they do. Who cares when the best things in life happen? Don't you see? You're getting everything you wanted. The packaging is a little unexpected and not ideal, but the stuff inside, the stuff that really counts, is just right."

Charlotte left the house early on Saturday morning so she could buy all the papers at the newsstand. She went straight to her father's store, where she sat behind the counter and went through them one by one, cutting out each mention and photograph and creating a stack of coverage off to the side.

It was more than she could have imagined. The *Daily News*! The *Brooklyn Eagle*! It all happened just as she'd planned. Some of the papers even printed the promotion that she came up with: buy one can of paint, get one free. Her father was especially traumatized by that particular lulu, but he didn't tell her to kill the plan.

Charlotte was so excited, she couldn't sit still in her stool behind the counter. So she busied herself organizing the new wallpaper books on the main shelf. When that was done, she made sure all of the paint can labels faced out. All the while, she would look out the window, expecting any minute for swarms of people to start lining up for the free paint. Or to see a real Miss Subways in the flesh. Or both.

Perhaps they're waiting until after lunch, Charlotte thought. At one point, the front door opened, and four young men walked in. Charlotte stood up and smiled as they approached the front desk. She stood a bit to the side so they could see her poster.

"How can I help you boys today?"

"Good morning, ma'am," the tallest one said. "My car broke down. Would it be possible for me to use your telephone to call for some help?"

"Of course," Charlotte said, trying not to let the surprise and anger enter her voice as she nudged the telephone closer to the boy. She waited to see if any of his friends noticed her poster. But they didn't.

And so went the day. A few customers here and there for typical Saturday needs. But no knocking down of the door in a mad rush. Charlotte chastised herself for thinking she could manipulate her situation. And she'd have no better luck on Sunday since the store was closed. On Sunday night, she endured a mostly silent dinner with her parents and looming looks from her father.

After dinner, Charlotte helped her mother with the dishes.

"You've shown a lot of maturity recently, Charlotte," Mrs. Friedman said, her hands deep in the suds. "Working for your father like that and doing what needed to be done for this family. You've got a good head on your shoulders."

"Thanks. I appreciate that," Charlotte said, drying a pot.

Mrs. Friedman suddenly looked up. "Charlotte, even though I haven't pried, I do realize you've got a lot on your mind. You don't have to tell me, but whatever it is, you know you don't always have to make things so serious, so grave."

Charlotte put down her towel. "What are you talking about?" she asked her mother.

"I sensed the tension between you and Sam the other day. I've noticed he hasn't been coming around, and I know you've been on the telephone with JoJo more than normal lately. I've learned valuable lessons from a lot of experiences: when I gave up my career, when Harry was killed, when your father and I were having problems—"

"Problems? What kind of problems?"

"Let me finish. And I learned more lessons when it became clear that the store was in trouble. Each of those scenarios seemed so important. Like nothing else in the world could continue as normal because I was experiencing something so critical. But you know what? Life goes on. The world outside does not stop a second for our little, and that's what they are in the scheme of things, little, individual problems. It took me a long time to learn that, and I don't want you to have to be my age when you figure it out."

"It doesn't make dealing with problems any easier though," Charlotte said.

"But it makes the experience of the problem easier. When I finally changed my perspective and accepted that those problems too shall pass, and life will go on, it was radically liberating. Hard times will always hurt, I'm not saying that.

But changing the picture frame around those hard times changes the way you see them."

Charlotte thought about how she could apply that thinking to her current circumstances.

"I also want you to know, Charlotte, that I think you're so strong. You're so much stronger than I was at your age. I think you can handle just about anything."

Charlotte looked at her mother, thankful for the vote of confidence. She had become so exhausted by all the decision-making and the heaviness of her situation. She didn't think she could take much more. Her mother dried her hands and put them on Charlotte's shoulders.

"I know our relationship has been strained recently. And I realize, and I'm so sorry, that I paid more attention to Harry when you both were little. It's inexcusable, and I know I can never make that up to you. But things have been looking up for me lately, I'm starting to see some sunlight, and I want you to know I'm here for you. I'm going to do better."

"Thanks, Ma." Charlotte knew that was difficult for her mother to say. It didn't wipe out the years of pain just like that, but Charlotte was open to developing a closer relationship with her mother. She smiled at the thought of moving on. "What did you mean when you said things have been looking up for you lately?"

"Well, you inspired me, Charlotte."

"I did?"

"Yes, with your Miss Subways. I felt so proud of you for having the confidence to do something like that. Rabbi Silverman at the synagogue has been asking me for years to sing at services. I've always been too timid, so I've repeatedly said no. But you know what I'm going to do, as soon as you and your father go to the store tomorrow?"

"What?" Charlotte was beaming at her mother.

"I'm going to walk myself down to that temple and tell Rabbi Silverman I will gladly sing at services. And you know what? I can't wait."

Charlotte sat in her bed and thought about what her mother had said. She was happy that her mother was finally getting to pursue her dream. And she realized her mother was trying to tell her that sometimes you need to play the hand that life dealt you and eventually things would turn around. Charlotte needed to accept that, for now, she would be working at the store, and perhaps someday she'd get to do her own version of singing in the synagogue. She took a breath and decided that come morning, she'd telephone Mr. Hertford and tell him she wasn't cut out for advertising after all.

CHAPTER 24

Olivia was in the conference room with Priya, Matt, and Pablo. Matt had asked Pablo to stay on to get through the pitch. When Pablo saw Olivia upon her return to the office, he apologized profusely and made her sit down with him so he could explain everything.

Olivia had worked on the plane ride home, and she thought they were in a good position. Mrs. Glasser had helped arrange for a handful of the Miss Subways alumnae, her handpicked choices, to be photographed for the new creative. Pablo had hired a freelance photographer, who was setting up in an empty office. Priya would manage the shoots.

Olivia was excited with the direction the pitch was taking, and she was also happy with how she and Matt were getting along. It almost felt completely natural, a normal coworker relationship, and the underlying and tension-filled hum that Olivia had always felt seemed practically unnoticeable.

Ben was supposed to bring Rose to his grandma's apartment at ten, so, starting then, Olivia began checking her phone regularly.

At 10:17 it finally buzzed. It was Ben calling.

"Hey, how did it go?" Olivia asked, stepping out of the conference room.

"My . . . Oh, Liv . . ." Ben was crying, unable to get the words out.

"Ben, what is it? What happened?" Olivia asked, frozen where she was standing.

"She had a heart attack. I'm on my way to Lenox Health."

"Who had a heart attack?"

"My grandma," Ben said, and started crying again.

"I'll be right there," Olivia said, and hung up.

Olivia grabbed her purse out of her office and told Chloe to tell the team that Mrs. Glasser was in the hospital, and she'd be in touch as soon as she could.

Lenox Health was less than a half mile away, so Olivia ran there. She had gone to work in casual clothes and flats, knowing they were just going to be working in the conference room all day and night, and she was thankful that she could move quickly on her feet.

Olivia went to the emergency room entrance on Seventh Avenue and asked at the desk for Charlotte Glasser. The woman at reception said she couldn't have any visitors, and directed Olivia to the waiting room.

While she walked, Olivia texted Ben that she was there. When she entered the waiting room, she found Rose sitting there, crying.

"What happened?" Olivia asked, putting her arm around Rose.

"She saw me and collapsed," Rose said. "I knew I shouldn't

have come. But it's been so many years. I thought it would be okay."

"What happened between you two?"

"It's not my story to tell, Olivia."

"What does that even mean?"

"Olivia."

Olivia turned and saw Ben standing at the entrance to the waiting room.

"I'll be right back," she whispered to Rose, and patted the woman on the shoulder.

Olivia went to Ben and put her arms around him. He held her tightly.

"Is she okay?" Olivia asked.

"They don't know yet," Ben said. His eyes were red. "The doctor said she just needs to rest."

"I'm so sorry. What happened?"

"When I got to her apartment, I told her I had a surprise for her. She came into the living room, took one look at Rose, and grabbed her chest. She was able to tell us that she felt pressure. Rose told me to call 911, that she thought it was a heart attack. I took out my phone, and Rose led my grandma to the couch. A few minutes later, the ambulance arrived and the EMTs started working on her right away. She looked so small and helpless. They took her in the ambulance, and I went in a taxi with Rose. We got stuck behind a tow truck, so it took forever to get here. They let me in to see her when I got here, but she was already sleeping. The doctor said they did an EKG on her when she arrived and they gave her some kind of clot-busting medicine. He said they'll transfer her soon to the ICU."

"That must have been terrifying, Ben. Are you okay?"

"I will be when she is. I just can't lose her, Olivia. She's all I have."

Ben's eyes teared up and she hugged him again. *This poor man,* Olivia thought, *to have lost so many people in his life.*

Eventually they pulled apart and went to sit with Rose.

Ben gave Rose the update, and she sat back in her chair with a long sigh.

"I guess she was so excited to see you," Ben said. Olivia imagined Ben was trying to assuage Rose's guilt at having caused this to happen.

Olivia, who was still holding her phone, felt it vibrate.

Priya

What happened? Is Mrs. Glasser okay?

Olivia

She had a heart attack. Being monitored. Doctor thinks she'll be okay. Do u need me to come back right away?

Priya

So sorry to hear. No, we're fine. Stay, and I'll let u know if we need u. Starting photo shoots now. I won't tell the ladies what's going on.

Olivia

That's a good idea. Okay, thx Priya. Thx for everything.

Olivia sat with Ben and Rose in the waiting room for the next couple of hours. She kept them hydrated and made sure that the television was tuned to something lighthearted. They didn't talk much. Everyone was absorbed in their thoughts.

Eventually the doctor came out to talk to Ben and told him he was pleased with how Mrs. Glasser's EKG looked and how she had been responding to the medication. He had transferred her to the ICU, but they had had to give her a small sedative because she tried to get up and leave.

Ben exhaled.

The doctor said that in his experience, a patient in this condition would sleep through the night, so he encouraged Ben to go home and he'd call if anything changed.

Rose said she wanted to go back to her hotel room and rest, that she was sorry she had caused so much trouble.

"Rose, please don't feel badly," Ben said. "I'm just sorry that this happened, because I know how much you wanted to see my grandmother. And I'm sure she felt the same. I think it was just too much of a surprise for her. I should have given her notice. I didn't realize her heart couldn't handle it."

Olivia said good-bye to Ben and Rose and walked back to the office. When she arrived, she reviewed the preliminary creative Pablo had mocked up using the photographs from the Miss Subways women. She loved how the treatment looked and was thrilled with both the creative and the copy one of the copywriters had written after he interviewed each of the women.

Olivia was pleased with how all the pieces were coming together. But she was incredibly worried about Charlotte.

MTA headquarters was all the way downtown near Battery Park. Olivia woke up early on Friday to get ready. She chose a fitted black skirt suit from Jenna's closet and an elegant white blouse. Matt picked her up in a taxi outside her apartment at eight. The presentation was to start at nine fifteen. They didn't know how traffic would be, and they didn't want to be late. Pablo and Priya would be coming directly from the office with the creative.

"You ready?" Matt asked Olivia when she got in the cab.

"I am," she said confidently. And she was telling the truth. Olivia loved giving presentations, always had. She felt powerful speaking in front of a crowd and always enjoyed the positive response she seemed to get. As long as she was prepared, public speaking was not a problem for her.

"How's Mrs. Glasser?" Matt asked.

"She's not out of the woods yet. But apparently she slept through the night and there don't seem to be any new complications. Ben, that's her grandson, the guy you met outside my apartment that night? He's been texting me with updates. I'm hoping to see her once the pitch is over."

"He seemed like a nice guy, that Ben," Matt said, looking at Olivia.

"He is," she said, turning away from him and looking out the window.

They rode in silence the whole way and then stopped in front of the MTA office at eight forty-five.

Pablo and Priya were on the sidewalk, waiting for them.

"You look great," Priya said, handing Olivia a latte when she got out of the cab. She handed Matt a cup of coffee as well.

"Thanks, Priya. You do too," Olivia said. She had been having thoughts last night about opening up a small consultancy with Priya. They worked so well together.

"I think we've gone over every contingency with this,"

Matt said, addressing them on the sidewalk. It would be reasonable to go inside fifteen minutes early, but a half hour early would appear a little too eager. "We've prepared as well as we could have, and I think we're going to ace this one. Thank you all so much for your hard work. I know there has been a little drama with this preparation, but we've come out okay, and this business is ours to win."

They conferred a bit longer, and then, when it was time, they went up the elevator in silence. When the elevator opened on the eighteenth floor, they all stood there, stunned.

"Oh my God," Olivia said quietly, and broke into a huge smile.

Olivia, Priya, Matt, and Pablo looked at each other, all questioning who was responsible for this. Each of them shook their heads in silence. There were at least thirty older women, each holding a Miss Subways poster, standing in the reception area of the MTA.

The women quieted down and Eleanor, who had been photographed for the pitch, came forward.

"Charlotte called a few of us Wednesday night to suggest we come down here this morning for moral support. I guess word spread." She shrugged. "We didn't realize we'd have such a turnout. I hope it's okay."

"Okay?" Matt said. "It's fantastic. Thank you all so much."

Matt pulled Olivia aside and whispered something to her. She nodded in agreement.

They all stood quietly, packed like sardines, in the waiting area. Ed Freck was the one who came out to usher the team into the conference room for the presentation.

"Matthew," Ed said, approaching Matt. "Looks like you brought your own cheering section."

"Something like that," Matt said, following Ed into the

conference room. Olivia, Priya, and Pablo walked behind Matt and Ed, who were making small talk. Matt turned around and noticed that the Miss Subways women were still in the waiting room.

"Well, come on, ladies!" he said loudly over his shoulder. "What are you waiting for?"

A little yelp rang out, and the ladies began following the team. When they got to the conference room, without a word, the women assembled around the perimeter of the room, each holding her poster in front of her midsection. Olivia didn't think they could have arranged it any better if they'd tried.

CHAPTER 25

CHARLOTTE
MONDAY, JULY 11, 1949

Charlotte dragged her feet getting ready. She'd had trouble sleeping the night before, thinking about the conversation she'd had with her mother. Thinking about the telephone call she would place to Mr. Hertford at J. Walter Thompson. And thinking about the decision she had to make regarding Sam.

She'd gone over every possible scenario. And though her head and her heart battled through the night, resulting in a life-threatening casualty for one of them, by the time she woke up, the blazing sun already warming her windows, Charlotte was certain of her decision. And she was prepared to share it with Sam.

There were people who wouldn't understand her decision. Wouldn't agree with it. She knew that for certain. And as life would have it, there were those who would. Charlotte decided to ignore the former group. And clink overfilled glasses with the rest. Who got to decide what path someone's life took? Was it foretold?

But it was time for Monday morning. The great arbiter

of fresh starts and calendars stretching for days on end. Office workers in Park Avenue corner offices and pattern makers in Garment District walk-ups were drunk with the possibility of a whole week set before them like a new school year to a class full of wide-eyed kindergarteners. The idea that there was so much time to make things happen.

For Charlotte, it was day one of settling into her life at Friedman's. One thing that had become clear during last night's duel was that in order for her to survive this new life she was embarking on, she would have to do two things: One, accept the reality that she had to help her father. This was not the time for her to have a career in advertising and an exciting and glamorous life out of Brooklyn. It would happen one day. Just not now. And two, initiate a thorough advertising plan for Friedman's so she could approximate a career. This she would do whether or not her father approved.

Charlotte walked to the store in a languid haze, precipitated by the suffocating air and her deep ambivalence toward how her post-graduation plans had turned out. Plus, she had big news to tell Sam. News that would change everything.

After preparing a cup of Maxwell House in the storeroom and pivoting the OPEN sign up front, Charlotte made herself comfortable behind the counter. Her father, as usual, was upstairs in his office.

Charlotte rehearsed what she was going to say to Mr. Hertford. She didn't plan on a long conversation. Rather, she feared he would be annoyed by her capriciousness, so she tried to come up with the perfect line to help him understand her predicament and ensure that if her station should change, he would be willing to give her another chance.

Gathering her courage, she picked up the phone and

started to dial but was interrupted by a young man in coveralls entering the store. Charlotte sighed in frustration and hung up the phone. The young man, holding a newspaper, approached Charlotte, looked at the Miss Subways poster, looked at his newspaper, looked back at Charlotte, and smiled. He was holding that morning's *Daily Mirror*, which contained this bullion from Walter Winchell:

> Who's not fawning over this month's Miss Subways, Charlotte Friedman? The golden beaut may be a lover of art, but most of the time she's locked up like a princess down on her luck at her father's paint store. Don't tell a soul, but if you want an audience with her, you can find her at Friedman's on Third in Bay Ridge. And if you just happen to have a bare wall, I hear they're offering a can of free paint for each one you buy. Sounds like this Charlotte may be brainy as well as beautiful.

Charlotte thought it was interesting to reflect on how a wave began. How it was impossible to notice the first tiny swell that would gain momentum and carry water and energy with it to create something bigger, something that would change landscapes and affect lives. And sometimes noticing the beginning dulled the impact, the beauty, of its final form. So it was with the young man in coveralls.

"Papa, can you come down here?" Charlotte yelled up the steps to her father's office before running back down to manage the swelling crowd.

"What is it, Charlotte?" Mr. Friedman yelled, annoyed as all get-out, halfway down the stairs before noticing what was happening on the floor.

"Walter Winchell wrote about us," Charlotte said, unable to contain her smile as her father came up next to her at the register.

Together they looked out at the store, at the crowd stacking paint cans in their arms, waving their papers, and pointing at Charlotte's Miss Subways poster.

"You should have seen it, Sarah," Mr. Friedman said as he and Charlotte entered the kitchen that night, side by side.

They told her all about the crowd. About the people who had come from as far as Staten Island to take a photograph with Charlotte and have her sign their autograph books. About the neighbors who told Mr. Friedman that his two-for-one promotion was a brilliant idea, and they would be stocking up on paint for renovations they'd been putting off. And about the developer who awarded Mr. Friedman the contract for a new building he was putting up in Brooklyn Heights because he wanted to keep the business local. Apparently, though Saturday's papers had given a small mention of Charlotte and the promotion, it took Walter Winchell's piece that day to make an impact and bring customers to the store.

"I'm proud of you, Charlotte," her father said.

Charlotte and her mother looked at each other, her mother with tears in her eyes.

"You've never said that to me before," Charlotte said, an edge in her voice.

"And I regret that."

"So why now?"

"Because today I saw you as a woman for the first time. And it startled me. I'm not too good with words, Charlotte.

And I know I haven't been too good as a father, but you have impressed me with your determination. So I've made a decision."

Charlotte looked at him expectantly and was happy she hadn't had a moment to call Mr. Hertford.

"I'm going to allow you to do the advertising for the store you've wanted to do. Business was incredible today. And it gave us a little cushion that will hold us for a bit. I know I've been stubborn in letting you execute your ideas, but if you come to me tomorrow with a plan, we can discuss it."

Charlotte exhaled and knew she was surprising her father by looking disappointed instead of elated. She looked at her mother and then her father, and then she stood up.

"I've been through more in the past few months than I've been through in my entire life. I've seen things and experienced things that have changed my perspective on life and my understanding of people. If I've learned one thing, it's that I need to make my life happen *for* me, not let it happen *to* me. Papa, I'm glad the press conference worked, and I'm glad today gave you a cushion, and hopefully the crowds will continue to come. But my last day working with you will be this Friday. Next Monday, I'll be starting my job at J. Walter Thompson." She held her breath, expecting her father to start shouting. But he didn't.

Dear Sam,

I'm sorry I'm writing this in a letter, but I was afraid I wouldn't have the

courage to tell you my decision if I was
sitting across from you.

This has been an excruciating decision
for me. If I reject the idea of adopting
the baby, I lose you in the process. If I
forgive you for your transgressions and
decide to marry you, I'm agreeing to raise
and be the mother of your and Rose's baby.
I know you're convinced that it would
someday become irrelevant that Rose is
the biological mother of the baby. I'm not
so certain.

Do you recall that Thoreau book we both
read in college and our favorite quote
about advancing confidently in the direction
of your dreams? I know I need to just do
that. And that way I can't go wrong.

The question is which dream do I pick?
The one where I'm married to you and we
have a family? Or the one where I become
an independent woman, pursuing a career,
experiencing life and the world on my
own for the first time? I can't pick both
dreams; that's just too much.

So I'm picking me. I know that by definition
means I'm not picking you, but please don't
feel that way. I hate that I am hurting

you with my decision. And please know that
I wish you all the best in health and
happiness with your new baby.

Love, Charlotte

On Monday morning, July 18, 1949, with a smile on her
face that hadn't subsided since she'd woken up, Charlotte
slipped on the new outfit she had bought for that day. She
tied the bow—a black-and-white polka-dotted number—at
the collar of the white short-sleeve blouse and adjusted the
matching belt on her knee-length black skirt. Looking into
her vanity mirror, she quickly applied another coat of ruby
lipstick and checked her eye makeup. Then she put on her
pumps, grabbed her gloves and purse, and skipped down
the stairs.

When she opened the front door, Charlotte laughed.
Nothing had changed: there were still twelve broad steps
leading from her door to the small wrought-iron gate and
then two more steps to the sidewalk. The silver maple in the
front yard still flaunted its glossy five-fingered leaves. The
windows of the brick two-family house across the street
were still cluttered with houseplants and religious statues.

But everything was different. The air hummed. The light
tingled on her skin. The sky smiled. Charlotte smiled back
and understood at once that this was what it felt like to finally be the author of her own precious life.

CHAPTER 26

"Tell me all about it," Mrs. Glasser said when Olivia walked into her room later that afternoon. She was doing so well—much to everyone's surprise and delight—that the doctor had transferred her out of ICU and into a regular room.

Olivia brought a chair close to Mrs. Glasser's bed and told her all about the pitch. Ben was sitting on the opposite side of the bed, so he was listening as well. He was holding his grandmother's hand and smiling brightly at Olivia.

Olivia told her about how surprised they were to see all the Miss Subways when they arrived at the MTA. And how the women stood proudly, a display of living history, in the conference room during the presentation. Having the women there, Olivia said, made for a compelling visual and deepened the impact of the message they were trying to send through the "Where Are They Now?" creative.

"When I wasn't speaking, I would glance around at the MTA people and watch them watching the Miss Subways. For some of the older people at the table, you could tell the memories of staring up at those girls throughout all the years of the campaign came flooding back. It was quite poignant."

Olivia said the MTA team asked all the right questions and completely seemed to understand the direction Olivia and her team presented. She didn't think it could have gone any better.

"I just wish you had been there to see it, Mrs. Glasser," Olivia said.

"Me too. But I'm glad I played a small role. It was a treat being back in the advertising world again, although so much has changed from my day. Anyway, I'm so happy it all went well. I knew it would, Olivia. You've got that special something," Mrs. Glasser said in a soft voice. "By the way," she added, "I think it's about time you called me Charlotte."

Olivia smiled. She was on a high. This always happened after she pitched new business. But to be able to share her feelings of success with Ben and Mrs. Glasser—Charlotte— made it feel extra special.

"Now that I'm feeling a little better, thanks to you and your wonderful account, Olivia, I'm ready to tell Ben something important," Charlotte said. And then to Olivia: "Will you excuse us, dear?"

"Of course," Olivia said, standing up. "Would either of you like something from the cafeteria?"

"It's okay, Grandma. I'd actually like Olivia to stay," Ben said, looking at Olivia.

Olivia saw Charlotte look from Ben to Olivia, catching the meaning of their glances.

"Suit yourself," Charlotte said. "Ben, there's something I need to tell you. Something very important. Something you deserved to know a very long time ago . . . ," she began.

She continued by telling Ben, and Olivia, about how she

had met Rose and about the circumstances the two of them found themselves in when Rose became pregnant by Ben's grandfather Sam. Throughout the whole story, Ben stayed silent, and Olivia, looking at him quite frequently, couldn't tell if he felt calm or on the verge of erupting. His face was quiet.

"But I don't understand," Ben said. "You and grandpa *did* get married."

"That's correct, but not right away. At first I went to work at J. Walter Thompson. It was exhilarating. Going into the city each day. Throwing my entire being into the work. I loved it. Eventually, I had saved enough money to move into Manhattan, into a tiny place with a couple of the girls I worked with. We had a ball. We went out to all the best places, the Stork Club, El Morocco. . . ." She trailed off, her eyes taking on a dreamy look.

"Are you okay, Grandma?"

"I'm okay, honey. Anyway, I did that for four or five years. I bided my time in the typing pool, trying to become indispensable to all the senior executives, hoping that they would see my worth and promote me. It was impossible to hide my fury every time I saw some pimply boy with a Harvard haircut being shown to his new office to start his career as an assistant account executive. One Sunday when I was back in Bay Ridge, visiting my parents, I ran into Sam on the street. He was walking with your father." Charlotte stopped, and her eyes were wet.

Ben fetched the box of tissues from the bedside table and handed a few to his grandmother.

Charlotte smiled. A radiant smile. "I realized I had been wrong. I had been so stubborn. So determined. Perhaps more like my own father than I'd ever wanted to admit to myself. All that time, I'd never stopped loving Sam. And the minute I met that darling boy, Henry, your father, I fell in love with him, too. I had been so convinced that I couldn't pursue my career and still thrive as a wife and a mother. But that day, I realized I didn't want to waste another minute of not having them in my life. Your grandfather and I began to *date* again and we fell back in love quickly, as if no time at all had passed. After a few short months, one of my roommates came into my bedroom one Saturday to tell me I had a delivery. When I went to the door, your father was there, all dressed up in a suit with a bow tie, looking darling. He was holding a bouquet of flowers and told me his daddy had a special present for me. Then your grandfather came around the corner, got down on one knee, presented me with a beautiful ring, and asked me to marry him. I didn't hesitate for a second. And that's how it all happened."

Charlotte paused and let out a deep breath. All the years of longing and loving seemingly rushing back to her. Ben opened his mouth to say something, but Charlotte had more to say.

"I kept working after that, but my career never amounted to much. It was a different time in advertising. There were a few female copywriters here and there, mostly working on beauty and fashion accounts, but it was still a man's world for account executives. I never made my way in. I'm glad things are so different for you, Olivia. And I hope you don't make the same mistake I made of believing that you can't fit a personal life into your career. And I've never told you this, Ben, but I admire you for hiring so many women for high-level positions at your company. Times have really changed."

Olivia turned toward Ben. "*Your* company?"

Ben smiled at Olivia and turned back to his grandmother.

"Why didn't you ever tell me any of this?" Olivia had been wondering the same thing. It wasn't like Ben was a child.

"I've asked myself that thousands of times. Your parents were going to tell you when you turned thirteen. I'm not sure how they chose that number, but I respected it. And then they died, and Grandpa and your mom's parents soon after, and I just couldn't bear, as you grew, to tell you that I wasn't your biological grandmother." Charlotte's voice caught, but she recovered. "You had gone through so much, and I didn't want you to feel like you had no one left who was technically related to you. But now I realize you deserve to know there's another person out there who you're related to. I'm so sorry, and I hope with all my heart that you're not angry with me."

"Oh, Grandma," Ben said. "I'm not angry. I'll be honest: it's overwhelming and I'm going to need some time to digest it all, but, no, I wouldn't say I'm angry. You clearly made your decision out of love. I know intellectually that it's not the person who gives birth to you who's your true parent. It's the person who raises you. And you raised my father. And you raised me." He squeezed her hand, and tears started to flow out of her eyes. "I just can't believe that story," Ben added, letting out a laugh of relief. "I thought times were simple back then. Boy, was I wrong."

"Rose was a character. She swooped into our lives and gave us a lot of heartache, but she also gave us your father. She had been in touch periodically with your grandfather when he was raising your father alone. He would send her photos once in a while. But when Sam and I married, we agreed that it was better for us to break ties with Rose. He wrote, told her our wishes, and asked her to respect them."

Olivia realized she was, though invited, intruding on a very personal family conversation. But she felt like she was in some small way a part of this family. And she was realizing that she hoped she'd be a larger part of it as time went on.

"I couldn't help seeing Rose's face every time I looked at your father. Luckily, he looked more like your grandfather, so that was helpful. But he was a sweet boy, an easy boy, and I ended up falling in love with him entirely, just like your grandfather knew I would. Soon enough, I began to see Rose as this troubled angel who brought us a gift. And I didn't hate her. I felt nothing for her, really. Gratitude for your father. But nothing emotional for her. She didn't contact us for years. She respected that we asked her not to. But then she started writing."

"The letters I found," Ben said.

"Yes," Charlotte continued. "I opened the first one out of curiosity, but I realized I wasn't interested in anything she had to say. I didn't need her reentering my life. I thought she would only bring uncertainty and . . . and here's where I feel a little guilty: I didn't want to share you with her. I didn't think she deserved any piece of you, and I thought she would want to take that. So I stuffed the letters into the scrapbook and didn't think of them again."

"I can see now why it was such a shock to see her," Ben said. "Actually, understatement of the year. I'm so sorry, Grandma. I never should have brought her here."

"As a matter of fact, I'm quite curious to talk to her."

"She's been in the waiting room this whole time," Ben said.

Charlotte smiled.

"Time has a really incredible way of dulling feelings that you think will be sharp for your entire life. One day you wake up, and sometimes it takes something like this for that to happen, but you realize that the point isn't so pointy. And the edge isn't so jagged. And you find in your heart a way to accept people for who they are, because it's not always entirely their fault. So if it's okay with the two of you, can you ask Rose to come up? I'd like to speak with her privately."

Olivia and Ben held hands in the elevator, and when they got to the waiting room, Rose stood from her chair and asked if everything was okay.

"She'd like to see you," Ben said.

"Are you sure?" Rose asked.

"I am. But first I'd like to tell you something. Henry, the baby you gave birth to, turned out to be a wonderful man," Ben said.

Rose gasped and took a step back. She covered her mouth with her hand and nodded at Ben to continue.

"He was kind and loving and fiercely intelligent. He was dedicated to his career, but more important, he was dedicated to my mom and to me. He was the most incredible father I could have asked for, and even though I only had a very short time with him, I know how lucky I was to have him in my life," Ben said.

Olivia could barely help the tears falling from her eyes.

"Thank you, Ben," Rose said, pulling him into her for a hug. "You have no idea how much those words mean to me. I want you to know that he was all of those things because your grandparents were the best of people. They raised their son with the values that they espoused. And they showered him with love. Something I was incapable of doing."

Ben nodded and they hugged again, and then Rose

walked toward the elevator to reunite with the woman she had met all those years ago in the conference room of the John Robert Powers Modeling Agency.

Olivia and Ben sat down and looked at each other. They were both laughing and crying and shaking their heads in disbelief at what they had just learned.

"You look at these older women and you just assume it's all sweetness and wisdom, but, man, these ladies have secrets. Deep, dark secrets," Ben said.

"I know," Olivia said. "That was epic." And then she turned to Ben with a serious expression. "Are you okay?"

He nodded. "I am."

"Why didn't you ever tell me UseYourWings was your company?"

"I didn't want to sound like a prick."

"You're the furthest thing from a prick, Ben," Olivia said, kissing him gently. Then she asked, "What now?"

"Well, now we let those two girlfriends talk it out. To-night I'll call you, because you seem to be the person I want to speak with all the time, and if you're up for it, I will invite you over for Scrabble and chocolate babka."

Olivia smiled. "That sounds like a perfect plan."

Matt brought breakfast into the conference room Monday morning so they could all wait for the call together. Ed Freck from the MTA had told Matt that they expected to make their calls first thing.

When the phone in the middle of the conference table

rang, Matt put it on speaker and told Layne to put the call through.

"This is Matthew Osborne," Matt said.

"Hi Matt, it's Ed Freck."

"Ed, good to hear from you," Matt said, looking around the room. They were all still.

"So, we were really delighted by your presentation on Friday," Ed said.

Delighted? Olivia mouthed in disappointment.

"It was well thought out," Ed continued, "certainly unique, and we all loved how you resurrected such an important part of our history in advertising."

"That's great, Ed, glad to hear it," Matt said, rolling his eyes.

But, Olivia mouthed.

"But," Ed continued, "we've decided to go with a larger firm, since this is an agency-of-record deal. If we were just assigning a project, you and your team would have won hands down. But the bigger agency has all the disciplines in-house to allow us to meet our needs fiscally and strategically."

"I see, Ed. Thanks for your honesty. Please consider using us if you're ever looking for out-of-the-box thinking for your specific project needs," Matt said.

And there it was. Done. Done-zo. Account lost. Again.

Olivia groaned and put her head facedown on the table.

"Tough loss," Matt said.

They were all quiet. They had put so much effort into the pitch, and now it seemed like it wasn't worth it.

"How would you feel if I told you I had some good news, though?" Matt asked, looking around the table. Everyone perked up. A little bit. Matt continued, "I happened to get a call from Shay Jones over at Y&R. As you know, she runs the Mini Cooper account for BMW. She said they were looking for a really outrageous promotional idea for the Mini to celebrate some milestone it has coming up, but they wanted to commission it out-of-house and she thought of us. I pitched her the 'Star Car' idea and she loved it. She's taking it to the client this afternoon. If they like the top line, they'll bring us in and we can pitch the full concept."

Matt put his hands out in front of him. Priya and Olivia looked at each other and smiled. Perhaps, Olivia thought, she might find a way to stick around The Osborne Agency after all. It would require a bit of a restructure in regard to her relationship with Matt, but it wouldn't hurt to get a few more years of agency experience before she and Priya, if it was meant to be, struck out on their own. She thought the "Star Car" idea was perfect for Mini Cooper, and decided right then to lean in wholly to this pitch and then negotiate a favorable raise for both herself and Priya when they won the business.

There was hope yet. And that wasn't the only piece of good news Olivia was to get that day.

Later that afternoon, Chloe lumbered into Olivia's office with an enormous package. It was about three feet square and wrapped in brown paper with a huge red bow on it. And she also had a smaller box wedged under her arm.

"It came by messenger with instructions to open the large box first," Chloe said. She smiled and walked out of Olivia's office, closing the door behind her.

Olivia broke into a huge grin and set the small box on

her desk. She leaned the large package against the wall of her office and gently pulled off the wrapping. Inside was a mounted and framed map of the world but without any glass covering the front.

Olivia took the small box from her desk and sat down in her chair. She wanted to savor this feeling. This feeling of knowing that she was special to someone who actually took time out of his day to do something kind for her. This feeling that she was falling for Ben. And that clearly he was falling for her too.

She unwrapped the small box and there were two smaller boxes inside, numbered one and two.

Olivia opened box number one and inside was a note that said, "You can start with LA." Taped to the note was a gold pushpin.

Olivia set that aside, opened box number two, and started to laugh and cry when she read the note: *And then you can move right on to Paris.* Stapled to the note was an itinerary on UseYourWings letterhead for a trip to Paris. Printed at the top it read: *Ben Glasser and Olivia Harrison / Paris, France / June 4–10, 2018.* And taped to the itinerary was another gold pushpin.

HISTORICAL NOTE

Miss Subways was a contest that took place in the New York City subway system from 1941 to 1976. During that time, approximately two hundred women held the esteemed title. The New York Subways Advertising Company developed the program, which featured glamorous photographs and short descriptions about the winners on placards in the subway cars, for several reasons. They wanted to show potential advertisers that subway advertising was an effective marketing vehicle, lure passenger eyeballs to the adjacent advertisements, and give straphangers something to look at during long and sometimes dreary rides. As it evolved, the contest took on local importance and a historical significance that endures to this day.

At the beginning of the campaign, John Robert Powers, head of the preeminent modeling agency of the time, chose the monthly winners—who were required to be residents of New York City and ride the subways—from his own stable of models as well as from the large pool of candidates who entered the contest by sending in head shots. The campaign changed throughout the years, and eventually John Robert Powers no longer led the charge.

In later years, winners were chosen by contest organizers, mailed-in postcard votes, and by telephone. And throughout the campaign, different—and sometimes Hollywood-famous—photographers were used, including Victor Keppler, F. A. Russo, Menyhert "Muky" Munkacsi, Michael Barbero, James J. Kriegsmann, and many more.

The contest took on varying significance to the hundreds of women who were Miss Subways. "Many dreamed of becoming models, actresses, and singers, but most quietly returned to their regular lives after their faces were plastered on as many as 14,000 posters seen by nearly 5 million pairs of eyes a day."[1] However, during their reigns, it wasn't uncommon for the women to be treated like celebrities, to be written up in gossip columns, and to receive attention in the manner of letters, proposals, and gifts from admirers. For instance, Ruth Ericsson, Miss Subways December 1941, received 278 marriage proposals, and Dorothea Mate Hart, Miss Subways June 1942, received 300 tea bags!

Today, Miss Subways lives on in many ways:

- In the memories of the women who had the honor and the aging city residents who remember admiring the posters on their commutes.
- In the play and movie *On the Town*, which featured a similar contest called Miss Turnstiles.
- In the original posters that still line the vintage subway cars at Brooklyn's New York Transit Museum.

---

1. To learn more about the history of Miss Subways and to read interviews with the winners, I recommend *Meet Miss Subways: New York's Beauty Queens 1941–1976* by Fiona Gardner and Amy Zimmer (Seapoint Books, 2013).

- In the decor at Ellen Hart Sturm's (Miss Subways March–April 1959) Ellen's Stardust Diner in Times Square, New York City.
- In Fiona Gardner and Amy Zimmer's book, *Meet Miss Subways: New York's Beauty Queens 1941–1976*.
- And now, in this novel.

Though antiquated and perhaps quaint, Miss Subways, according to historian Kathy Peiss in *Meet Miss Subways,* "opens to view hidden histories of everyday life in New York that touch upon the changing ideals and aspirations of women, the struggle for civil rights, and the rise of a modern culture of beauty, consumption, fashion, and image-making. These are, in fact, significant themes in the annals of New York and America's history."

AUTHOR'S NOTE: Although I honored the true history of Miss Subways, many of the details of the selection process, photo shoots, etc., are from my imagination, as records of these specifics are unavailable. Charlotte, Rose, and the other contenders for Miss Subways July 1949 are fictionalized, but all of the other Miss Subways mentioned are based on actual winners. I took the liberty of changing Thelma Porter's Miss Subways month to March 1949 for the purposes of the story; she was actually April 1948.

The frontispiece photo and photos on pages 298–99 are courtesy of *Meet Miss Subways: New York's Beauty Queens 1941–1976* by Fiona Gardner and Amy Zimmer, Seapoint Books.

MEET MISS SUBWAYS

JULY 1946

Creative
ENID BERKOWITZ

Art student at Hunter College—interested in advertising and costume design— makes own clothes—plugging for B.A. but would settle for M.R.S.

John Shaw Powers
247 PARK AVENUE

PUBLISHED BY NEW YORK SUBWAYS ADVTG. CO., INC. • 630 FIFTH AVENUE, NEW YORK 20, N. Y.

PHOTOGRAPHED BY **F. A. RUSSO**

MEET MISS SUBWAYS

MAY-JUNE 1953

Sparkling
MARY GARDINER

Thank County Mayo parents for this Washington Heights beauty. An Aquinas graduate, she loves her secretarial job in airline office. Now 19; stands 5' 7½"; skates, swims, paints in oil.

John Shaw Powers
247 PARK AVENUE

PUBLISHED BY NEW YORK SUBWAYS ADVERTISING CO., • INC. 630 FIFTH AVENUE, NEW YORK 20, N. Y.

Photographed by Michael Barbero of **F. A. RUSSO**

MEET MISS SUBWAYS

APRIL 1948

Vivacious
THELMA PORTER

Psychology student at Brooklyn College and part-time nurse receptionist in dentist's office. Is active in social welfare work and ardent church worker. Sings in a choral group and is a Gershwin devotee.

John Robert Powers
247 PARK AVENUE

PUBLISHED BY NEW YORK SUBWAYS ADVTG. CO. INC. • 630 FIFTH AVENUE, NEW YORK 20, N. Y.

PHOTOGRAPHED BY **F. A. RUSSO**

MEET MISS SUBWAYS

MARCH-APRIL 1952

Blue-eyed
PEGGY BYRNE

This petite Brooklyn-born colleen is studying to be an insurance broker. Plans to wed her childhood sweetheart, an Army Private. Her older brother is a Tank Destroyer Pfc. in Korea.

John Robert Powers
247 PARK AVENUE

PUBLISHED BY NEW YORK SUBWAYS ADVERTISING CO. • INC. 630 FIFTH AVENUE, NEW YORK 20, N. Y.

Photographed by Michael Barbera of **F. A. RUSSO**

ACKNOWLEDGMENTS

I first heard about Miss Subways while listening to a *Radio Diaries* episode called "'Miss Subways': A Trip Back in Time to New York's Melting Pot," produced by Samara Freemark on NPR's *All Things Considered*. It was the fall of 2013, and I nearly had to pull my car over. I was immediately fascinated by this slice of New York City history, and as I delved more deeply, I became smitten and thought it would make a wonderful topic for a book.

It wasn't until 2016 that I began writing *The Subway Girls,* so I had plenty of time to let the story marinate and evolve into what you've just read. After researching Miss Subways online, I devoured the book *Meet Miss Subways,* by Fiona Gardner and Amy Zimmer. Fiona and Amy tracked down forty-one Miss Subways and photographed and interviewed them about their experiences. The result was pure gold for my research, so my first thank-you is to Fiona and Amy for all their hard work creating such an important and comprehensive tribute to the history of Miss Subways. Fiona, thank you so much for meeting with me and sharing your experience. I'm delighted to be the next torch holder. If you are interested in learning more about Miss Subways, I highly recommend Fiona and Amy's book.

What an honor to speak with past Miss Subways Ruth Lippman (January 1945), Enid Berkowitz Schwarzbaum (July 1946), and Mary Gardiner Timoney (May–June 1953), who generously shared their memories and impressions about both the Miss Subways program itself and what it meant to them. Peggy Byrne (March 1952) graciously invited me into her home to tell me about her experience.

My research also brought me to the wonderful New York Transit Museum in Brooklyn, where I had the opportunity to sit on historic trains and look up at preserved Miss Subways posters as if I were back in the 1940s. I was lucky enough to meet a museum-goer who remembered Miss Subways and shared his memories with me. Thank you to Desiree Alden-Gonzalez, archivist and acting collections manager of the New York Transit Museum, who answered my inquiries skillfully and with great enthusiasm.

Thank you, Carly Watters, literary agent extraordinaire, who gave me the wonderful author experience of "The Call." I have loved working with you and appreciate everything you have done for me. I'm so excited to be on your team.

Thank you, Alicia Clancy, for acquiring the manuscript for St. Martin's Press. And thank you to my editor, Lauren Jablonski, for grabbing the torch and taking us through the finish line. I'm thrilled to be embarking on this journey with you.

Thank you to the incredible marketing and PR team at St. Martin's Press: Brant Janeway, Jordan Hanley, and Brittani Hilles, and to Chrisinda Lynch, Anna Gorovoy,

Kerri Resnick, Kaitlin Severini, Yolanda Pluguez, and everyone else at St. Martin's who made this book a reality.

Thank you, Crystal Patriarche, my first book cheerleader, for all of your confidence in me and encouragement over the years and for giving me your blessing to fly out of the nest. And to the whole team at BookSparks, a tremendous thank-you for your hard work, dedication, and enthusiasm.

Thank you, Nicola Kraus, for your brilliant and constructive early insight into the manuscript and your tremendous support.

Thank you to my friends and early readers/supporters/venting recipients/book-deal celebrants, especially Marcia-Elizabeth Baker-Thompson, Rene and Mike Benedetto, Sharon and Andrew Cooper, Karen Cousin, Jill and Larry DeLuise, Penny Kosinski, Beth and Larry Lipman, Lauren Mandell, Bets Miller, Elizabeth Moyer, Sally Paridis, Richard Rosenzweig, David Shorrock, Cherylanne Skolnicki, John Thomas, Allison Wohl, and Lauren Zucker.

Special thanks to Annabel Monaghan, my "coworker," who has been a true rock for me throughout this process, an astute and encouraging first reader, and an excellent and hilarious friend. "Chicago is good. Paris is great." I owe you a trip!

I am fortunate to be part of such a supportive industry and I treasure the friendships I have developed with other authors in the last few years through events, The Balance Project interviews, and online. Thank you, Cristina Alger, Jenna Blum, Jamie Brenner, Kristin Contino, Fiona Davis, Elisabeth Egan, Abby Fabiaschi, Liz Fenton, Elyssa Friedland, Kristin Harmel, Brenda Janowitz, Emily Liebert, Lynda Cohen Loigman, Sarah McCoy, Eileen Palma, Amy

Poeppel, Lisa Steinke, and Beatriz Williams for your guidance, referrals, and support.

And the bloggers and book champions! So much love especially to Andrea Peskind Katz (you are incredible), Jenny O'Regan, and Melissa Amster.

Thank you, readers. You are so wonderful and motivating.

Thank you to my family (thanks, Dad, for your edits!). I am lucky to have such a loving team behind me.

And, most of all, thank you, Judson, William, Jason, and Rick, for absolutely everything good in my life.